CONFEDERATE
VAMPIRES
IN SPACE

CONFEDERATE VAMPIRES IN SPACE

a novel

Havelock Mandamus

d r u m h e a d

Copyright © 2017 by Havelock Mandamus

First printed 2017

ISBN 978-0-9993825-2-3 (hard cover)
ISBN 978-0-9993825-1-6 (paperback)
ISBN 978-0-9993825-3-0 (mobi)
ISBN 978-0-9993825-0-9 (epub)

Sections of this book were inspired by
Death Comes for the Archbishop
by Willa Cather

Cover art and design by Havelock Mandamus

www.drumheadbooks.com
www.havelockmandamus.com
havelockmandamus@gmail.com

For my mother
and in memory
of my father

It is only with the heart that one can see rightly;
what is essential is invisible to the eye.

-The Little Prince

1

TWO YOUNG MAIDENS, of which you will recall, the one being fair with flaxen hair and the other dusky and raven dark, came climbing quickly with great exertion and much effort over the rocky escarpment. Under different circumstances, the two maidens might have lingered in their traversing to admire the austere beauty of the windswept canyon and the cerulean brilliance of the clear western sky, but on this day, at this desperate hour, the maidens did not tarry, for their very lives were in danger.

Just as it seemed circumstances could not conspire in a more calamitous manner, one of the unfortunate maidens, the fair young lady with flaxen hair, caught her delicate foot on a gnarled root and fell to the ground.

"Alas," she cried out to her companion. "I cannot persevere in this madness. I am hobbled and well nigh unto despair." Her eyes were wild with a rampant terror, and she awkwardly turned to look over her shoulder as if she expected to find her tormenters mere steps away and stalking closer still.

The maiden with raven-dark hair paused in her flight and, too, cast a fearful glance down the winding path they had so arduously ascended. If their pursuers were there in cunning ensconcement among the rocks and junipers and sagebrush, she could not them espy. The raven-haired maiden knelt quickly by the side of her prostrate companion.

"Do not leave me," the flaxen-haired maiden implored, grasping the sleeve of her companion's calico dress. "I would rather depart this life than endure the horrendous debasements that I will most surely suffer at the hands of those remorseless savages."

Her wild eyes spied a rock on the path nearby.

"Look yonder at that fateful rock. You must spare me. I beseech you. Strike that rock unto my brow and free me from this impending doom."

The raven-haired maiden wore a pendant on a necklace around her neck. It was carved from quartz, a white serpent in a closed circle, with its tail in its mouth. The pendant dangled in the distances between them.

The raven-haired maiden looked down at her desperate companion. Her dark eyes were steady and grave. She laid a comforting hand against the flaxen-haired maiden's temple and answered her with a slow shake of her head.

At that moment, there came the unmistakable call of a bird from below among the rocks and sparse trees where they had so recently idled. An ominous silence descended over the canyon, and the two maidens became like unto breathless statues and strained mightily with all their being to hear what further song the unseen bird might sing. Hearing nothing further of the bird, if indeed that was what they had heard, the raven-haired maiden offered her hand to her companion and assisted her as she rose unsteadily to her feet.

The two maidens gazed intently toward the shadows in the copse whence the call of the bird had come. In their minds, they could not forswear that the shadows did not teem with the foulest abominations of their imaginations, and for a vertiginous moment, a great whirlpool seemed to tug at the very fabric of the canyon and to pull down into the depths of that darkness, faster than the maidens could assail, the rocks, the blazing sun, and the last of the clear, cerulean sky.

But Time ticked on implacably, and the ground did not yield, and the sun continued to shine with comforting constancy. The two maidens summoned new reserves of womanly fortitude and resisted the icy fingers of terror that grasped at their souls. The raven-haired maiden pointed toward the rocky horizon and circled her arm firmly round the flaxen-haired maiden's waist. She offered her shoulder to her companion, and with a tentative, halting locomotion, the two maidens resumed their determined ascent.

Unbeknownst to the two maidens, as they pressed onward into the labyrinth of stone, two figures emerged from the shadows in the copse below and with a swiftness that belied sinew and bone came bounding on in a straight, silent demarche along the path the maidens had trod.

The maidens climbed for long minutes with all the deliberate haste they could muster. Soon, they topped the crest and paused to recover their breath and to reconnoiter the way ahead. The trail cut back and threaded past a great boulder that all but blocked their forward progress. A sheer cliff fell away to one side, and a false step would most assuredly send a hapless pilgrim hurtling to certain oblivion. There was but one way forward betwixt the boulder and the canyon wall. A sliver of sky beckoned with the promise of a more forgiving terrain. Seeing no other course of action, the two maidens resolved to limp and stagger on in stoic persistence toward the eye of the needle before them.

As the maidens drew closer to the boulder, a seeming shadow began silently to move and then to slide away from the surface of the boulder.

Before the maiden's horrified eyes, the shadow resolved into the figure of a man.

"Look now," the flaxen-haired maiden warned in a tremulous voice. "I fear we are beset."

The figure of the man stole forward as noiselessly as a creeping panther. The sun fell full on his face, and the maidens were stricken as they beheld the fierce countenance of a red-skinned savage. The Indian's eyes glittered darkly with an inhuman light that pierced the maidens to the marrow of their bones.

The maidens recoiled at the sight of the Indian and staggered back on quaking limbs. The Indian came pacing closer. His bare limbs were roped lean with muscle. The maidens could see his skin with its mottled and scarred patterns of mud, ochre and charcoal. As he came closer, he began to crouch down nearer to the ground, bracing in anticipation of an encounter.

The maidens were frightened most sorely and had no time to settle upon a stratagem other than a sudden and precipitous retreat. They knew the chance of escape would be slight. They would have only a few moments at best, but those moments might suffice to steal away on the flank and avoid the menacing Indian.

But there was no escape to be had. As the imperiled maidens stepped back and turned from their fearsome adversary, they confronted two more stealthy Indians creeping up from the rear. The maidens' hearts leapt in their chests. Circumstances had turned most unexpectedly against them.

The Indians closed in on all sides, and the maidens backed slowly towards the wall of the canyon.

Indians on their front, Indians on their flanks, the maidens were surrounded.

"Help! Indians!" the flaxen-haired maiden cried. "Save us from the unspeakable predations of these pitiless fiends."

If anyone was there in that desolate canyon to hear the maiden's fervent entreaty, their rejoinder was not immediately forthcoming.

The Indians had no intention of retreating. They held forth with visages of the fiercest description. One carried a hefty, misshapen club of a dubious, ruddy coloration. Matters could not remain thus stationary for any appreciable length of time.

The flaxen-haired maiden cast about with a blind urgency not unlike that of a drowning woman. She sought to grasp hold of any nearby object that might serve as a crude weapon. Her frantic hand fell upon a small rock, and she clutched the rock in her fist and brandished it wildly back and forth in a semi-circle toward the ever-encroaching Indians.

The first Indian who had lain in wait against the boulder was now crouching to the left of the maidens. With the speed of a serpent, he dodged the rock-wielding maiden and reached deftly to the girdle round his waist. He drew an obsidian knife from its sheath and held it with practiced ease low at his side. The black blade glinted in the sun.

Upon seeing the obsidian blade, the flaxen-haired maiden ceased flailing about with the stone and commenced to trembling from head to toe. Unable longer to endure the shock and horror visited upon her, she fell back fainting and unconscious against the raven-haired maiden, who was much perturbed.

The Indians seized upon their advantage. The largest Indian among the three stepped over the flaxen-haired maiden and laid his hand firmly on the wrist of the raven-haired maiden. He thrust his face close to that of the maiden who had cast her gaze askance in the vain hope that her captors would somehow return to the stygian pits whence they surely had crawled.

The Indian reached toward her neck and lifted the quartz pendant from her bodice. He held the figure of the small, white snake delicately between his fingers and inspected it closely. He uttered strange words in his harsh tongue, and the maiden felt his fetid breath hot against her cheek. She slowly turned her face toward the waking nightmare beside her and forced herself to meet with a forthright steadiness the red-skinned savage's bestial gaze.

To her surprise, she found there not the eyes of the monster she had conjured, but rather eyes uncanny in their ordinariness. In truth, they were eyes not so very different from her own. For a fleeting moment, they shared something inchoate, a hovering curiosity. She held his gaze and tried to shape what was to come despite knowing that it would all too quickly resolve into an intolerable vulnerability, some pale underbelly, the one missing scale.

Thinking: *After the intravenous tessellation? The linen-white attainder? The chemo? The neuroplasty? What then? What happens next?*

The Indian with the obsidian blade drew close beside her, and, as she had known all along, the moment was lost. He seized her hair and yanked her head back exposing the soft of her comely neck. She sank to her knees. The third Indian loomed over her, and she saw now that he held a hatchet in his hand. The big Indian still held her arm in a grip tight as a vise. The first Indian raised the obsidian blade and held it poised above the quick of her neck, the sharp edge glinting in the sun. His cruel lips spoke strange words, and she fixed her eyes on the clear, cerulean sky.

Asking: *What happens next? What happens next? What happens next?*

"Stay your blade, you bloodthirsty cur," a booming voice thundered, and a brawny hand reached out and seized the

Indian's forearm and abruptly arrested the terrible arc of the obsidian blade.

A new figure had arrived to engage with the Indian brutes, and the course of the skirmish was perforce greatly altered. A strapping figure in buckskin had seized the Indian with the obsidian blade and was tossing him to and fro as if he were nothing more than a rag doll filled with straw.

The two Indians who had heretofore bedeviled the raven-haired maiden were filled with dismay, and the maiden dared entertain the hope that a brave paladin had come in all due haste to deliver her from the loathsome villainy of her wicked oppressors.

With tremendous force, the big man in buckskin launched the bewildered Indian through the air towards the canyon wall. The Indian struck against the rocky surface with such force as to render a man insensate. The big man in buckskin rounded on the two Indians beside the maiden and in two great strides came close enough to grapple with his over-matched foes. He grasped the awestruck Indians round the neck, one in the crook of each of his mighty arms, and knocked their heads together with a resounding thump. The Indians fell stunned to the ground and staggered back from the vigorous onslaught of the big man in buckskin.

The man leaned forward to address the red-skinned savages.

"Best turn tail and run, you wretches. And when you recollect this day and speak of it to others, know that it was Kit Carson that spared yer miserable hides."

The Indians' mouths fell agape and their eyes grew wide with amazement. They cowered in a manner most unbecoming and stumbled away in their haste to turn and flee from the big man in buckskin.

"Go on and git!" Kit Carson said with a dismissive wave of his stout arm.

The Indians hied away into the enfolding arms of the vast, unknown wilderness, and Kit Carson watched their retreat with narrowed, flinty eyes.

The flaxen-haired maiden was still aswoon, and the raven-haired maiden knelt by her side and endeavored to comfort her fallen companion. Kit Carson moved to join the raven-haired maiden, but as he came closer, with an unexpected suddenness, the Indian with the obsidian blade resumed his attack.

The Indian had recovered from the earlier encounter, and stepping swift on silent soles, the crafty Indian came now with deadly intent at Kit from behind. The Indian leapt from the concealment of the nearby rocks and raised high the obsidian blade to strike a killing blow.

How Kit Carson sensed the Indian's cowardly assault is as unknowable as the Eluesinian mysteries. Perhaps it was a premonitory zephyr blowing soft against his nape. Or perhaps it was the ineffable play of light and shadow dancing at the edges of his perception that alerted him to the Indian's evil presence. Or perhaps it was some innate goodness ever vigilant at the vital core of his mighty, beating heart. Who can say? For us, dear reader, the answer is obscured, and it must be enough for now to know that Kit Carson somehow sensed the Indian's treacherous debouch and lived to tell the tale.

While the Indian with the obsidian blade was still in the midst of his leap, Kit spun around and met the other in midair and dealt him a mighty blow that laid him prostrate to the ground. Kit then vaulted over the other, and a pitched battle ensued. Kit suffered the other to rise properly, then rained a multitude of swift, heavy blows down upon the other's head, neck and shoulders, uttering at the same time vociferous maledictions and adroitly frustrating the other's feeble endeavors to seize hold.

Now, Kit Carson was not a man given to the quick dispensation of death. Indeed, if the truth be known, he had a grudging respect for the physical bravery of the Indian warriors with whom he had tangled on occasion in the past. But circumstances had answered the last of any charitable doubt. Kit knew the Indian before him sought an honorable exit. Kit pinned down the Indian's weapon, drew his knife from its sheath and thrust the sharp tip deep into the Indian's beating heart.

Once he was sure the Indian had breathed his last breath, Kit cleaned his knife and returned to the side of the flaxen-haired maiden. He splashed water from his canteen on her ashen face. The maiden's blue eyes fluttered open, and she quickly came back to her senses.

"We are rescued," she exclaimed, a hand at her bosom. She gazed up adoringly at the tall, broad-shouldered man in the fine-tanned buckskin hunting frock.

"To whom do we own our everlasting gratitude?" she asked in a voice at once both astonished and demure.

"They call me Kit Carson."

"The famous mountain man?" she exclaimed. "With the strength of a grizzly bear? Who vanquished a dozen Indians with but a single blow?"

Kit laughed his hearty, booming laugh, and his great, white teeth gleamed in his round, ruddy face. He doffed his ring-tailed cap and inclined his head, displaying a shock of thick, brown curls.

"Lady, I am but a humble trapper."

"I know personally several red-skinned savages who might disagree," the flaxen-haired maiden quipped, struggling to arise.

Kit stooped down and placed one strong arm beneath the lady and gently raised her to her feet.

The raven-haired maiden stood silently aside, a witness to all that transpired.

"By what stroke of good fortune did such a humble trapper as you come to find us so wanting and in need of protection in this hard and barren hinterland?" the flaxen-haired maiden asked gamely, as she steadied herself against the burly man's arm.

A dark cloud passed over Kit's jovial face.

"Word came to the garrison at Taos," Kit said in a serious tone. "We pursued them from Point of Rocks past Tucumcari. After we found their encampment, I tracked you here."

Kit paused.

He frowned and rested his hand reassuringly on the hilt of his big knife. He looked then discreetly at the raven-haired maiden standing so quietly behind. His sharp eyes glimpsed the quartz pendant carved in the shape of a circular serpent hanging round her neck. The raven-haired maiden turned subtly, shifting away from the mountain man's eyes.

"Something scared those Indians like nothing I ever seen," Kit said, shaking his head. "Two of them had their throats slit from ear to ear, and the rest had run off and high-tailed it toward the river."

The flaxen-haired maiden turned, and she looked at the raven-haired maiden. The raven-haired maiden said nothing, and her face was as if cut from stone. The flaxen-haired maiden looked at the ground near her feet.

"We fled. Into the night," the flaxen-haired maiden said softly.

She looked up into Kit's trusting eyes. Her lip began to tremble.

"There was naught else we could do."

He placed a comforting arm around her shoulders.

"Do not be troubled, good lady. I give little credence to

the superstitious vexations of the addled Indian mind," Kit said and glanced over his shoulder at the raven-haired maiden. He tried to read the expression on her face, but her face was impassive and inscrutable, and she showed him nothing in her outward appearance that would indicate the substance of her inner thoughts.

"You ladies are welcome to accompany me," Kit said brightening considerably. "I am expected at the Rendezvous to the North. We will find shelter and sustenance at Fort Bent four or five days hence, and there you may secure safe passage onward."

Then Kit placed his coon-skin cap back atop his flowing hair and raised one mighty arm and gestured expansively toward the horizon.

"Good faith and fair dealing!" Kit exclaimed, and his cheeks were ruddy, and his teeth glinted in the sun.

He turned back to the two maidens.

"I will show you the way," he said

Gratitude and admiration glistened in the upturned eyes of the flaxen-haired maiden.

"Our fearless protector! Thank you, Kit Carson. We will long remember this good deed and bear witness to others of your stout arm and your brave heart."

2

A PLUME OF BLACK SMOKE drifted eastward across the sky. Towards the river, the smoke grew diffuse, and the wind took the last of it, and the sun shone through with a weak, brown light. Where the fire still burned, the smoke billowed skyward in thick, black gouts. Cinders and ash had tinted the yucca blossoms pale blue.

Two men stood at some distance upwind from the fire. The larger of the two wore an oilcloth duster. The smaller man wore a muslin poncho. The man in the duster held a charred book in his hands and was reading aloud to the smaller man. They leaned in close over the open book, their heads bowed together, hatless, almost touching. The man with the book spoke in a deep, clear voice, and the man in the poncho listened closely.

"Gratitude and admiration glistened in the upturned eyes of the flaxen-haired maiden.

" 'Our fearless protector! Thank you, Kit Carson. We will long remember this good deed and bear witness to others of your stout arm and your brave heart.' "

The man in the duster stopped reading. The man in the poncho looked up at him.

"What happens next?"

The man in the duster closed what was left of the blackened pages.

"I can't make it out," the man in the duster said.

The man in the poncho took the charred book in his small hands and looked again closely at the cover. On the cover was a four-color illustration. A tall man in a coon-skin cap and fringed buckskin was thrusting a large knife toward a band of frightened Indians. The Indians wore feathers on their heads and their faces were painted with garish shades of red and white and green. Within the seared edges of the pages, the big letters of the title were still legible: Kit Carson and the Mountain of Gold.

"So that's supposed to be me," the small man in the poncho said.

The man in the duster smiled a wry smile.

"It's just a fiction, Kit. Like a campfire story."

The small man in the poncho put on his broad-brimmed, felt hat and looked to the west. The high mountains were lead-colored, and shadows were moving across the surface of the earth. The man in the poncho watched the play of light and shadow on the land. The deserts and mountains and mesas seemed to drift in an out of the sunlight, and it appeared as if they were constantly being reformed and recolored, as if, beyond the next rise, the whole world, everything, was fluid and insubstantial.

The small man in the poncho nodded his head toward the fire behind them.

"Ask those two about their fearless protector."

On the ground near the smoldering ruins behind them were the blackened skeletons of two human bodies. Even from a distance, it was clear they had been tied to the ground and had burned alive. The structures of the trading post around them and all they had held had burned almost entirely to the ground. Great cedar beams, ox-drawn from the mountains, the fire had rendered to ash. Only blackened adobe heaps and the crushed shell of an oven remained.

The man in the duster adjusted the round lenses of the spectacles on his nose.

"It's actually rather ironic. In a perverse sort of way."

The man in the poncho turned and looked at him. His eyes were set deep and in shadow beneath the brim of his hat.

"Spare me the lecture, Professor," the man in the poncho said without emotion.

He spat in the dirt.

"Let's get those bodies in the ground while we've still got daylight."

*   *   *

They rode for a day to the red mesa. The wind shifted, and a line of dark clouds massed along the horizon. The horses watched with rolling eyes and listened with pricked ears. The sky was with them then like a third rider, and the man in the duster spoke to the sky as if it might answer. The man in the poncho, Kit Carson, said nothing, but, like the horses, he turned his eyes often to the changing sky.

When they reached the mission, the wind was blowing hard, and something metal in the distance was pealing like a bell. The horses were skittish, and Kit talked to them in a soothing voice and stroked their necks, and they settled down once they reached the stable.

The rain began and beat down without mercy. Reddish-brown water filled the arroyos and ran down the ruts in the road. They walked on weary legs through the mud to the old rectory. It was dark now, and the light of a lamp filled the square window of the low, flat adobe house.

The old woman met them at the rectory door, a lamp in one hand. Stooped and gray beneath a dark shawl, she stood in the doorway and stopped them with an open palm.

She pointed a bony finger at their muddy boots.

"Take those off."

The Franciscans had built their church on a sandstone bluff near fresh water. The people living in the pueblos and the nomads from the plains had relied on the water for a thousand years or more. A long succession of priests had come and gone, some more violently than others, and it often seemed as though the mission had survived more in the defiance of any authority, earthly or otherwise. The parishioners were again awaiting the arrival of a new priest. Their ostensible leader, a novice friar, was bedridden.

Inside the rectory, Kit and the Professor sat on benches at a table built from piñon pine. The surface of the table had been dressed with a hatchet. It was uneven and showed the marks from the edge of the blade, but it was a sturdy table. The smooth adobe walls were washed white with lime, and the oil lamp on the table cast shadows across the rounded ceiling. Against one wall, a votive candle burned on a pine shelf altar beneath a carved retablo of the Virgin Mary.

In the shadows, a large green parrot perched high atop a wooden stand. It watched them, occasionally cocking its head or shifting subtly on its clawed feet. The parrot had roosted there in the rectory since before Kit had come for the first time, since before even the earliest memory of the old woman, who remembered more than anyone.

It was said the parrot had been carried on long trails over high mountains from far south of the Rio Grande and had been a gift from the people of a nearby pueblo to one of the first priests at the mission. That priest was long dead and the pueblo all but abandoned, but the parrot had somehow persisted, living on in the rectory, passed from each new priest to the next.

The old woman poured hot chicory coffee into clay mugs and set them before the men. She drew back a blanket hanging over a doorway and stepped into the soft lamp light of the next room. As the blanket closed over the doorway, the men glimpsed a plain pallet and, beneath the covers, the shape of the bedridden man.

The old woman spoke softly and said little. She possessed a furious energy, and her wiry limbs and spotted, veined hands seemed to be in constant motion. Her dour, wrinkled, brown face bore the scars of the pox. Immune, she found herself often at the side of the dying. She had seen many people perish over the years.

The Professor had fallen uncharacteristically silent. The formidable old woman and the ill man in the adjoining room had subdued him.

The flame from the lamp illuminated their faces. The Professor had a bald head and a blunt, round face. The round lenses of his spectacles reflected the lamp's wavering flame. Kit, the smaller man, had delicate, freckled features. His reddish hair was thin and wispy on top. His eyes were sunken deep within their sockets.

The old woman emerged from behind the blanket. She stood next to them at the table, arms akimbo, and looked at Kit.

Kit opened his leather saddle bag and ferreted out an object wrapped in thick felt. He set it on the uneven table and carefully unfolded the square of felt.

"Ah," the old woman said softly.

At the center of the square of felt was a milky-colored figurine. It was carved from quartz in the shape of a serpent in a circle holding its tail in its mouth.

The old woman carefully picked it up between the tips of her thumb and middle finger and held it close beside the sconce of the lamp. Her dark eyes were cloudy with gray cataracts, and she inspected the figurine for long moments, turning it to catch all the details of its surface in the light of the flame.

The old woman looked to Kit and nodded. Kit folded up the felt and put it back in his leather bag. The old woman took the figurine, drew back the blanket covering the doorway and left them alone.

Kit and the Professor drank from their cups and listened to the sound of the rain falling on the roof.

Then the parrot spoke.

"Penicillium notatum."

The two men turned slowly and looked at the parrot. The parrot bobbed its antic head and subtly shifted its hooked beak. The flame from the lamp glittered in the bird's large, dark eyes. It seemed to be amused.

Kit looked at the Professor.

"What the hell was that?" Kit said.

The Professor shrugged.

"Latin?"

They turned back to the bird and waited.

The parrot cocked its head.

The old woman came back into the room. She was carrying a basin and towels.

The parrot squawked an unintelligible syllable, and the old woman looked at the parrot with her cloudy eyes.

She turned to the two men.

"Wash up," she said, nodding at the basin and towels.

After they had washed, she placed clay bowls on the uneven table and poured more coffee. The bowls held goat cheese, dried apricots and cold corn bread. The stooped old woman stood with her arms akimbo looking down at them with her cloudy almost blind eyes and waited until they bowed their heads to pray.

The two men ate and drank quietly. Rain drummed on the roof, and the old woman's shadow lurched across the ceiling. The two men stole curious glances over their shoulders at the parrot, and the parrot watched them with dark, antic eyes.

*   *   *

Weeks later, in Washington D.C., Kit picked up the charred book and looked again at the cover. Kit Carson and the Mountain of Gold. He could recognize the letters of his own name, but the rest of the letters on the page were like strange glyphs drawn on the face of a boulder.

Kit regretted his illiteracy, but it did not shame him. There were other fluencies. For many years, the best map of the territory between Santa Fe and the Pacific Ocean could be found only in the mind and memory of Kit Carson.

Kit set the book aside on the table and watched the Professor as he finished chewing the last bite of their porterhouse steaks. The hotel restaurant wait staff weaved smoothly across emerald-colored carpeting between the linen-covered tables. A murmur of conversation came from the fashionably dressed people seated around the room. A bright chandelier hung from a rococo ceiling. A mirror reflected rows of bottles behind the dark walnut and polished brass of a long, crowded bar.

"So this man earns his livelihood writing these . . . fantasies?" Kit said.

His red hair was slicked back. His little ears stuck out, scrubbed and pink.

The Professor wiped his mouth with a linen napkin.

His round, bald head seemed comfortable above a starched

collar. Kit thought he looked like an otter. Friendly. But shrewd. With sharp teeth.

"No stranger than a trapper who profits from the sale of beaver pelts," the Professor said.

Kit nodded his head.

"I'd hate to see those poor folks in Paris go bare-headed," he said with a quick smile.

The Professor laughed.

A member of the wait staff, a woman with raven-dark hair, emerged from the bustle of the dining room and hovered at the Professor's elbow, poised to remove the china plate. The Professor glanced at the woman's face, and, for an instant, their eyes met. The Professor seemed to recognize the raven-haired woman. Her face remained impassive.

The raven-haired woman gracefully took the plate and withdrew with downcast eyes. She carried a round tray balanced on the fingertips of one hand. The Professor turned his head and watched from the corner of his eye as she receded into the interior of the crowded restaurant. The Professor turned back to Kit and was silent.

"Friend of yours?" Kit said.

The Professor drummed his fingers on the table top.

"No," he said.

An abrupt smile filled his blunt features. He seized the wine bottle and poured burgundy into their glasses.

He held his glass up.

"What shall we drink to?"

Kit thought for a moment.

Kit picked up the charred book.

"Words," Kit said.

"To words," the Professor said.

Kit tossed the book on the table, picked up his glass, touched it softly to the Professor's glass, and they drank.

Kit watched the rivulets of wine collect at the bottom of the glass.

"Words . . ." Kit said.

He set the wine glass on the table.

"My first wife was Arapaho," Kit said.

He looked at the Professor

"Did you know that?" Kit asked.

"No."

"She taught me her words. Her people's words."

The Professor listened closely. He laced his fingers together and rested his hands on the table.

"It was like seeing a new country," Kit said. "A new world."

"You understand them. Her people."

"I respect them."

"And they trust you."

"Perhaps."

Kit paused.

"It is an ugly business," Kit said.

The Professor sighed.

"Ugly indeed for those two dead women."

Kit nodded.

He picked up the charred book and held it up where the Professor could see its cover and the four-color illustration of the coon-skinned figure and the cowering Indians.

"This . . . don't help."

"Just a tall tale, Kit. A fable."

"I've told tall tales. I never got paid for them."

Kit tossed the book on the table.

"How many people have read this? A dozen? A hundred?"

"Whole cities, my friend," the Professor said.

"These words . . . My wife would be ashamed. These

words are the wrong words. People will take this as fact."

"What would you have written instead? Dry history?"

"That's my name right there on the front for all to see, but inside, what you read . . ."

Kit shook his head. His voice was soft but steady.

"No sir," he said. "That ain't my story."

"Artistic license."

Kit frowned.

"Look here, Professor. You've studied in the universities. What does the law say on this?"

The Professor leaned back in his chair and steepled his blunt fingers.

"You cannot stop it, Kit. You may advance an argument in a court of law, but I fear you will not have much success. They are businessmen. You cannot stop the course of commerce. It is like the river in spring."

"Progress," Kit said.

"Indeed," the Professor said.

The Professor poured the last of the wine into their glasses.

"Drink with me, Kit."

The Professor raised his glass.

"It is an exciting time to be alive."

*   *   *

That night Kit rested his head on a down-filled pillow, and he dreamed. He dreamed of the fastnesses of the canyon and the last unconquered remnant. He dreamed of towering walls of red sandstone and hidden fields of corn and sheep grazing beneath the cottonwoods. He dreamed of the cool waters of the unfailing spring and the peach trees on the terraced slope and bees thrumming in the shade near the ground where the heavy fruit had fallen. He dreamed of the inaccessible white houses set in caverns in the face of the high cliffs which were older than history which no living man had entered. He dreamed of the last unconquered remnant and the stream of the survivors and their faces as they passed.

3

THE PROFESSOR STOPPED READING and looked up from the pages of the manuscript. He adjusted the round lenses of the spectacles on his nose. The students were sitting in their various postures in their usual seats around the long oak table.

Each year's class arrived at an unspoken agreement regarding seating usually by the second or third meeting, and they more or less stuck to it for the rest of the semester. By the last class, each student, even the quiet ones, had so inhabited their seat around the table, strewn with their bookbags and scarves and coats, they each left a presence that persisted like a ghost. When the time came to mark down final grades, which the Professor did reluctantly and only because the University required it, he could sit in the empty classroom and look to each empty chair and see the faces and feel somehow the personalities as if the most recent class were still gathered around the table.

Some, like Robert, were always reliably present, hanging on his every utterance. Some, like Marcel, would fade in and out, their eyes glazing over as they mentally wandered away. Some, like Zach, by the end of class, were in a visible struggle to maintain consciousness.

When he began teaching, the other teachers had often remarked that the students never age, and as he watched his own classes gather and disperse year after year, it did seem that only he among them was growing older. It made for a heavy yoke, he told his tenured friends, but each year's fresh faces still filled him with anticipation and hope and yearning. There were always a few students who set themselves apart for one reason or another, whether it was an affinity for putting words on the page or some other interesting aspect of their character. They kept his writer's antennae busy invisibly twitching above his bald head, and it was still a joy for him to discover each of them as they revealed themselves, from the first day when they filed in and selected a seat, until the last day at the farewell dinner at his home.

The Professor looked back to the typed pages of the manuscript before him on the long oak table and continued reading.

"He dreamed of the inaccessible white houses set in caverns in the face of the high cliffs which were older than history which no living man had entered. He dreamed of the last unconquered remnant and the stream of the survivors and their faces as they passed."

He ceased speaking, and the sound of his voice faded, and a silence filled the small white room with the narrow windows.

"So," he said and looked to the students around the long, oak table.

*   *   *

The Professor's seminar was titled "Writing the Long Narrative" but could be more accurately titled "Listening to the Long Narrative" and, by long narrative, Marcel meant, at this point in the semester, almost without exception, *The Iliad*, which, first of all, is an epic poem and definitely not a novel, and, second of all, she, Marcel, like the ten or twelve other students who, in various states of alertness, might, at the appointed time each week, fill the unforgiving wooden chairs spaced randomly around the long oak table in the small white room with the narrow windows, she, like the others, had submitted her writing sample to the Professor many months before — a story she had written in high school about an old boyfriend and their mutual cynicism in the face of the conformity and the hypocrisy and what, at the time, had seemed like, well, yes, the horror, really, of growing up in a small midwestern town — had submitted it carefully typed with a fresh ribbon with her roommate's typewriter on the bonded stationary she brought from home, sealed with saliva and glue tasting of ritual and adulthood, of college applications and invitations and thank you notes, on her knees submitted in a plain brown envelope beneath his office door, launched across the tiled floor into what was then unseen and unimagined with trembling hands on her knees and then a quiet moment after, standing, to tamp down the rising fear, her words offered on her knees not to hear a weekly recitation of *The Iliad*, but because she believed she had something important to say, and not just about her sad old boyfriend and their benighted small town, but because Winston Straw, Winston Straw, because she wanted to study writing with Winston Straw, who was not just a successful novelist but also a sort of cultural hero, an icon, a legend, really, Winston Straw, with the criminal prosecution and his exoneration, or as he would say, vindication, and perhaps that was the problem, the root, as it were, of what seemed to Marcel like a sort of deception when in class so often it seemed they sat listening to the Professor reading, reciting, in that deep, mesmerizing voice, *The Iliad*, which, frankly, Marcel had come to loathe, *The Iliad*, especially when they could be spending more class time in critique of each other's work, and, yes, specifically, of her work, which Professor Straw only allowed, strategically it seemed, the time devoted to critique, toward the end of class when her mind had started to wander, falling behind the dusty ranks of Greek warriors and their gleaming shields and pikes, and outside the narrow windows the autumn leaves were spiraling down, and the Professor's voice had lost all meaning, and she heard the words without understanding, and her classmates in the seats around her seemed to fade away, and the Professor's voice carried her away to those solitary hours sitting on the cool tile floor in the empty hall outside the door waiting for the precious minutes of one-on-one criticism, just the two of them, expectant, alone, sitting in the hushed white room with the light from the narrow windows and her thin manuscript before him on the long oak table.

*   *   *

"I liked the verbs."

"All of them?"

"The ones when they're doing something active in the natural world. Here, I wrote them down."

"Ach. You always write them down."

"I think there's an interstitial playfulness that has intimations of the Kantian sublime."

"Uh . . ."

"Like reconnoiter. I love that."

"I'm not sure what the author's trying to do."

"Reconnoiter is very specific, but it conveys a whole world of information."

"I agree. It's kind of muddled."

"Kant wrote about an epistemological category that was inexpressible."

"Uh . . ."

"Is there more?"

"Yeah, what comes next?"

"Maybe that's the point. The nested stories could go on and on."

"Ad infinitum."

"Ad nauseam."

"And pealing. Like a bell. That's beautiful."

"Then it's just a gimmick, a distraction."

"More style than substance."

"Same thing. Style. Substance."

"Not for me."

"Or me."

"And ferret. That was a good one."

"I like the writing, but I think the nesting would be very hard to sustain in a lengthy piece like a novel."

"As Kant observed —"

"It would definitely be hard to develop the characters."

"Characters? Please."

"Maybe the author is deliberately trying to draw attention to the artificiality of the narrative."

"And thrumming. That was good."

"Maybe the author is just lazy and is using scraps to sew a crazy quilt."

"Maybe the author is forcing the reader to deal with the radical contingency of language."

"Yeah, but murder? Racism? Misogyny? Those are real."

"Wait —"

"Colonialism? Genocide? That's historical."

"The sublime —"

"I agree. This isn't satire from what we've got so far. It's not a farce per se. I don't think it works."

"Ach. There's blood in the water."

"Just being honest."

"Circle the wagons!"

"The fact that Kit Carson is an historical figure does make it harder to read this as just an exercise in technique."

"I mean, people are still arguing about Kit Carson, right?"

"But that's the point."

"Kant —"

"No, it isn't."

"Wait . . ."

". . ."

". . ."

"I liked some of the adjectives, too."

*　　*　　*

Marcel heard the party before she saw it. The crowd had already spilled out the front door and was backing up onto the front porch. Behind the darkened windows, the interior of the house seemed to seethe and throb. A cacophony of voices roiled above the relentless beat of the music. The sound grew larger as she approached, and suddenly she was within it, and the bass from the huge stereo speakers made her body vibrate all the way into her bones and her crotch and her brain, and her ears tightened, and she knew they would be buzzing the next day, and faces came at her in blurred waves, and she noticed how hot it was and how she was beginning to perspire, and the room smelled of stale beer and sweat and lust, and she wanted a drink, and someone she did not know and did not want to know was yodeling something incomprehensible in her ear, and she began to elbow her way through a swirling tumult of hawaiian shirts, bare torsos, blue plastic cups, zinc-oxide noses, and cheap plastic leis. A styrofoam surf board struck a glancing blow on her head. Bamboo fronds slapped her and other oblivious young men and women in the face as they passed through a large doorway. The bamboo stalks had been spirited away with faces burnt-cork black under cover of night from the grove in the University president's back yard. Much of the bamboo had found its way to the floor where it had been trampled into a gooey, beer-soaked mush.

I come in peace, Marcel thought. *I mean you no harm.*

A theme party was meant to be a dignified affair, a step up from the so-called cattle drives which were designed primarily to facilitate young men and their careful appraisal of recently matriculated first-year women. Marcel herself had participated in a cattle drive. She remembered it now like something embarrassing from her distant childhood. In her memories, she glided through it all unscathed with a serene, ironic detachment. She still marveled at her peers' ability to devise insidious catherine wheels of intoxication out of the most innocuous objects — dice, funnels, ping pong balls, bottle caps, quarters.

Within a large room, at the clustered center of an ersatz polynesian village, the beer kegs weighed. Petite, blond women in grass skirts eyed Marcel nervously. They smiled at her with lips stained kool-ade-red from cups of germicidal grain punch. One woman was wearing fruit on her head like Carmen Miranda. She could be seen from any point in the room. Her headdress was listing badly.

A group of bodies crowded around one of several small bars. A large, inflatable shark suspended from the ceiling was slowly succumbing to gravity. Brown, sticky goo was solidifying on the sides of several abandoned blenders. Behind the bar, a young, bare-chested man in a grass skirt was whacking coconuts with what proved to be a very sharp machete. He paused long enough to catch his breath and announce, *We're out of daiquiri mix*, and resumed whacking the round, brown coconuts. Behind him was a trash can full of coconuts. White coconut halves had tumbled into piles around his feet.

Somehow a cup of beer found its way into her hand, and she was speaking words to a boy that might have been a conversation in the language they spoke on the curious island on which he dwelt. She began to wonder how exactly she had come to be marooned on this uncharted, beer-soaked shore. What strange winds had blown her so far off course.

Then she saw Robert across the room.

"What is it?" the boy said and turned to look over his shoulder.

"Nothing," Marcel said, but she was squelching laughter and smirked with the side of her mouth.

Robert, steady Robert, with his square jaw and his square toes, his serious face and his solemn voice, Robert with his knee-high white tube socks and his shirt tucked neatly in his shorts, Robert with his near-to-bursting red book bag the size of a small refrigerator on his back marching off to the library, Robert who paused to remove his wire-frame glasses before he kissed her, Robert who cracked the joints in his ankles after the first time they made love. She could not but laugh now at the sight of him, Robert, steady Robert, in a hawaiian shirt with a blue plastic cup full of warm beer, talking with that serious face in his solemn voice, and the boy in the grass skirt was whacking the coconuts, and the petite blond girls were smiling, and the music was thumping within the darkness of the house, and she smirked again with the side of her mouth.

She drank the rest of her beer and held the empty cup where the boy in front of her — Sam or Seth or something — could see it and smiled into his restless, narrow-set eyes. He had been braying in her ear something about a constitution, French Polynesia, American Samoa. The braying ceased, and he took the empty cup from her outstretched hand.

He smiled, tentative, with red, wet lips.

"Will you be here when I come back?" he shouted.

"Of course . . ." she said, feigning surprise.

She paused, wavering.

"Maybe . . ." she said.

She sighed and shook her head.

"No," she said and offered an apologetic shrug and walked away.

She weaved through the crowd until Robert saw her, and they looked at each other for an instant with the bodies passing between them, and she turned and began to tack her way out of the room.

She stumbled into some inner sanctum where three young men were mixing up another bucket of grain punch. They were pouring in the grain alcohol and kool-ade and stirring it with the handle end of a broom. All three stopped and stared at her as if she had stumbled into the middle of a solemn ritual. They saw her looking at the broom, and one of them said, *Don't worry, the grain'll kill the germs*, and they started laughing. Not knowing what else to do, Marcel joined their laughter and slowly backed out of the room.

She found another place, ignored and almost hidden, beyond the bar with the inflatable shark. Bamboo stalks festooned the doorway and the walls. Inside, there was a small hot tub flanked by two small plastic wading pools filled with sand. In one corner, a stuffed, green parrot perched awkwardly atop a battered, wooden coat stand. One of the wading pools had split open and was leaking sand onto the floor. A few coconuts bobbed in the swirling bubbles of the hot tub's water. The air was unbearably warm and stuffy and smelled somehow of lavender and pine. Marcel thought it looked like a department store window display.

Someone had placed rickety card tables in the middle of

the sand-filled wading pools. At the center of one card table was a framed black-and-white photograph, a portrait of a toothy man with a crew cut. Marcel almost laughed out loud. The man in the photo exuded an almost comic sense of probity and rectitude. A halo of white sand dollars was glued around the edge of the picture frame. Arranged around the portrait on the card table were two large conch shells, several starfish and smaller seashells. The table was illuminated by several fat, scented candles.

Marcel stepped closer to the card table. Something about the man with the crew cut seemed familiar, but she could not place him. She watched the wavering candle flames. The beat from the music thudded dully somewhere behind her, and the floor shuddered regularly like a bowling alley. *What could possibly go wrong*, she thought, ironic. She licked her fingers and began to pinch out the flames.

On the other card table amid more fat, burning candles was a velvety pedestal on which rested a curious carved figurine. Marcel picked it up and held it close to the flame. It was carved from quartz, pale like the moon, in the shape of a serpent in a circle with its tail in its mouth. She turned it in the candlelight. She could see the scales along the serpent's body, the tiny eyes carved on each side of its triangular head.

Robert came through the bamboo fronds into the stuffy lavender-pine scented air. Marcel put the snake figurine back on the little pedestal and pinched out the last of the candles. Steady Robert stood beside her and looked down at the card table.

She smiled to herself.

"Wanna dance?"

In the throng with the others, they danced, sweating, until their hair was plastered to their foreheads. The music was familiar, reliable. Funk, mostly, with a beat that shook the building. Songs like Burn Rubber, Super Freak, Flashlight. Dancing was freedom, freedom from chemistry labs and thesis papers, from job interviews and medical school applications, from parents and friends, from the future, from life, from being.

Then the music stopped mid-song, and the dancing ceased, and they stood in the abrupt silence. Steady Robert found his handkerchief and blew his nose. The sound of voices rose from a murmur to a steady grousing din, and then there was the sound of a turntable needle dropping on record vinyl. Some well-intentioned person was playing a song from an album.

They waited, silent now, sweat trickling down their bodies. They listened, and a lush orchestral swell began to play, and then *Bali Hi is calling, Bali Hi* from the huge stereo speakers facing the expectant crowd, and it lasted just long enough to penetrate their heads and reach into their brains. A huddle of distressed young men bolted out of the crowd, and seconds later the speakers jumped with the seismic rumble of a turntable needle ripping across record vinyl followed almost immediately by the deafening throb of the dance music, and the dancing resumed, slowly at first and then with a near frenzy.

Zach and the strange, red-haired girl Marcel had dubbed Pippi Longstocking came swimming out of the dancing throng and accosted them. Zach was glassy-eyed and wore a cardboard pirate hat from a fast-food restaurant, and his long brown hair was hanging loose around his face, and they began to dance together gleefully, Steady Robert, Marcel, Zach and Pippi, with their arms around each other, stumbling against the crowd, and Zach started singing, started bellowing, *Some Enchanted Evening*, and they were arm in arm, facing each other in a circle swaying together in the throng, and they were singing, *Once you have found her*, and then everyone was singing, and the whole room was singing, shouting, a drunken wordless chorus more or less in tune with Some Enchanted Evening.

*   *   *

Marcel looked at herself in the mirror. She pulled the fast-food pirate hat from the top of her head. Tangled hair. And not in a good way. Her face looked waxy. Like death warmed over. Scary, she thought. That's what her sister would say.

The restroom was filled with foul smelling smoke. Someone had thrown kerosene tiki torches in one of the commodes. The contents of someone's stomach had come to rest on the floor near a trash can in the corner. Marcel splashed cold water on her face. She looked at herself again, and thought about her sister and her parents and home.

When she came out of the restroom, she was still thinking about her parents and the work she had to do for her classes, and then she noticed a crumpled photograph among some debris against the wall. She picked it up and smoothed it out, and it was the black-and-white portrait of the toothy man with the crew cut. She recognized in the debris on the floor the remains of the rickety card table, the photo frame, the sand dollars, the scented candles. The man in the photo looked so familiar. She remembered the same restless, narrow-set eyes, remembered dimly someone telling her earlier that their father had drafted the constitution of some Pacific island principality and that was why they called it the founder's party, *Because of my Dad*. She had the urge to do something with the picture, to keep it because maybe someone wants it back. She looked at the photo and waited for some moment of clarity, but the longer she looked at it, the less certain she became. A wave of emotion had come over her. It was a drunken sort of sadness, sudden and inexplicable. Someone brushed past her on their way to the restroom. She carefully folded the photo and slipped it into her pocket and walked back to find her friends.

The crowd had thinned, and Some Enchanted Evening was blasting from the stereo speakers. Carmen Miranda was sitting against the wall, her fruit hanging limp from her head. The inflatable shark had completed its descent and was flattened and unrecognizable in a puddle of latex and beer. There was sand everywhere, and it crunched beneath her flip flops.

The bare-chested boy who had been chopping coconuts with the machete had passed out on a couch. His friends were carefully, lovingly balancing a small tower of objects on top of him. A male voice yelled, "Let's throw him in the hot tub." Zach and Pippi were gone. With a sense of relief, she saw Steady Robert waiting near the door.

*   *   *

Robert and Zach and Marcel each had a stretch of free time after the Professor's seminar, and on days when the sky was clear, they would walk down the fieldstone paths past the tremendous water oaks to the edge of campus and to the sagging, wooden steps at the back door of Old Grundy where the sun was warm, and they would sit on the steps and face the playing fields and watch the tiny clots of players in the distance, and inside Old Grundy, the dancers would be practicing, and they could hear the music, and the notes of the melody would begin and abruptly end and then begin again, and the leaves would come drifting down from the water oaks, and they would talk about writing and college and their classmates and the Professor.

They fell into an easy intimacy during those hours after the Professor's class. They could finish each other's sentences and trigger paroxysms of laughter with the arch of an eyebrow or a single, well-timed syllable. They began to speak that secret language, and Robert and Marcel were falling in love. Zach would stop talking sometimes and look at them, at their faces in profile in the late afternoon sun, and Marcel felt his eyes on her, but what Marcel did not sense, or perhaps what she chose to ignore, was that Zach was looking at them on those clear fall afternoons sitting on the sun-bleached steps, not with envy, but only with affection, with an overwhelming happiness, in his eyes.

"I need to tell you something," Zach said.

"Not again," Marcel groaned.

"Out with it," Robert said and gestured with his fingers toward his chest — come on — like they were fighting.

"Professor Straw wants to introduce me to his agent."

Robert, usually quick with a riposte, fell silent.

A faint cry carried from the playing fields.

Marcel raised her head from where it rested against the wooden steps behind her. She turned to Zach and peered over the top of her dark sunglasses. Her face slowly lit up, and she seized him by the shoulder.

"Seriously?" she said.

Robert was still processing the information, still taking it in, still watching the leaves drifting down from the water oaks.

"That's . . . that's huge," Marcel exclaimed.

She started shoving his shoulder until his head wagged back and forth, and he started grinning.

"When did he tell you?" Robert asked in his serious, just-the-facts-ma'am voice.

"At our last meeting."

"Your last piece was pretty amazing," Marcel said.

"It was . . ." Robert said, as if someone were arguing with him, as if he were conceding something, as if he wanted to add *and yet* but left it unspoken.

"We should celebrate," Marcel declared.

Zach demurred.

"Let's not get carried away," he said.

Marcel sat up and slapped her hands to her knees.

"And why not?" she said, brooking no dissent. "What better reason to get carried away?"

"She's right," Robert sighed.

"We should get totally carried away."

Robert massaged his forehead with the fingers of one hand.

"She's totally right," Robert said.

"We should get absolutely totally completely thoroughly and absurdly . . . carried away."

She had seized the crown and placed it firmly on her head.

"Straw is going to open doors for you," Robert said.

"I don't know . . ." Zach said.

"This is such a big deal," Marcel said, drumming her feet on the steps.

She threw her arm around Zach's neck.

"He's taking you under his wing. It's like the Winston Straw good fiction-writing seal of approval," she said.

"Mentor," Robert intoned, like a judge.

"We are so going to celebrate," Marcel said encircling him with her arms, hugging him tight.

"Mentor," Robert intoned again, poking Zach's leg with an index finger.

*   *   *

Winston Straw occupied a unique place in the University pecking order. Not a peer-reviewed scholar, not a doctor of philosophy, he was the writer-in-residence. He was a broadly-learned autodidact who could translate Greek and Latin — he had been working on a translation of *The Iliad* for years — but his credentials were mostly honorary. He was not the product of a fine arts program or a well-established workshop. His literary reputation rested on a smattering of essays, short stories, novels and a memoir. He had been categorized variously as a realist, a fabulist, a penitent, a prophet. The University had come to regard him as a sort of non-sectarian voice of conscience. Never a scold, he amused people, a genial bald man in a bow tie with his expressive hands and delicate, stubby fingers. He often punctuated his speech with an extended little finger, like a conductor's baton, leaving invisible curlicues floating in the air long after he finished talking. He had become an expected presence at official gatherings where he would speak in his deep, smooth voice and offer polite words and conjure ceremonial thoughts of work and love and memory and time. The circumstances of his earlier life had grown increasingly indistinct, living on in low murmurs in quiet corners of the faculty lounge, in soft whispers behind the cabinets of the card catalog.

* * *

Robert dribbled the basketball, got a step on Zach and drove past him for a lay-up. The ball dropped smoothly through the hoop. Robert returned to the top of the key and faced the basket. Zach retrieved the ball and tossed it to Robert.

"That shot was weak," Zach said.

"Kit Carson taught me that shot," Robert said.

Zach and Robert were playing a game of one-on-one in the Bubble. The Bubble was an old, neglected basketball court in the pine trees behind the business school. The surface was a slab of cracked pavement littered with brown pine needles. The white paint that had once outlined the boundaries of the court and the foul lanes was faded and barely visible. The hoops were bare metal and rusty brown. The old nets hung by their last few strands, frayed and dirty gray. The hoops and backboards were mounted on concrete slabs that arched over each end of the court. Someone had spray painted a jagged, red graffiti tag on the side of one of the arches. Zach and Robert had the Bubble all to themselves.

Zach and Robert had already played a game of full-court pick-up on one of the several crowded outdoor courts alongside the athletic field house. Zach and Robert had allied with three strangers and took to the court with all the evanescent confidence of an obvious underdog. Their opponents were a lean and hungry crew all of whom had played in high school. Zach and Robert's team was summarily dispatched. Their alliance, briefly undefeated, flew apart. Zach and Robert found they had little value as free agents. They congratulated themselves in subdued tones for at least getting a few shots off and trekked across campus to the Bubble for some one-on-one, which was what they had really wanted all along.

Robert and Zach had played organized sports in the years before college. Robert had played soccer, lettering his senior year. Zach had wrestled, losing in the state tournament to the eventual champion. It was an extracurricular activity, of course, one that filled a section of their application to the University, but Robert and Zach were not such cynical competitors. They both played baseball as boys and if asked would have said it was their favorite. When they had played basketball, it was usually in a neighbor's uneven driveway on goals mounted on the roof of the garage. And that was still how they liked to shoot hoops, the way they had played it in the driveways in their safe, middle-class neighborhoods in the lengthening shadows before dinner when that one big family began to ring their dinner bell and you knew your own mother would soon begin patiently to call you home.

Robert was a few inches taller. He wore a blinding, plain white tee shirt and tight green shorts and spotless tube socks pulled up to his knees. His thighs and upper arms were shockingly pale, like something that lived in a cave. He had a separate pair of glasses that he wore for basketball — black horned rims with an elastic strap. He kept his good pair of glasses off the court behind the concrete arch in a little pile with his enormous wristwatch, his brown leather wallet, his keys, rabbit's foot fob, and some pocket change.

Zach was heavier with broad shoulders and thick thighs and calves. He wore baggy, cut-off sweat pants and a pale-blue jersey that had been stained and discolored with splashes of undiluted bleach. The discolored jersey had been a careless laundry mishap, but Zach decided he liked the dreamy, cloudy way the discolored jersey looked, like a chest-shaped piece of the sky, and always wore it for basketball. He wore a dark blue bandanna tied around his head with his long brown hair tied back behind his neck.

Robert checked the ball with Zach and dribbled from hand to hand a few times facing Zach and the basket. Zach was wearing his game face. His eyes seemed to focus on a spot somewhere around Robert's waist. Robert took a few exploratory steps towards Zach, feinted a drive to his right towards the hoop, and then pulled up for an abrupt jump shot. The ball left his fingertips, spinning backwards, rising skyward, arcing on a trajectory towards the center of the rusty-brown metal hoop.

Zach was deceptively fast and could elevate. He leaped in front of Robert, stretched his arm above his head, fingers splayed against the sky, and swatted the shot out of the air. After a brief, stunned moment, Robert retrieved the loose ball.

"Kit Carson taught me that block," Zach said when Robert faced him again.

Robert gripped the basketball firmly with both hands. He felt the pebbled surface beneath his fingertips. A bead of sweat was hanging from the tip of his nose. Zach's eyes were on the ball. Robert wetted his lips. His square-jawed face hardened.

Robert put his head down, turned his shoulder to Zach and started to drive toward the hoop. Zach's eyes stayed on the ball, and he bodied up next to Robert, put one hand almost gently on the small of Robert's back and leaned hard against him. Zach's tennis shoes were sliding on the gravel and pine needles. Taking a charge was out of the question, totally disrespected, the sort of thing that could bring a pickup game to a disputatious standstill. They moved together as one for a moment across the court toward the goal. Robert muscled closer and prepared to take the shot, and as he positioned himself against Zach, he swung his arm around, and his elbow struck Zach in the face. Zach recoiled and covered his mouth with his hand. Robert continued sweeping toward the basket and finished. A soft baby hook shot. The ball boinked off the backboard and dropped smoothly through the hoop.

"Gah," Zach cried.

Zach removed his hand from his mouth and saw bright red running down his arm.

Robert spun around and saw the blood dripping from Zach's mouth.

"Carnage. Mayhem," Zach mumbled.

"Oh, man. My bad. My bad," Robert said.

Robert dropped the ball and rushed to Zach.

Zach spat out a mouthful of blood, wiped blood on his cloudy blue jersey.

"I've been tomahawked."

"Let me see."

Robert put one hand on his friend's shoulder and looked at Zach's bloody mouth. He made a pained expression.

"I gotta call this one," Robert said.

"TKO?"

"Yep. We're done."

*   *   *

Robert and Zach sat on the bench. The basketball was on the ground next to their feet. Zach was holding a towel full of ice against his lip.

"This feels like one of those moments," Robert said.

"Easy for you to say," Zach mumbled through numb, swollen lips.

"No, I'm serious. This is one of those moments you know you're going to remember."

"Couldn't we maybe pick another moment?"

"It's like in high school when everything is changing and you're leaving your friends and family, and there are these moments you know you'll remember, but you don't know how or why exactly because you don't know what's coming."

Zach took the towel from his mouth and turned and looked at Robert.

"What is wrong with you?" Zach said.

Robert looked at Zach and smiled a tight smile.

"Have you read Straw's memoir?" Robert asked.

"No. Why?"

Robert sighed.

"I read it. The whole thing. The summer before freshman year."

"Okay. Congratulations."

"I was working at my parents' country club. In Jersey. In the canteen by the pool . . . dressing hot dogs . . . toasting little pepperoni pizzas . . . fetching cold cans of soda and a straw for the freckled girls in their pastel tennis shorts . . ."

"Sounds nice."

"It was, I guess. There was this wooden stool in the shade, and when it was slow, I would sit in the shade and read. I think I read just about every book on the stupid summer reading list."

"Of course you did."

"But I also read the Professor's memoir."

"Goodbye to all that . . ."

Robert nodded.

It was the title of Straw's memoir. *Goodbye To All That: A Political Epitaph.*

"So, he writes about Smoothstone, right? The scandal. And that's what people remember. The Formula One crash, the congressional testimony —"

" 'Senator, I still can't program my VCR,' " Zach said, imitating the Professor's bass voice.

"Right. But he also wrote about his childhood in West Virginia. And, Zach, it's . . . it's the real thing. Like, solid. Like an anvil. He grew up poor in the Depression. He writes about working on his father's farm and . . . and the War. His father was illiterate. His mother wanted him to be a preacher, to . . . you know . . . hear the call. She fought for him so he could go to school. Literally came to blows. His brothers died in Europe. He tried to enlist. He was too young . . . too young to . . ."

Robert stopped.

Zach was watching Robert's profile. Robert was looking down at the ground, his face solemn and grave.

"I . . . I can't do it justice," Robert said.

They were silent for a few moments.

Zach shifted the ice in the towel against his numb lips.

"So I'm sitting there in the shade on this wooden stool with the smell of chlorine wafting on the breeze and the girls with their pastel shorts and the sounds of splashing and screams and laughter and yet another cannonball off the diving board. And I'm sitting there, and I'm reading these . . . incredible sentences. These . . . primordial words . . . dark rooms and corn-shuck bedding and sun-dappled forests and rifle-squinted eyes . . . river bottoms and train depots and radio static . . . and . . . and . . ."

"And that's when you knew you wanted to take Straw's class."

Robert looked at Zach and nodded.

"Yeah. Exactly. I made a promise to myself."

Robert paused.

"So . . ."

Then he sighed.

"So I want you to remember this moment, Zach. I'm happy for you. You've worked hard. You deserve this. Don't let any of us hold you back."

"What are you talking about?"

"You. Me. Marcel."

"Oh."

"Marcel's kind of been . . . I don't know . . . drifting."

"Hey, Robert. C'mon. Nothing's going to change."

"Of course it will."

Zach looked at his friend. He thought of the three of them sitting side by side on the steps in the afternoon sun. The happiness he had known in those moments.

Robert was watching a spot on the ground near his feet. His face was so serious, Zach felt like laughing.

"All right, whatever," Zach said, smiling at his friend. "Just don't tomahawk me in the face again."

Robert laughed.

"Okay?"

"Okay."

Robert turned to Zach, and Zach held out his fist, and Robert bumped it with his fist. Zach threw the ice on the ground and picked up the ball.

"Come on, Kit Carson."

Robert laughed.

"No, you're Kit Carson."

"You are."

They stood and left, tossing the ball back and forth as they went.

*　　*　　*

Marcel was lying in the dark waiting for him to fall asleep and thinking that the hardest part of college was not the sudden, heady escape from the vise grip of parental authority or the at times overwhelming academic demands or the psychotic strangers masquerading as your classmates, no, the hardest part was learning to share a single bed with a man, a bony man with toe nails like scimitars who left mystery bruises on your thighs roughly the size of his knee cap so that what at first seemed romantic quickly became an excruciating exercise in body contortion and sleep deprivation and only when it was too late and he was sleeping like a baby did you realize you had not stretched out on a bed but had willingly subjected yourself to something far more procrustean when what you really wanted in all honesty was just a good night's sleep but instead you're wide awake wondering if it is possible that the administration purposefully furnished the rooms with the smallest, squeakiest single beds on the market knowing all along that the seemingly innocuous single bed is in fact the most insidious instrument of torture known to man, or perhaps more accurately in this case, to woman.

She rolled her eyes just enough to peer painfully at the red glow of his digital clock. There had been a time not so long ago when she thought a man's profile outlined in the dim glow of a bedside digital clock or a stereo console display was arresting and significant somehow, not the face so much as the moment, the closeness of being intimate in the same bed, imagining a tenderness beneath the sleeping flesh and bone, but then it occurred to her as she was lying there motionless in the dark that sleeping with a man in a small single bed was probably not so very different from being married to one — a lot of maneuvering and negotiating and the occasional intercourse and her floating there wide awake folded up inside herself and him sleeping soundly only inches yet galaxies away.

It was a precise feeling, the one she felt after she had made love, fucked, whatever, and she was lying next to him, together, almost touching, but at the same time, there was somehow this immense distance like an ocean between them. She suspected it was a feeling more women had experienced, and perhaps that explained why there were no words — no good words — to describe it. At least no words that she knew. Not enough women had written about it. Otherwise, there would be a better word than distance or distress or angst or alienation or estrangement or fear or anxiety or hysteria or melancholia or dissociation or temporary spatial post-coital dementia or any of the other inadequate words men might use to label such a feeling for their own psychiatric or legal or familial purposes. If enough women had tried to define that telescoping distance, that whistling void, that unbridgeable chasm, that windward shore, she would have a specific word. One that would convey the sense of being alone with being alone, of not knowing if the person next to you, not knowing if anyone, can understand what you are feeling.

Being alone with being alone.

She was sure he was asleep, but she waited a little longer, then she carefully began to ease herself, wincing with each tick and ping of the mattress, out of the small, single bed. She stood over him for a moment, but he did not stir. He looked comfortable, boyish, a happy labrador dreaming of rabbits and footballs and food.

A streetlight from outside was shining through the open window. It was casting shadows of tree limbs across the walls and the ceiling. She silently gathered her underwear and clothes. The shadows slid across her bare legs like pale-blue zebra stripes.

At the door, she took one more look around his room. A fetid compost heap of clothes was piled next to the bed. She looked for a long time at his high-top tennis shoes and the socks. The shoes rested where he kicked them off, one on its side, with limp frayed laces and worn tongues and slick leather. One long-fingered hand dangled over the side of the bed. She wanted to remember the shadows on the ceiling and tried to fix their wild, spidery lattice in her mind.

Outside his door, she quietly dressed herself and padded down the hallway. Her shoes hung from two crooked fingers. The rest of the dormitory was quiet, stunned with sleep. She slipped out the back door into the coolness of the night.

The dormitory was off the main quadrangle. It was a white wooden building, older than the other dormitories. The radiators clanked like a construction site. One side of the building was high and flat, and the streetlight in the parking lot threw the shadow of an oak tree over its white, slatted surface. It was a huge stencil of a tree spoiled only by the dark rectangles of the windows. She glanced up where the tree shadows fell across his dark, empty window. She turned and set out for her dorm.

She cut across the flat, grassy expanse of the main quadrangle. Emptied of students, the quadrangle seemed immense. She felt like a solitary ant crawling across its surface. The grass was damp, and soon her favorite pair of red Chuck Taylors was soaked. She was tired and sore, and she wanted to be in her own bed and her own bathroom. Tears came to her eyes. Stupid, foolish tears. Hot tears ran down her cheeks, and she wiped them away quickly, and the cool night air dried her face.

She vowed to herself that she would not make this walk again.

The sky arced above her. The stars whispered their cold, brittle mysteries. She stopped and craned her neck, gazing up at the sky, trying to take it all in, turning in place, pirouetting, but it all just kept getting bigger and bigger, and she knew she must quit or fall down or go mad.

She thought of when she was a little girl and she had snuck around the neighborhood and hoarded treasure in a tree. She had been Marcel the Pirate Queen, and all had feared her, and none would meet her gaze. Only the stars, her oldest friends.

The Pirate Queen walked on, careful to leave no sign of her passing.

*   *   *

"It's refreshing to see you conscious," the Professor said.

"I blame Homer," Zach said.

The Professor smiled a patient, tolerant smile.

"Just Homer? Not Herr Budweiser? Or maybe the nameless fellow who discovered fermentation?"

Zach cleared his throat, somewhat chastened.

"They may have had a hand in it, too," Zach said.

The Professor and Zach sat facing each other across one

corner of the long oak table in the small white room with the narrow windows. It was just the two of them, the Professor at the head of the table, leaning back in his captain's chair, relaxed, legs crossed at the knees, and Zach two seats away, elbows resting on the table. The rest of the chairs in the room were empty, still in positions of disarray, kiltered around the edges of the table, swept toward the door in the haste of departure.

The Professor used the small white room for his office-hours meetings with the individual students. The meetings were voluntary, but the students rarely passed up an opportunity to meet with the Professor. The Professor left the florescent ceiling lights off, preferring the shadows and the diffuse light from the narrow windows. The darkened room was quiet and still, and once the door was closed, the world outside fell away, and the room seemed to dilate and transform. The Professor would speak in his deep voice in soft and measured tones, and in the moments when no one was speaking, the sounds from beyond the closed door would intrude, distant echoes on hard surfaces, footsteps down the hallway, the rustle of a bookbag settling against the wall. Shadows would pass across the tiled floor visible beneath the bottom edge of the door, and when the inevitable knock came, it was always too sharp, too soon.

"What happened?" the Professor said.

Zach was momentarily lost.

"To your lip," the Professor said.

"Oh, uh, sports related."

"I didn't know you were an athlete."

Zach gave him a quick smile and shook his head.

"I'm not."

He circled a hand in front of his face.

"Hence the disfigurement," Zach said.

The Professor laughed, nodded.

"You should see the other guy," the Professor said.

Zach was puzzled.

"The other guy?"

The Professor quickly shook his head and waved it away.

"It's an old joke. Never mind."

"Oh, right," Zach said, with a polite laugh.

"The other guy," Zach murmured.

When the class met during the seminar, Zach usually spent the majority of the time in a gravity-defying posture designed to come as close as physically possible to a prone position while still remaining seated at the table. He would invariably rouse himself from a seeming coma by the end of class and manage to make at least one insightful contribution. With his paint-stained clothes and unkempt hair and irregular shaving habits, he often seemed insolent, defiant, uncivilized. It did not help that Zach had big bones and thick limbs that were suggestive to the Professor of a farm animal. On those occasions when he was alert and focused, his whole face seemed to bristle. The other students seemed to tolerate Zach, like a beloved pet at the dinner table. The Professor suspected he was the sort of student who would clean up well, appearing alongside his parents at graduation, nearly unrecognizable, smiling, with shorn hair and a coat and tie. If his written work had not shown such promise, the Professor might have been more insulted. In truth, despite his unpredictable hygiene and circus-act deportment, Zach was the student the Professor most looked forward to seeing during office hours. All of the students in the seminar could write well, but Zach had that intangible quality. Sometimes you could tell immediately, from the moment a diffident student stopped hovering in the hall-way and took the first tentative step through the open door.

"Have you thought about what we talked about?"

"I have," Zach said.

"And?"

"What if I'm not ready?"

The Professor thought about this for a moment. He slid the top onto his fountain pen and set it on his yellow pad of lined paper.

"And what if you are?"

"Carpe diem?"

"Yes, exactly. Carpe diem."

They were silent.

Zach looked down at the table. There was a knot in the swirl of the grain of the wood.

The Professor picked up a manuscript from the table, black words printed on white pages fastened together with a staple at the top corner. He gestured toward Zach with the manuscript.

"Tell me about The Quarry," the Professor said and tossed the manuscript onto the table between them.

The Quarry was a short story Zach had written as an assignment for the class. The story grew out of Zach's memories of the summer when his father taught him how to swim and dive. In the story, the quarry was a swimming hole near one of the succession of military bases where the family in the story had lived while the boy was a child.

Zach drew a breath and exhaled loudly.

"Well . . ." Zach said. He frowned, not sure how to respond.

"What's it about? How would you describe it?"

"It's about a hole in the ground."

"Yes, and Moby Dick is about a whale. What else?"

Zach spoke softly.

"It's about truth. I guess. What is true. How do you know."

Zach looked at the Professor, not sure how to go on.

"Res ipsa loquitur," Zach said and shrugged slightly with his big shoulders, opening briefly his empty hands.

The Professor slowly nodded.

"Yes, quite so."

The Professor leaned forward and placed one stubby index finger on the manuscript on the table. He looked steadily into Zach's eyes.

"It's a good story, Zach."

He tapped the manuscript gently with his fingertip.

"The Quarry is ready."

Zach looked at the pages beneath the Professor's finger. He could see the title floating in the middle of the space at the top of the page. For a moment, it all seemed like a dream, and he feared the Professor would ask him to read from the manuscript, and he would look at the pages, and the words would be changing on the page, cascading down into some strange language, Ancient Greek or Sanskrit or Klingon, and his name would vanish, and the manuscript would no longer be recognizable as something he had created or had even understood or comprehended, and anything he had ever tried to mark down would be irretrievable, untranslatable, lost, gone.

The knot in the wood was dark brown, almost black. Zach grasped the edge of the table with his thumbs.

"I don't know if I can do it again," Zach said.

"Balderdash," the Professor said mildly and flicked the fingers of one hand like he was brushing dust away.

Balderdash, Zach thought.

Who says that?

Zach laughed nervously.

"Balderdash?"

"Zach, I came to writing late in my life, but I've gleaned a few things. . . . Writing is a job just like any other. You've got to stay in the hitch. Do you know what I mean?"

"I think so, yes."

"It's not about inspiration or talent or having a gift. It's about being curious and observant. It's about telling a story. What happens next. If you do the work, the material will find you. The stories won't let you rest. But I think you already know that."

The Professor spread the fingers of his hand apart and held it over the manuscript on the table. Zach could see where the tips of each of the Professor's fingers were lightly touching the paper.

"This could be part of a novel. Or a collection of other stories."

The Professor sat back in his chair and laced his blunt fingers together.

"Agnes is very good at her job. I've known her a long time."

His round face was smiling, friendly.

"It's just a meeting," the Professor said. "Listen to what she has to say. Get to know each other."

They were silent for a long moment.

The air in the hallway outside the room shifted, and the door bounced gently against the frame.

Zach's gaze drifted back to the dark knot in the tabletop. It was round but irregular, lopsided, not quite a perfect circle.

"I'm grateful, Professor. But I still need to think about it."

A frown settled onto the Professor's face.

"Zach, let me ask you a question."

"Okay."

The Professor leaned forward. He gestured with one hand, elbow on the table, his fingertips touching and his little finger extended. It was a gesture Zach knew well, one that any of his students immediately associated with the Professor.

Zach and Marcel and Robert had often used the gesture themselves in conversation, pointing their little finger at the other for comic emphasis.

The Professor's hand was poised in the space between them, his little finger pointing at Zach.

"What is most important?" the Professor said.

The Professor was watching him closely.

"To me?" Zach said.

The Professor paused, waited until Zach looked him in the eyes.

"What is most important?"

The Professor sat back and raised a hand and arranged his fingertips around his mouth and chin. The round lenses in his eyeglasses caught the light from the windows.

"I . . . I don't know," Zach said. "It depends, doesn't it? Love? Work? I don't know."

"You need to answer that question."

There was a knock at the door.

It was time for Zach to go.

Waiting in the hall was the quiet young woman with the raven-dark hair who sat in the back of the seminar. Zach nodded as she passed. She went into the room, and Zach glanced back. As she turned to shut the door, her eyes briefly met his, and her face was without expression, and the raven-haired woman closed the door.

*   *   *

Zach faced the blank page.

It curled around the smooth roller of his manual typewriter and rose above the straight edge of the inky black ribbon and presented the uncluttered white field waiting so patiently for his fingers to strike the lettered keys.

For days, he had watched the deadline inflating on the

horizon, the slack tether moving slowly through his hands. Now the deadline was aloft, and the parade was leaving, and the tether had grown taut in his grasp.

Zach preferred his manual typewriter to the newer electric typewriters. He liked the idea of being self-sufficient. He could envision himself surviving in a cabin in the woods with his trusty manual typewriter and a wood-burning stove, trekking into town for paper and ribbons, visiting the post office to drop off another phone-book-sized manuscript.

Zach faced the blank page.

He contemplated the intricacies, the ingenuity of the manual typewriter, the way when he struck a key a typebar flew in an arc toward that one spot on the blank page, and the ribbon rose to meet the metal face of the typebar, and the raised letter struck against the ribbon and snapped it against the page leaving an impression of black ink in the shape of the letter on the smooth fibers of the paper's surface, and the typebar fell back down neatly in line among the semi-circle of other typebars with the other letters and symbols side by side, and the carriage advanced just enough to print another letter, and the ribbon spools turned just enough to keep the ribbon ink fresh and pristine, and if you typed quickly and firmly and smoothly, without error, the letters formed words, and the words covered the inches of white space that ran across the page until the line was full, and a soft bell rang in your ear, and you would pause to slap the return lever with your hand and slide the carriage back to the beginning, and the roller would turn just enough to move the page up, and the whiteness of the paper rose to meet the typebar and the black ink of the advancing ribbon, and a new line began, and you struck the keys with your fingers and slapped the return with your hand and filled each line with letters and words and symbols until you had filled the page.

Zach faced the blank page.

The University made electric typewriters available in various grim, haunted locations around campus. A few students brought electric typewriters from home, hauling them out of the back of their parents' Suburbans and mini-vans, piling them like treasure with their tennis rackets and golf clubs on the curb at the beginning of the semester. Some students brought even more exotic devices — desktop computers that connected with dot-matrix printers and consumed with a hot, dry breath reams of paper edged with perforated strips with holes that tore free to leave neat, clean printed pages that Zach thought were suspicious somehow, not quite authentic. Some students paid other students, or even professional typists, to do their typing for dissertations, thesis papers, term papers. Bulletin boards around campus fluttered with hand-lettered notices offering typing services. The bottoms were fringed with carefully cut tabs with a phone number, usually with one or two tabs torn off.

Zach faced the blank page.

Among the clutter on Zach's desk was an IBM Selectric typeball. It was silver-colored and metal, about the size of a golf ball. Its surface was covered in raised letters. It clicked into place in a Selectric typewriter and whirled and struck unerringly against the paper. When a fast typist was using a Selectric, the ball was just a blur spinning too fast for the eye to follow. The Selectric and its patented typeball had become the prevailing typing machine in offices across America. Switching fonts was as easy as switching typeballs.

On his desktop, alongside the typeball, there were buckeyes and pine cones and sycamore bark, oak leaves from the back of Old Grundy, bottle caps and colorful, plastic fast-food figurines, a tiny Doctor Tempus astride his winged steed Tachyon, miniature race cars, empty tubes of paint, a metal piggy bank in the shape of a red Shriners fez, the pale-blue mosaic of an ashtray he had painstakingly pieced together in summer camp, a bottle of Tabasco hot sauce.

Zach liked the shape of the Selectric typeball. Detached from the typewriter, it was like a piece of found art. Among the clutter that had come to rest on his desktop, the Selectric typeball was like the future. A spaceship. Alien technology. The monolith among the cavemen. Sometimes Zach envisioned the typeball as a giant sculpture, an installation, big enough to walk inside with stenciled letters cut in a domed roof where the light could shine through.

Marcel's roommate had a Selectric typewriter, and Marcel had taken a class in typing in high school, or rather her mother had made her take a class in typing, always reminding her that it was a skill she could fall back on. Marcel was blindingly fast, like 120 words-a-minute fast. The Selectric ball was just a silver-gray blur when she was at the keyboard.

Zach faced the blank page.

He wondered if Robert and Marcel were also working on their assignments for the Professor's class. He thought again about how their paths had been crossing and re-crossing for months, how they each had realized, like when jigsaw puzzle pieces fall unexpectedly into place, that they had seen each other on many occasions in many places before they had come to sit in their usual spots around the long oak table in the small white room with the narrow windows. It seemed they had been traveling unknowingly their whole lives toward those warm fall afternoons after the Professor's class, the moments spent sitting side by side on the sun-bleached steps behind Old Grundy looking out toward the water oaks and the playing fields.

Marcel was the serene girl with the red beret and the gauzy skirt, just after sunrise in the long shadows that morning first year, riding a bicycle with a wicker basket, gliding straight down the middle of University Drive. Robert was the oblivious guy with the enormous book bag who almost knocked you over the wall at the Center. Zach was the broad-shouldered dude with the pony tail who seemed to roll smoothly, invisibly, in his apron and hat, out of the kitchen at the grill with a perfectly-timed basket of fresh chicken strips. Marcel was the friendly usher with a flashlight who seated you and then disappeared up the aisle into the darkness though you kept searching for her face even after the play began. Zach was the guy softly snoring, sound asleep in a carrel deep in the bowels of the library who awakened to the sound of your retreating foot-steps. Robert was the guy in the sleeveless argyle sweater in the front row who raised his hand and asked the question about widows and orphans in your British lit survey that caused an eruption of laughter that lasted for five minutes, and, for the rest of the semester, the professor referred to Robert as the widows-and-orphans guy.

Zach faced the blank page.

The deadline was overhead, and the ropey tether was slid-ing through his fingers.

Zach had assembled the fragments of a rough draft in a meager pile on the cluttered desk top. They formed a bizarre flow chart — unwadded colored pages and torn folded scraps scrawled with coiled, crawling paragraphs, dog-eared index cards with transcribed quotations, a coffee-stained napkin with barely legible handwriting recording snatches of drunken conversation, a match book with a name and a phone number and other bits and pieces of seeming detritus.

Zach imagined Robert and Marcel toiling away like factory workers on an assembly line, like bees in a hive, and the parade was leaving, and the deadline loomed overhead, and he was tangled in the tether, and it was lifting him off the pavement, and he floated past an apartment building and inside the apartment building he could see the three of them, Robert, Marcel and Zach, older, in the future, neighbors, old friends, living each on a different floor, and it was a splendid, old, art deco building with a nice view, and he could see through the big windows as he floated skyward, and Robert was sitting at his neat desk with a cone of buttery light shining from his draftsman's lamp clamped to the side of the desk and a stack of fresh paper waiting beside the typewriter at his elbow, and in the apartment above, there was Marcel sitting cross-legged on the floor against the bed, index cards spread neatly on the floor, hair tied back in a ponytail, yellow Ticonderoga No.2 tucked behind one ear, her roommate's Selectric humming expectantly beside her, and higher still in another apartment, through another window, there he was, Zach, sitting behind his cluttered little desk next to a pile of fire wood and a cast-iron stove, pecking away on his trusty manual typewriter, long hair in his eyes, but, wait, there was the Professor, too, calmly at work with his fountain pen and ink well and his yellow pad of lined paper and a cup of tea at his tasteful desk and a leather chair with Remington cowboy sculptures and Bierstadt landscapes, and Zach thought of each of them, the way Robert would touch his forehead and knit his brow, the way Marcel would crinkle her nose, the way he, Zach, threw sharpened pencils unerringly like darts into the ceiling, the way the Professor pointed with his little finger, and the parade was leaving, and the air had grown thin, and the tether was burning through his hands, cutting to the bone, and he was hitting the space bar repeatedly, typing one key and then stopping with his finger poised above the keyboard, staring slack-jawed at the page, and the desperate need to find the tennis ball and throw it repeatedly against the wall, the siren call of pizza, an apple, the day-old sub in the fridge, broken pencils, the rising piles of eraser dust, shredded index cards, crushed aluminum soda cans, the urge to flee, to be doing anything else, your hair between all of your fingers, firmly in your grasp, the nausea, the pacing, such pacing, the nap, just for a few minutes, your head cradled in your arms, your knees weak, leaping out over the emerald green and falling, falling toward the white blossoms below, and the typing, the furious typing, and the words coming, the words, in a torrent, the words.

*   *   *

Zach was playing guitar when Marcel let herself into his room.

He was sitting behind his cluttered writer's desk in front of the manual typewriter. A page drooped over the top of the roller. Marcel could see the blocks of black text on the white surface of the page.

Zach was facing away from her. He strummed a few chords, hummed the tentative notes of an unfinished song.

"Is the guitar part of your process?" Marcel said.

Zach stopped playing and turned around.

He smiled, surprised.

"What? You don't use a guitar?"

She took measured steps toward him and touched him on his shoulder.

"Actually, when I get stuck, I take a walk."

She tilted her head and looked in his eyes.

"Want to tag along?"

Zach met her gaze and held it for a while.

"Yeah, sure," he said.

They walked to the main quadrangle. It was a chilly night, and Marcel was wearing her old pea jacket and a red scarf. Zach had thrown on a faded blue denim jacket over a heavy wool sweater. She had linked her arm with his, and he could see her breath when she spoke. The large, grassy lawn was empty, and the dome of the auditorium seemed to hover in the darkness. They were talking about the Professor's class.

"You know, like when the author says this character is me and has the same name as me and writes like me and is more or less reliable, or, you know, as reliable as any other third-person narrator, but you know it's still mediated, and it's still a character, and they're not speaking with the same voice, you know what I mean?"

"Oh definitely. When it's fiction. But what about a memoir? Kit Carson wrote a memoir."

"In the third person?"

"I don't know, but why not?"

"So is it supposed to be like a multiplicity of viewpoints or is there a single narrator?"

"I think the answer is yes," Zach said.

"Bah," Marcel said with irritation.

They walked in silence for several steps.

"Marcel is not amused."

They burst out laughing, and Zach watched the laughter playing across her open lips, her quick, sharp eyes.

Marcel stopped. She turned and looked at him, grinning.

"Hey, have you ever climbed the dome?"

"I am not climbing the dome."

She took him by the hand and pulled him towards the auditorium.

"Come on, it'll be fun."

She pulled him with her, and they began to run together, and the night air was cold against their faces, and he felt his heart beating in his chest and the blood rushing in his ears, and he was caught up in her mood. She broke away from him and sprinted ahead, and he watched the soles of her shoes rising and falling until she had vanished in the darkness, and he felt an old, childlike giddiness. He ran ahead for several yards until he saw a low brick wall that seemed to materialize out of the darkness, growing more substantial as he approached it. The brick wall was perpendicular to the corner of an arch over a fieldstone path. The arch abutted the auditorium. Zach stopped and took a few breaths. He looked around for Marcel, but he could not see her.

"Marcel," he said in a loud whisper.

"Up here."

Marcel was above him, hanging over the edge of the top of the arch. Zach looked up. He could see the dark silhouette of her head and shoulders. Behind them, the dome rose pale against the clear, starry sky.

"Shouldn't we be getting back?"

"Would Kit Carson turn back?"

"I think you may have missed the point of that story."

"So yer yellah."

Zach was silent, smiling in the dark, watching her silhouette above him.

"Fine," he said.

He moved to the wall, found handholds and began to climb. He climbed to the top of the wall and pulled himself up on top of the arch. The arch supported a larger wall that abutted the main roof of the auditorium and, above that, the dome.

A new terrain emerged as Zach stood unsteady in the dark. It was a second landscape of shadow and light. It floated above the expanse of grass and fieldstone paths below him.

"This way," he heard Marcel say.

He searched for her among the unfamiliar shapes before him and found her standing in her pea coat and red scarf at the edge of the roof of the auditorium.

"Come on," she said.

Zach stood on the arch and held his arms out for a moment, testing his balance, looking at the pale flat surfaces and deep shadows in front of him. He stepped carefully across the top of the arch and the wall and the roof. As he was crossing, Marcel disappeared into the shadows around the bottom of the dome.

Zach paused for a moment and looked out at the sleeping campus. There were a few lights in the windows of the dormitories. The stars were bright in the sky. A mist seemed to hang over the lawn in the distance. He could see dimly a dark statue on a pedestal standing at the front of the quadrangle. Over his shoulder, the dome rose, huge now, white and distinct.

He took a deep breath and focused his attention on the way before him and continued carefully across until he reached the edge of the roof.

"Marcel?"

He hopped down off the wall onto the edge of the roof and then down into the shadows.

"Annie Oakley?"

He took a few steps.

"Sacagawea?"

He stepped past a large fixture, and as he passed it, Marcel stepped from behind it. She circled her arms around him from behind and rested her head on his shoulder.

Zach turned around, and Marcel put her arms around his neck. He felt the warmth of her body against him. She started to kiss him.

"Wait. My lip. I split my lip playing basketball."

"I'll be careful."

She kissed him on the lips.

He gently pushed her away.

"What about Robert?"

She dropped her arms to her sides.

He could feel her glaring at him.

When she spoke, her voice had changed.

"You need to decide what you want."

Zach was thinking of her profile in the sun on the steps, thinking of Robert and the blood on his cloudy blue shirt.

Let me see, Robert had said, his eyes searching, his brows drawn together with concern.

"I want you both," Zach said. "The way we are now."

She folded her arms around her stomach.

Her face was in shadow, just a smudge above the red of her scarf.

"Grow up, Zach," she muttered.

In the distance behind her, a light in a dorm window winked off.

His lip hurt and tasted of blood.

"Why me, Marcel?"

She made an exasperated sound in the dark.

"Are you that insecure?"

Am I, he thought. *Am I that insecure?*

"Maybe I am."

She turned away, facing the quadrangle. She was looking toward the sky.

Zach tried to see her face. The light and shadows around them were unreal, disorienting. Zach felt adrift, untethered, a faceless spectator in a dark balcony listening to words spoken someplace offstage, prompts for the understudies.

Zach thought of the Professor in the white room with the narrow windows. He thought of the Professor leaning towards him over the oak table, gesturing, pointing at him with his little finger.

"What if I told you writing isn't important to me?"

She spun toward him. He could feel her, coiled, confused, looking at him in the dark.

"That's bullshit. Your Honor."

"What if I told you I just took Straw's class to meet women?"

Her face was hidden in shadow. She watched him in silence for a moment.

"I'm leaving."

Zach watched as she climbed down.

The red of her scarf grew faint as she walked across the lawn until she disappeared entirely into the darkness beneath an arch on the other side of the quadrangle.

*   *   *

Zach did not attend the next meeting of the Professor's class, which was unusual, because Zach never missed class.

"Anybody know where Zach is?" the Professor asked, looking pointedly at Robert and Marcel.

"No," Robert said.

Marcel looked away and shook her head.

Years later, Robert and Marcel would remember that time sadly and wonder what exactly had been going through Zach's mind. Years later, Marcel in her curator's office at the museum would see something familiar in a new acquisition, a splash of emerald green or cerulean blue, and she would lean back in her comfortable chair and think of something she had read long ago back in college in that writing course she took with Winston Straw and the clever boy, the writer, she had walked with arm in arm on the fieldstone paths across the green lawns past the tremendous water oaks.

Years later, Robert would set aside the actuarial tables and leave his corner office at the global conglomerate where he worked to reinsure the reinsurers, and he would take the train home to the dinner table in his sprawling brick colonial and ask his children what they had learned that day in school, and the boy, the shy one with the square jaw and freckles and the red hair, would say something amusing, and his wife would laugh, and Robert would remember that interesting fellow in Winston Straw's writing seminar, something funny he had said about Kit Carson and the obsidian blade and the cool waters of the unfailing spring, and Robert would wonder whatever became of him and think how sad it is the way people lose touch and drift apart and how strange it is the way life happens.

"There are many ways to tell a story," the Professor said. "Artists will always experiment with new ways of telling stories, and when an experiment works, it might shed some light on who gets to tell the story, or even on who decides what a story is."

"On privilege."

"Yes, that's one way of looking at it, but it's more complicated than that, isn't it?

"It's about language. . . .

"It's about words. . . ."

The Professor was turned toward the narrow windows. The round lenses of the spectacles on his nose reflected the light. He seemed to be looking toward something in the distance far beyond the small white room.

"I read something recently," the Professor said. "Or perhaps it was a dream. I don't remember now. . . .

"Certain breeds of dogs can be trained to smell cancer in the byproducts, the metabolites, in human urine. . . .

"In the same way a bomb-sniffing dog can be trained to alert in the presence of a bomb, a cancer-sniffing dog can be trained to alert in the presence of urine from a person with a malignant tumor. . . .

"Maybe what the science-fiction writers say is true. Maybe one day we will create machines that can tell stories, and the machines will write stories for other machines in ways we cannot foresee or understand, and we'll find we aren't that special after all. Maybe the machines will create sonic art for dolphins and whales, olfactory art for the canine nose, textural art for the feline whisker."

The Professor paused. Someone's chair creaked as they shifted their weight. The Professor turned back to the students gathered around the table.

His smile seemed wistful.

He steepled his stubby fingers.

"For me, new types of fiction are only interesting in the way they vary from traditional storytelling. It's still about sitting around the campfire and passing the time. It's still about wanting to know what happens next. Otherwise, it's poetry or art or something else, isn't it? Not prose, not fiction. . . .

"Tell me a story. . . .

"Tell me what happens next."

After class, Robert and Marcel walked to the steps behind Old Grundy, thinking that Zach might meet them there, but the steps were empty. They sat together, just the two of them. The absence where he usually would have been seemed unnatural, and their conversation was awkward and halting without him.

"My mother wants me to stop thinking about writing," Marcel said, her arms circled around her knees.

"She wants me to go to law school," Marcel said.

Robert was sitting forward with a forearm on each knee. He was turning an oak leaf by the stem, watching it rotate back and forth as he rolled it slowly between his thumb and index finger.

"Do you want to go to law school?"

Marcel sighed.

"I don't know. My sister got some stupid job selling toothpaste for Pee and Gee."

"Literally selling toothpaste?"

Marcel rolled her eyes. She leaned back on her elbows.

"You have square toes."

Robert dropped the leaf and leaned back on his elbows.

"Be that as it may . . ."

The sun was warm on their faces. In the distance, on the playing fields, the tiny figures clustered together and scattered apart.

"What are you doing for break?"

"Nothing. Going home. You?"

"Home probably. Yeah. Home."

*   *   *

Marcel was sitting at a small, wooden desk tucked away in a gloomy, secluded corner of a subbasement of the library. She was softly crying. She wiped away her tears with a tissue and composed herself. She gathered her possessions, zipped up her bookbag and prepared to leave. She stood and heaved a big sigh. Hours of study had left her fatigued and spent.

She began to wind her way through a labyrinth of aisles, corridors and narrow stairwells. The paint was curling and peeling from the walls. At the edge of her vision, the walls seemed to vibrate with fantastic shapes and vivid colors.

She passed carrels covered with academic graffiti — post cards, photographs, doodles, doggerel, handwritten musings, dialogs that scrolled down the wall. The art and handwriting and photos seemed to change every day, like something organic creeping up from beneath the floor.

She passed the doorway of a room. Inside, she glimpsed oversized folios flat on tables like bodies in a morgue. Two library workers in gas masks and rubber gloves were draping a sheet over one of the tables.

Marcel began to climb the narrow stairs between the floors of the stacks. Other students were emerging from the darkened aisles and began to climb alongside her. They were shouldering their backpacks, zipping up their jackets.

Down one book-lined aisle, a face painted bright red and black floated out of the gloom. On the stairs below her, she glimpsed someone wearing a head dress with feathers flowing down the back. At the far end of one floor, beneath a low ceiling, harsh florescent light fell briefly on what appeared to be a boy with a leering, fleshless skull.

Marcel and the other students trickled out of the stacks and joined a larger group flowing together into the main lobby of the library. There were masks and painted faces scattered throughout the throng. She walked with them, and they filed steadily through the doors to the campus.

Outside, they came down the library steps onto the main quadrangle. Distant music was playing somewhere. Whipping Post by the Allman Brothers. It was night, and their breath fogged the chilly air. They walked in small groups down the fieldstone paths. She listened to their voices murmuring. There was soft laughter in the darkness around her.

Then Marcel heard, in the distance, a sound like something howling. The sound was drawing closer. A young man came running out of the darkness across the quadrangle. He was yelling at the top of his lungs in a strange, whooping cadence. He was wearing khaki pants and a collared oxford-cloth shirt with the tail untucked and hanging loose down past his waist. Like the faces from the library, his face was painted bright red.

The whooping boy ran toward Marcel and crossed in front of her. Marcel stopped and watched him running. He disappeared into the darkness. She listened as the sound of his rhythmic whooping drew farther and farther away. She looked in the direction he was running.

On the horizon were the dark silhouettes of buildings. The sky behind the buildings was a murky, shifting color of orange. There were trees and shrubs nearby. Other students were moving toward the orange glow. Marcel joined the stream of other students and started walking toward the strange orange glow.

As she drew closer, she heard a distant drumbeat. Suddenly, in front of her, an Indian came walking out of the darkness. He was bare-chested with feathers on his head and his face painted in garish colors. He did not see her, and Marcel watched as he walked silently past.

Marcel rounded a corner and saw the bonfire burning in an open field. The drumbeat was deafening. Dozens of students had gathered around the bonfire, and dozens more were joining them. Many of the students had their faces painted or wore masks. Some were wearing costumes. A few were dressed like Indians. The whooping boy was carrying a spear. He howled toward the sky.

The students had encircled the bonfire. They were laughing and drinking. It was like a carnival. Many students had shed layers of clothing. Some of the men were bare-chested. A few women stripped down to their bras. One young woman was sitting on the shoulders of a man. The intense light from the fire shone weirdly on their faces and the skin of their bodies. The whooping boy burst from the crowd, bare-chested with his spear, and began to sprint around inside the circle of bodies near the flames.

The bonfire was raging now. It was quickly consuming logs the size of telephone poles. The logs were glowing white hot, and the embers were red like blood.

Marcel made her way to the edge of the crowd. She searched the wild faces. Many of the students had painted their faces and were wearing headdresses with feathers. One or two carried tomahawks. Another young man wore a coonskin cap. A grotesque human effigy was swinging above the crowd. At the back fringe, for an instant, she thought she might have seen dark bodies tumbling across the sky.

Then she saw the raven-haired girl from her writing class, silent, expressionless. Moving bodies blocked her sight, and then the raven-haired girl was gone. The whooping boy sprinted past, running faster and faster round the hottest edge of the flames.

Then Marcel saw Robert in the crowd and tried to get his attention. He saw her, and they began to maneuver through the crowd. They reached each other, and Marcel hugged him, relieved to have him there, to have found him in the crowd. They looked at each other, and the light from the fire was moving on their faces.

A hand tapped Robert on the shoulder.

Robert and Marcel turned to see Zach standing next to them. He was carrying a sheaf of manuscripts and spiral-bound notebooks under one arm. Robert was happy to see Zach, but Marcel was wary and uncertain. Robert clapped him on the shoulder.

"Old man! Where have you been?"

Zach's face was strange in the light of the bonfire. The bruise under his eye was muddy brown. The shrunken scab on his lip was hard and black. He was oddly focused, unsmiling. He showed them the stack of his manuscripts, grasped the stack with both hands and shook them.

"I want you both to see this," Zach said.

"What's that?"

"Every word I've ever written."

He gathered the stack and stepped toward the fire.

Marcel grabbed his arm.

"Zach stop."

Zach broke free from Marcel and ran as close as he could to the edge of the bonfire.

He turned and faced them.

"I renounce it," he shouted. "All of it."

Then, in one swift motion, he flung the manuscripts into the maw of the bonfire.

Robert did not fully grasp what was happening. He was half laughing.

"What? Renounce what?"

Zach bolted away into the crowd.

Marcel was crying and started after Zach, but Robert grabbed her by the arm.

"What just happened?"

"Writing," Marcel said. "He's renounced writing. He's giving up. He's quitting. "

*   *   *

The manuscripts landed in the fire, and it quickly began to consume the white, typewritten pages. They rushed up in a column of cinders and flame and smoke, and the fine, black ashes began to drift in a plume across the night sky. The bonfire below dwindled to a bright circle, and the students' cries grew distant and faint. The ashes, still burning at the delicate edges, drifted higher until a strong wind took them and carried them ever farther away.

4

INT. MARCEL'S OFFICE – DAY

On a dark, polished, wood credenza, we see a vase with cut flowers, a squash racquet and a stack of law books.

> CLIENT (O.S.)
> (filtered)
> (agitated)
> Is it too late to shred everything?

MARCEL

Marcel raises an eyebrow, mildly surprised.

> MARCEL
> Or . . . we could quash the
> subpoena and seek a protective
> order.

OFFICE

Marcel is sitting in a comfortable leather chair behind her tidy desk. The credenza is behind her against the wall. An open laptop computer and a sleek telephone are arrayed in front of her. She is wearing a stylish, professional suit, tasteful jewelry, nice shoes. She is confident, successful, coolly competent. Her eyes are sharp and quick. Her office is elegantly furnished, not huge, but with a window and a modest view of the city sky-line.

Facing Marcel, sitting in the chair in front of her desk, is TREVOR. Trevor is in his late twenties, pale, thin, nervous, exhausted. Trevor is busily taking notes on a legal pad.

> CLIENT (O.S.)
> (filtered)
> (pauses a beat)
> Quash the subpoena . . .

> MARCEL
> And seek a protective order.

> CLIENT (O.S.)
> (filtered)
> (long pause)
> That might be better.

> MARCEL
> I'll have Trevor draft the motions.

Trevor protests silently, vigorously shaking his head. He is waving frantically, trying to get Marcel's attention.

She ignores him.

Marcel's secretary, BERNICE, knocks on the door and leans into the office. Bernice is in her late fifties, small, fierce, un-flappable, with bold lipstick and eye shadow.

Marcel raises a cautionary index finger and lifts the telephone from its cradle and holds it to her ear.

MARCEL

Can we talk about that later?
I've got to go. Okay . . .
Don't worry . . . Talk with
you then.

Marcel hangs up the phone and glowers at Bernice. Bernice has violated one of Marcel's unwritten rules regarding the closed door and the speaker phone.

Bernice is unperturbed. She enters the office and closes the door. Marcel's face is expectant, her chin raised, waiting to hear what justified the interruption. Bernice speaks in a flat, gravelly monotone.

BERNICE

You have a hand delivery at
reception.

MARCEL

From whom?

BERNICE

Winston Straw.

Marcel is surprised. Trevor spins around and looks at Bernice.

TREVOR

The writer?

BERNICE
You know Winston Straw?

Trevor spins back around facing Marcel.

TREVOR

The writer?

                    MARCEL
Calm down, Trevor. I took his
writing class in college.

                    TREVOR
Really? You? Creative
writing?

                    MARCEL
Is that so hard to believe?

                    TREVOR
It's just that you're so . . .

                    BERNICE
Not creative.

                    TREVOR
At all.

                    MARCEL
Trust me, there's a lot you two don't
know about me.

                    BERNICE
              (in a fake whisper
              behind her hand)
I know she hasn't had a date in
three months.

                    MARCEL
              (through gritted teeth)
Boundaries, Bernice. Boundaries.

INT. LAW FIRM RECEPTION AREA – DAY

Marcel walks down the hall toward the law firm's hushed
reception area. Standing at the marbled front desk is the

woman with raven-dark hair. Her face is without expression. Her hair is gathered in an elegant, elaborate french braid. She is wearing a white silk blouse and a navy-blue pencil skirt. She is carrying a black leather attaché.

As Marcel approaches, the raven-haired woman opens the attaché and removes an envelope and offers it to Marcel. A brief, quizzical expression passes over Marcel's face. Marcel takes the envelope, and the raven-haired woman bows her head slightly and leaves. Marcel watches her go. Marcel looks at the envelope.

ENVELOPE

The envelope is made out of thick, creamy paper. Marcel's name is inked in calligraphy on the front. She turns it over. It is sealed with melted red wax and impressed with a signet of the entwined letters W and S.

* * *

INT. ROBERT'S OFFICE – DAY

The bottom of a tee shirt rises on a young woman's bare lower back, exposing part of a large, ornate tattoo. The tattoo is of a serpent in a circle with its tail in its mouth. The tattoo covers most of the lower back of the young woman. The lower half of the tattoo dips beneath the top of her black yoga pants.

ROBERT

Robert reacts with mild surprise. His eyes open wider, and he tilts his head slightly to one side. Robert's face is square jawed, and he has a sober mien. His hair is long but neat in a way that suits his face.

ROBERT'S POINT OF VIEW

Over Robert's shoulder, we see that the young woman with the tattoo is unselfconsciously leaning over in front of him, dropping her bookbag, preparing to sit in the chair facing him.

ROBERT AND JOLENE

Robert clears his throat and fastidiously looks away before the young woman turns around.

Robert is sitting in his cramped office beside a small, institutional, metal desk. He wears a button-down oxford-cloth shirt, khaki pants and a wedding ring. On his shelves, among the rows of books about literary criticism and the stacks of academic journals, is a baseball glove, a Rubik's cube, a gleaming brass plumb-line weight.

The young woman is JOLENE. She settles into the chair across from Robert. She has bleached shoulder-length cornrows and a large metal ring in her nose. She has the grace and posture of a dancer. She has intense, crazy eyes.

> JOLENE
> So I wanted to get your
> input.

She pauses, waiting for Robert to respond. She speaks in bursts, in a rapid, lilting, sing-song voice.

> JOLENE
> Because I've enjoyed your class.
> And the way you've stressed the
> importance of effective written
> expression.

She pauses again, waiting for Robert. She smiles sweetly, patiently and blinks her eyes several times.

> JOLENE
> I try to solicit and synthesize relevant
> viewpoints and opinions from a
> diversity of sources to assist me in my
> decision-making process.

She smiles again and nods her head several times. Robert is not sure what she wants.

> ROBERT
> Well, as I wrote in my comments,
> your analysis of marriage as metaphor
> in the novels was very well done. In
> the poetry, not so much. Overall,
> though, a very solid effort.

Robert pauses and kneads his forehead with one hand.

> ROBERT
> Is this about your grade?

Jolene blinks at him several times and then bursts out with a high pitched, staccato laugh.

> JOLENE
> Oh, no. I'm planning my own
> curriculum. Self-directed. I sent you
> an email.

> ROBERT
> Oh, okay. I never received it. My
> computer. Something is wrong with
> my computer.

Jolene gives him a brief, sympathetic frown.

                    JOLENE
          Probably a virus. I don't open
          attachments from anyone. Do you
          have an anti-virus software?

                    ROBERT
          Uh, yes. I do. So, tell me, Jolene, what
          is it you want to do?

Jolene nods, composes herself, clears her throat.

                    JOLENE
          When I was a child, my mother
          thought I was having a problem with
          depth perception, so she took me to a
          neurologist, and they stuck this thing
          on my head like a metal salad colander
          with electrodes and wires on top, and
          they decided I was spatially
          challenged, and I ended up doing a lot
          of therapy which eventually led to
          yoga and dance, which I love, but I
          also developed this fascination with
          distance.

                    ROBERT
          Distance?

                    JOLENE
          Yes. From here to there, point A,
          point B, nanometers, inches, fathoms,
          furlongs, miles, clicks, parsecs, as the
          crow flies, knotted up with space and
          time, Xeno's paradox. It gets
          complicated.

ROBERT
Sounds like . . . What? . . . A calculus
problem?

JOLENE
Well, yes, but what interests me is
the language people use to describe
distance, not the numbers. How
humans come to perceive the world
as being positioned and oriented in
time and space. Not just stuff like
how far light travels from a distant
star or the distance between
subatomic particles, but also like
when a flock of birds is wheeling in
the sky, or a school of fish is
swimming downstream, or the way
people spread out on the floor in a
yoga class, or even the way a writer
arranges columns of text on a page,
because the words we choose to
describe those distances are
important to the way stuff gets
organized in our minds, or to the
way we perceive it as being
organized. There's all this space
around us, dark matter we can't
explain, the parts of the human
genome that don't seem to do
anything. Instead of thinking of it as
negative space or a void or
emptiness or randomness or chaos,
I want to understand myself as
being a part of it or even as one with
it, not in a significant way, but
without significance, you know,
without ego, without self.

ROBERT

Those are challenging ideas, Jolene. And I think you deserve a lot of credit for the disciplined way you're thinking about them. I guess I'd suggest that perhaps you might want to narrow your area of inquiry.

JOLENE

Yes, I agree. I want to design a clinical study that will determine whether gender and race have any effect on not only the accuracy of the perceived distances, but also on the words people use to describe the distances. The experiment would elicit written descriptions from the participants about their perception of the fixed distance between people and objects. The race and gender of the people will vary, the setting will vary, but the distances between the people and objects will be constant. The participants would write a narrative of the experiment. I want to take some classes at the law school, evidence or jurisprudence. Psychology, obviously. Maybe gender studies. But I'm not sure yet whether there are linguistic or maybe english or philosophy courses that might apply.

INT. ROBERT'S OFFICE - DAY

It is later in the day. Robert is seated behind his desk, head bowed, focused on the task at hand. He is grading his students' papers with a pen. Jolene is gone. Robert is alone.

There is a knock at the door. Robert looks up.

ROBERT
Come in.

The door opens, and we see standing in the hall the woman with raven-dark hair. She appears the same as she did in Marcel's law firm. She is wearing the same white silk blouse and navy-blue pencil skirt.

When Robert sees the raven-haired woman, he recognizes her and stands. His face is a mixture of surprise and confusion.

The raven-haired woman steps into the office. Her face is without expression. She opens her black leather attaché and removes an envelope and gracefully offers it to Robert. Robert steps toward her and hesitantly takes the envelope from her extended hand.

ROBERT
How . . . how is he?

The raven-haired woman does not reply. She bows her head slightly and leaves. Robert stands in his office looking at the front of the envelope.

* * *

INT. COMIC BOOK STORE - DAY

Behind a glass counter displaying rare first-edition comic books in clear plastic sleeves and bowls of colorful twenty-sided dice, on a shelf beside a cup full of pistachio shells and a discarded rare Boba Fett figurine, there is an IBM Selectric typeball.

We hear two voices, high pitched and precise.

FIRST NINJA (O.S.)
You realize, of course, that Doctor
Tempus is but a pale imitation of the
original Timekeeper.

SECOND NINJA (O.S.)
That's absurd. Doctor Tempus is the
Guardian of the Circle of Time. The
Timekeeper is an evil synthezoid bent
on world domination.

The glass counter and the shelf are surrounded by a riot of
colorful figurines, cards, games, models. A life-size inflatable
superhero hangs from the ceiling. The fantastic covers of the
latest comic books beckon, one after the other, from neat
stacks on racks against the walls. On tables in the middle of
the store are row after row of narrow cardboard boxes filled
with old comic books in sealed plastic bags.

FIRST NINJA (O.S.)
The Galactic Orb placed the original
Timekeeper in a suspended animation
pod and cast him into the cosmic
singularity.

SECOND NINJA (O.S.)
Before the Nano-War?

In the back of the store, there are several long, folding tables.
A fluorescent light burns above one corner. The rest of the
tables are in shadow.

Two young boys, FIRST NINJA and SECOND NINJA, are
playing a card game at one of the tables. They are wearing
identical black ninja outfits. They wear masks that cover most
of their faces.

ZACH is sitting at another table, directly under the light. They are the only people in the store.

The First Ninja turns and looks at Zach.

> FIRST NINJA
> Hey, Zach. Did the Galactic Orb put the original Timekeeper into suspended animation before or after the Nano-War?

Zach is wearing high-top tennis shoes, cargo shorts and an old tee shirt printed with a faded, almost illegible logo reading "Terra Incognita." His hair is a mess. It looks like he cut it himself. He has several days growth of whiskers.

Zach is reading a book.

BOOK SPINE

The title is printed on the spine. Zach is reading something like "The Archaeology of Knowledge" by Michel Foucault.

BACK TO SCENE

Zach speaks without looking up from his book.

> ZACH
> Before. The Galactic Orb created the synthezoid Timekeeper to be an exact duplicate of the original Timekeeper.

> FIRST NINJA
> With all the original Timekeeper's powers to manipulate the space-time continuum.

The Second Ninja gravely nods his head.

SECOND NINJA
But in service of the Galactic Orb's
diabolical plans.

Zach turns a page in his book.

ZACH
Exactamundo.

FIRST NINJA
Told you.

The First Ninja turns back to the card game.

RAVEN-HAIRED WOMAN

The woman with raven-dark hair is standing still and silent behind the Second Ninja. She is wearing the same white blouse and navy-blue skirt. She has silently approached the ninjas and Zach. The First Ninja sees the raven-haired woman. He is startled and gasps.

FIRST NINJA
Gah!

The First Ninja falls out of his chair onto the floor. The Second Ninja spins around out of his seat and assumes a defensive martial arts posture. The First Ninja bounces back up and also assumes a martial arts posture.

The raven-haired woman calmly watches the little ninjas. Her expression does not change.

Zach stands up and moves to restrain the little ninjas.

ZACH
Hey. Guys. Do not assault the
customer. I repeat. Do not. Assault.
The customer.

The little ninjas exchange tense glances.

> FIRST NINJA
> Set up a perimeter.

The Second Ninja nods, and they scuttle away from the raven-haired woman into the shadows of the room.

Zach approaches the raven-haired woman.

> ZACH
> I'm sorry about that. They get a little
> carried away sometimes.

The raven-haired woman removes a envelope from her black leather attaché and offers it to Zach. Zach takes it. The raven-haired woman bows her head slightly.

Zach examines the letter and looks up.

> ZACH
> Wait . . .

But the raven-haired woman is gone.

Zach stands in the light from the florescent bulbs above his head and looks at the envelope.

From the darkness in the comic book store around him, one of the little ninjas hoots like an owl, HOO HOO, and from another place in the darkness across the room, the other little ninja answers softly, CAW CAW, like a crow.

*   *   *

INT. SQUASH COURT – DAY

Marcel and Trevor are playing squash. Marcel is serving.

                    MARCEL
          I could have been a really good
          novelist.

                    TREVOR
          Just serve it already.

Marcel lobs a perfect serve into the corner. Trevor flails help-
lessly several times at the ball as it floats over his head. He
stumbles and falls backwards in a tangled heap.

INT. SPORTS BAR - NIGHT

Marcel and Trevor are sitting at a table drinking a beer. There
are several empty bottles on the table. Everybody else in the
bar is standing, watching sports on television.

                    MARCEL
          Winston Straw said that I was one
          of the best students he'd ever
          taught.

The bar erupts in CHEERS. Trevor looks over his shoulder at
the crowd.

INT. SPORTS BAR - NIGHT

Marcel and Trevor are playing as a team on one side of a
foosball table. On the other side are two men with their neck-
ties hanging loose and their shirttails untucked. Trevor is
unsteady. Marcel is somewhat disheveled.

                    MARCEL
                (slurred)
          It's not that I don't love the
          law . . .

Marcel confidently takes a shot, and there is a THOCK as the ball hits the back of the goal. The two men groan. Trevor takes the two $20 bills from the top of the table and smiles. The men have had enough and stagger away. Marcel guzzles the last of another bottle of beer.

INT. SPORTS BAR - NIGHT

Marcel and Trevor are standing beside a billiard table. Marcel is somewhat more disheveled. They are holding billiard cues and are playing against two other men. Marcel sinks the winning shot, an improbable bank shot, but she hardly notices. Their opponents are dumbstruck. One is agape. The other smacks himself on the forehead.

> MARCEL
> (badly slurred)
> You think about what might have
> been. The whole road-not-taken
> scenario . . .

Trevor collects their winnings from the edge of the billiard table and starts counting through a sizeable stack of money.

INT. SPORTS BAR - NIGHT

Marcel staggers back and forth in front of a dart board with a dart in her hand poised to throw. She is obviously intoxicated. A small crowd is watching.

> MARCEL
> I could have taken . . .the road not
> taken . . .

She narrows one eye. She tosses the dart. The dart hits the bullseye. A small crowd cheers. Their opponents groan. Trevor collects the winnings.

INT. SPORTS BAR - NIGHT

Marcel and Trevor are sitting at the bar. Marcel is quite drunk, a total mess.

> MARCEL
> (rambling)
> And that has made all the difference.
> (intense)
> And that has made all the difference.

Marcel looks around the bar. Everyone else is ignoring her.

> MARCEL
> Thank you. Thank you very much.

The BARTENDER steps toward them. He is a burly man with a bristling mustache.

> BARTENDER
> Last call, folks.

> MARCEL
> I will arm-wrestle you, nancy boy.

Trevor gathers her in and pulls her away from the bartender.

> TREVOR
> Let's get you a cab.

INT. MARCEL'S KITCHEN – MORNING

Marcel is sitting in her apartment at a small kitchen table with a cup of coffee. The sun is shining through a window. She is very, very hung over.

MARCEL
I could have been a really good
novelist.

Trevor sets a plate of scrambled eggs and toast in front of her
and sits down across from her. Marcel is surprised to see
breakfast. She squints across the table at Trevor.

MARCEL
Tell me again, why are you in my
apartment?

TREVOR
I slept on the couch. I've never seen
you so drunk. It's like you turned
into Norman Mailer.

He puts a wad of money on the table.

TREVOR
We made two hundred and thirty
dollars, by the way. Is this how you
paid for law school?

MARCEL
When I wasn't stripping.

Marcel pushes the money toward Trevor.

MARCEL
Listen, Trevor, thanks for your help.
I probably don't need to tell you
this, but getting drunk and gambling
are probably not the best ways to
advance your legal career.

TREVOR
Hey, it happens. So . . . what's this all (more)

TREVOR (cont'd)
about? What was in that letter?

MARCEL
(reticent)
Winston Straw wants to have a
reunion. He's invited our class to his
home for dinner.

TREVOR
And you don't want to go?

MARCEL
Let's say I have mixed emotions.

INT. CEDAR CHEST - MORNING

Inside the darkness of a closed cedar chest, the sound comes
of someone outside opening the chest. The top of the cedar
chest cracks open and lets the light in. Two hands swing the
top up, and we see Marcel's face leaning over the chest,
peering into the chest, and behind her, looking over her
shoulder, Trevor's face. Marcel's hand comes closer and
reaches into the darkness of the chest. She pulls several
objects out of the chest. She is looking for something near the
bottom, buried under sweaters and shoe boxes and photo
albums.

MARCEL
It's in here somewhere . . .

She finds the old typed manuscript. It is several inches of
white paper bound with a metal clip. She pulls it from the
bottom of the chest.

MARCEL
Here it is.

She holds it with both hands, pausing to look at it. Trevor's face is hovering over her shoulder as he also peers at the manuscript.

Marcel smiles, her thoughts far away.

                    MARCEL
          Marcel is not amused.

INT. MARCEL'S KITCHEN - MORNING

Marcel and Trevor are seated at her kitchen table. Marcel is reading from the manuscript. Trevor is listening

                    MARCEL
          They rushed up in a column of
          cinders and flame and smoke, and the
          fine, black ashes began to drift in a
          plume across the night sky. The
          bonfire below dwindled to a bright
          circle, and the students' cries grew
          distant and faint. The ashes, still
          burning at the delicate edges, drifted
          higher until a strong wind took them
          and carried them ever farther away.

                 *   *   *

EXT. BICYCLE RACK – DAY

Robert is unlocking his bicycle. He puts metal clips around his pant legs. He dons an enormous helmet. The helmet has a flashing light. He has several mirrors on the helmet and the bike. He puts on a neon orange safety vest. He mounts the bike and pedals away. A student waves as he is leaving. He waves back, almost crashes.

INT. ROBERT'S CONDOMINIUM – EVENING

Robert comes in the front door with his bicycle. Robert and his wife live in a modest condominium decorated in an eclectic, arts-and-crafty style. Robert's wife TILDA is standing beside a dining table. She is facing away from him. He stops for a moment and contemplates his wife.

> ROBERT
> I just had the strangest idea.

Tilda turns and faces him. Tilda is an attractive mixture of simplicity and self-assurance. She radiates focused energy and polite insistence. She wears her blond hair very short.

> TILDA
> Make it quick. We've got the condo
> board meeting in an hour.

> ROBERT
> We should get tattoos.

> TILDA
> On our bodies?
> (frowns)
> Don't be absurd.

She walks out of the room.

> ROBERT
> I just don't want us to . . . you know,
> get in a rut.

Robert drifts over to the table where she was standing.

> TILDA (O.S.)
> We're not going to get in a rut. Did
> something happen at work today?

Robert looks at the table.

TABLE

On the table are neat stacks of glossy brochures with Tilda's picture on them. She's running for condo board president.

BACK TO SCENE

> ROBERT
> Oh, no. Not really. I mean, I got this letter. From my old creative writing professor.

> TILDA (O.S.)
> The Gloaming guy?

BOOKSHELF

Three of Winston Straw's books are on a book shelf. The titles are legible on the spines: "Before the Gloaming", "Into the Gloaming" and "After the Gloaming".

BACK TO SCENE

> ROBERT
> Yes, the Gloaming guy. Winston Straw.

Tilda comes out of the bedroom with a large campaign poster with her likeness on it.

POSTER

She is smiling stiffly in the poster photo, and it looks a little frightening.

BACK TO SCENE

> ROBERT
> You're running for condo board
> president?

> TILDA
> I told you. Like a month ago.

> ROBERT
> I guess I wasn't expecting . . .
> > (picks up a brochure)
> campaign literature.
> > (joking)
> Is there a debate?

Tilda steps past him.

> TILDA
> Just one.

> ROBERT
> Seriously?

> TILDA
> > (unsmiling)
> Seriously.

Tilda puts the poster aside and stacks the brochures in a box.
She sits on the couch and pats the seat next to her, indicating
that Robert should join her.

> TILDA
> So what did the letter say? From your
> old teacher.

Robert awkwardly sidesteps the campaign poster, almost trip-
ping over it, and sits next to Tilda.

TILDA AND ROBERT

ROBERT
It was an invitation. Dinner with my
old classmates.

TILDA
And tattoos are required?

ROBERT
(joking)
Yes. Yes, they are.

Tilda smiles at her husband's joking tone.

TILDA
You should go.

ROBERT
You don't want to come?

TILDA
I really need to focus on this election.

ROBERT
For condo board.

TILDA
You gotta start somewhere.

ROBERT
Sweetheart, this was a really important time
in my life. Winston Straw was like a father
to me. I want to share this with you.

TILDA
Oh, Robert. Was it really that
important? Isn't this just . . .nostalgia.
Shouldn't we . . .   (more)

> TILDA (cont'd)
> put aside childish things?

Robert reacts, stands up. He raises an index finger in mock umbrage, but there is the suggestion of real irritation beneath the surface when he speaks.

> ROBERT
> The child is father to the man, my
> dear wife.

He walks over to an antique secretary and opens a drawer.

OPEN DRAWER

The drawer is full of Tilda's campaign brochures, row after row of her smiling face.

BACK TO SCENE

Robert is surprised.

> ROBERT
> What . . . what happened to my old
> manuscripts?

Tilda covers her open mouth with one hand.

> TILDA
> Those were manuscripts?

> ROBERT
> (emphatic)
> Yes.

> TILDA
> (grimacing)
> I think it's under the ficus.

FICUS

The ficus is growing in a pot in a sunny corner of the room. The pot is resting on top of a stack of Robert's manuscripts. The manuscripts are dirty and waterlogged.

*　　*　　*

INT. COMIC BOOK STORE – DAY

Zach is sorting new comic books and putting them into folders. Behind him, across the room, is a trash can.

TRASH CAN

In the trash can is the Professor's letter, wadded up and unopened.

LITTLE NINJAS

The little ninjas, still wearing their black outfits and masks, are hiding from Zach. The First Ninja is watching Zach while the Second Ninja is crawling on his belly towards the trash can. The First Ninja nods to the Second Ninja. The Second Ninja's hand rises above the trash can and carefully removes the letter from the trash.

INT. COMIC BOOK STORE - EVENING

Zach is preparing to close the comic book store. At the front door, he flips the closed sign and turns off the lights. He turns around, and the little ninjas are now standing behind him with their arms crossed on their chests.

                    FIRST NINJA
          We need to talk.

INT. COMIC BOOK STORE - EVENING

Zach is sitting at one of the folding tables in the rear of the store. The little ninjas are standing on either side of Zach. They are directly underneath the florescent light. It is the only light on. The ninjas are grim and serious. It looks like an interrogation.

                    ZACH
          Aren't you guys going to be late for
          dinner?

                    FIRST NINJA
          You've been holding out on us.

                    ZACH
          About?

The Second Ninja tosses the letter from the Professor onto the table in front of Zach.

                    ZACH
          Not cool, guys. Really not cool.

                    SECOND NINJA
          Sorry. We needed the intel.

                    ZACH
          I think this might be just a little
          outside your jurisdiction.

                    FIRST NINJA
          How come you didn't tell us about
          the Professor?

                    ZACH
          Nothing to tell.
               (sadly)
          It's ancient history.

SECOND NINJA
He invited you to dinner at his
house.

Zach picks up the letter.

ZACH
(unsure)
Really?

FIRST NINJA
You've got to go.

The First Ninja nods to the Second Ninja. The Second Ninja
unzips his backpack and pulls out a homemade graphic novel.
He carefully positions it on the table in front of Zach.

GRAPHIC NOVEL

The graphic novel has a lurid cover with garish colors. The
title is "Confederate Vampires in Space." The quality of the
art is poor.

BACK TO SCENE

ZACH
Winston Straw isn't going to look at a
comic book.

LITTLE NINJAS
(together)
Graphic novel.

ZACH
That's not a graphic novel.

The little ninjas are stricken. They gasp.

FIRST NINJA
(hurt)
Why would you say that?

SECOND NINJA
Maybe you should try reading it
first.

The First Ninja turns to one side, and the Second Ninja puts a
consoling hand on his shoulder.

ZACH
All right, all right. I'm sorry. You're
right, okay. You're right. I should
read it.

The First Ninja stoically brushes away something in his eye.

SECOND NINJA
Philistine.

ZACH
Look, let me give you guys some
advice.
(pauses, thinking)
You remember how the Galactic Orb
tricked Doctor Tempus into looking
at his reflection in the Narcissus
Chamber?

The little ninjas nod in unison.

ZACH
Writing is like that. If you aren't
careful, you get trapped. You stop
caring about other people. You lose
your friends, forget your family.

FIRST NINJA
Is that what happened to you?

ZACH
Winston Straw said I was one of the
best students he had ever taught. But
I saw what it was doing to me, to my
friends.

Zach pauses, lost for a moment in the past.

ZACH
So I quit. I burned everything I ever
wrote, and I haven't written a word of
fiction since.

*   *   *

EXT. THE PROFESSOR'S BROWNSTONE – NIGHT

Marcel, in a wool overcoat, is standing at the front door of a
brownstone in an upscale neighborhood. The door opens,
and the raven-haired woman greets Marcel and gestures for
her to enter. Marcel goes inside, and the door closes.

INT. THE PROFESSOR'S PARLOR – NIGHT

Robert, in a coat and tie, is sitting alone on a couch in a small,
comfortable, tastefully furnished room. There are Remington
sculptures of horses and cowboys. A Bierstadt landscape hangs
on the wall.

The raven-haired woman leads Marcel into the room. She
takes Marcel's coat and leaves.

Marcel is beautiful in a flattering dress. Marcel stops when she
sees Robert.

Robert stands. Marcel hesitates, then sits at the opposite end of the couch. Robert sits back down. It is awkward.

COUCH

Marcel looks at her hands in her lap. Robert gazes at her for an uncomfortable moment. Finally, she turns and forces herself to look at him. That breaks the spell.

Robert exhales, smiles. He shakes his head, amazed to see her again.

Marcel smiles. It is a smile that is tentative and unsure at first, but it slowly ripens into a knowing, radiant grin.

Robert shakes his head again and laughs ruefully. He holds up his wedding ring.

> ROBERT
> My wife is running for condo board
> president.

Marcel sighs.

> MARCEL
> My secretary is trying to fix me up
> with her neighbors.

They both laugh, and Marcel reaches across the couch toward Robert, and Robert reaches out and takes her hand.

DOORWAY

The raven-haired woman leads Zach into the parlor. She has his coat, an old ski jacket. Zach has cleaned up, shaved, combed his hair. Zach sees Marcel and Robert. The raven-haired woman leaves.

ZACH

Whoa. Uh, surprise.

COUCH

Marcel and Robert quickly pull their hands back. They are both surprised to see Zach.

PARLOR

Marcel and Robert stand up and meet Zach in the middle of the room. They face each other for a long moment, three sides of a balanced triangle. When they begin to speak, it is with a strained, arch civility.

MARCEL

I can't believe Professor Straw invited you.

ZACH

I can't believe I came.

ROBERT

Still at the comic book shop?

ZACH

Yes I am.

MARCEL

No Pokemon tournament tonight?

Robert smirks. Zach simmers for a beat.

ZACH

Look, could we maybe try to put the past behind us for just one night?

ROBERT

I don't think so, Zach.

                    MARCEL
          Nope. Sorry.

               THE PROFESSOR (O.S.)
          Behold!

Marcel, Robert and Zach turn to face the Professor.

The Professor is standing in the doorway to the parlor. He is
using a cane. He has aged. His skull is more pronounced beneath his bald head. He seems imperious, but with a
mischievous gleam in his eye.

                  THE PROFESSOR
          My three greatest disappointments.

                    ROBERT
          Are you talking about us?

                  THE PROFESSOR
          Regrettably yes. You three had more
          talent than all my other students put
          together.

The Professor walks into the room.

                  THE PROFESSOR
          The rest of your class will not be
          joining us tonight. I have brought you
          here under false pretenses.
               (pauses dramatically)
          I am dying. I have assembled you
          three because I have a special request.

INT. DINING ROOM – NIGHT

The Professor, Marcel, Robert and Zach are finishing their
meal at a table with linen, flowers, candlelight, wine.

THE PROFESSOR
So I thought, what can I do in the
face of this relentless technological
onslaught? What can be done to save
the genre?

ROBERT
I share your concern, but isn't it
possible that the Internet will make it
easier for people to publish a novel?

THE PROFESSOR
Perhaps. But it won't matter if fewer
and fewer people are reading them.

MARCEL
So what exactly are you proposing?

The Professor leans forward, looks them each in the eye.

THE PROFESSOR
A live, online writing competition.

ZACH
Like a reality show?

THE PROFESSOR
Yes, I suppose. Viewers would vote
based on what each competitor wrote.

ROBERT
And the winner would receive . . .

THE PROFESSOR
The majority of my estate. Several
million dollars.

They are silent for a moment.

THE PROFESSOR
Yes, yes, I know what you're thinking.
How crass. How commercial. Well, yes.
Writing has always been competitive. I
say drastic times call for drastic measures.

MARCEL
How can we help you?

THE PROFESSOR
I want you to be the first three
competitors.

They all react with surprise. They quickly exchange glances
across the table.

ROBERT
Are you sure? We aren't exactly on
the best of terms.

ZACH
I'll do it.

The Professor sits back and smiles with satisfaction. Marcel
and Robert are stunned.

ROBERT
What?

MARCEL
What happened to Mister "I renounce
writing forever"?

Zach looks at the Professor, and they hold each other's gaze
for a beat.

ZACH
People change. Plus, I need the money.

                    ROBERT
          You're assuming you'd win?

                     ZACH
          Like either of you is going to beat
          me.

                    MARCEL
          That's it. I'm in, too.

The Professor claps his hands with glee. They all turn and
look at Robert.

                    ROBERT
          I've got classes to teach.
                    (weakening)
          My wife is running for condo board.
                    (gives up)
          Fine. I'm in, too.

Marcel and Zach cheer.

                    MARCEL
          So how will this work?

                 THE PROFESSOR
          I've arranged for something I believe
          you denizens of the Internet call a
          website.

WEBSITE

We see a computer screen displaying the website. The website
is called "Deathless Prose Gladiators". It has a grand prize
amount displayed and a section for the score. Below that, it
has three sections. Each section has a profile picture for Marcel or Robert or Zach.

THE PROFESSOR (V.O.)
You each can log in and upload your
work. The rest is self-explanatory.

BACK TO SCENE

THE PROFESSOR
My publicist is handling the
marketing. People will vote every
week. You must finish to win.

ROBERT
It's like King Lear.

MARCEL
No, it's like the Judgment of Paris.

ZACH
No, it's like Confederate Vampires in
Space.

Zach's comment annoys and puzzles Robert and Marcel.

The Professor raises his glass.

THE PROFESSOR
(toasting)
To writing . . . To words.

ZACH AND MARCEL AND ROBERT
(toasting)
To words.

They raise their glasses and drink.

*   *   *

ROBERT (V.O.)

And so the contest began. The next few weeks were exciting. Robert arranged for a sabbatical from his teaching duties and avoided his politically ambitious wife. Marcel scheduled a much-needed vacation and quietly shifted most of her cases to Trevor and Bernice and to the other attorneys at her firm. Zach hired the little ninjas full time at the comic book shop and holed up in the back with last summer's movie merchandise and other forgotten figurines . .

5

AT THE FAR EDGE OF THE SOLAR SYSTEM, where the solar wind meets the interstellar sea, a transmodal transfer station swept smoothly through the icy silence of outer space. The nearest human outpost with a self-sustaining biosphere was millions of miles away on the terraformed structures orbiting high above the methane seas of Saturn's moon, Titan.

The transmodal transfer station, or TTS, was one of many semi-autonomous satellites designed to be a router for the transfer of faster-than-light data launched from a quantum catapult. The TTS was not an endpoint, but rather a relay station, a conduit, one point in a network designed to receive data and to speed it on accurately to another destination light years away. The TTS was a large satellite by human scale with huge gossamer sails that turned like leaves toward the distant Sun. Maintenance robots crawled the satellite's skeleton and made the frequent repairs and necessary updates. Unmanned convoys docked periodically and delivered containers full of supplies in the TTS's compact cargo hold. At the fringe of deep space, the TTS was not intended to support human life for an extended period of time. Only a small section of the

TTS could maintain an atmosphere and gravity. Long and narrow, the section revolved like a needle at the center of the petals of the satellite's blossom.

Inside the TTS needle, in a small, windowless cabin, a man was sitting on a bunk. He was wearing simple, black, loose-fitting garments cinched at the waste with a crude belt tied in a knot. His brown hair was cropped close to his head. His square jaw and serious face made him seem somber and grave. He appeared slight and almost frail, but something in his shoulders and the way he held his head suggested discipline and a preternatural calmness. He looked like an ascetic or a monk. A ninja, perhaps, from some lost time on ancient Earth.

Across from the man, another figure was sitting on another bunk. She appeared to be human, but her gender was not immediately apparent. She wore clothing that simulated tanned deerskin, carved and beaded with an intricate design. Her skin was distinctly rufescent and was inked with swirls of bold tattoos partially visible on her arms and chest. Her jewelry — rings and bracelets and armbands and chokers — was exquisite, crafted from silver and turquoise. She wore an elaborate necklace with pendants and gems carved in the shape of bear claws and boar tusks. Her hair was dark and straight, and she wore a circle of feathers like a crown on her head. Her face was long and serene and majestic, colored like a mask with vivid streaks of pigment.

The man was holding a strange artifact, a sheaf of white parchments with black text printed in ink on each dog-eared page, all bound together with a metal clip at one corner. A manuscript, he had called it.

The man was reading from the manuscript:

"And so the contest began. The next few weeks were exciting. Robert arranged for a sabbatical from his teaching duties and avoided his politically ambitious wife. Marcel scheduled a much-needed vacation and quietly shifted most of her cases to Trevor and Bernice and to the other attorneys at her firm. Zach hired the little ninjas full time at the comic book shop and holed up in the back with last summer's movie merchandise and other forgotten figurines."

The man stopped reading and looked at the figure seated across from him. They were facing each other, knee to knee, almost touching.

"Go on," the other said. "What happens next?"

A soft chime sounded, and a pale blue light briefly glowed around the edge of the door. There was a pneumatic hiss, and the door slid open.

Outside the doorway was Jeb Stuart.

Stuart was wearing a spotless gray uniform with silver buttons and epaulets, a scarlet-lined cape, a bright yellow sash, a hat with a brim. On one side of his hat, he wore a flawless, white ostrich plume. His black gloved hand rested on the glittering hilt of a long sword hanging in its scabbard at his waist. His black boots shone with polish. On his lapel, he wore a fresh, fragrant, red rose, held firmly in place with a pearl-headed pin. His face was bloodless and pale. A neat, gray beard obscured his mouth. The seated man glimpsed Stuart's eyes briefly in shadow beneath the brim of his ostrich-plumed hat. They were strange, liquid eyes, almost solid black. When he spoke, his voice was soft and watery and cold.

"It's here," Jeb Stuart said. "We're ready for you."

The seated man nodded and set the manuscript aside. He and the figure wearing the feather crown stood and followed Jeb Stuart out of the room. They walked through the close, tight passageways in the needle at the center of the TTS. The artificial gravity diminished as they proceeded through several open air locks. When they reached the entrance to the cargo hold, they grasped firmly the handholds on the walls, and their feet barely touched the floor.

The cargo hold was small and very cold, but it had a higher ceiling. After the cramped rooms and passageways in the needle, it felt like they were entering a much larger area. On the far wall was a large air lock. On the other side of the air lock was the inhospitable edge of interstellar space. In the wall near the airlock, there was a dark and frosty porthole. The man tried to see what was outside the porthole, but he could only see darkness. He guessed there was some sort of starcraft docked outside the airlock, one he hoped to see with his own eyes.

The cargo hold was almost full with very little wasted space. There were several interlocking, modular containers stacked neatly up to the ceiling against one wall. An idle maintenance robot squatted against another wall, locked in place, its blunt appendages sprawled loosely on the floor.

In front of the air lock was a single container. It appeared that it had only recently arrived. Standing in front of the container were four figures that appeared to be human. Two of them, a man and a woman, were clothed in deerskins and feathers in a similar fashion to the feather-crowned woman. A third figure, thin and pale, wore a plain gray uniform similar to that of Jeb Stuart.

And there behind them, the man saw a welcome sight — the bald head and round glasses of his mentor, the Professor.

They stepped toward each other and grasped each other's arms firmly in a happy greeting. The Professor was wearing the same dark, monk-like clothes as the man.

"Deadly Robert!" the Professor said, beaming. "I knew I'd see you again, old friend."

Jeb Stuart nodded to the others, and they opened the container.

Inside the container was a bizarre object roughly the size

of a human being. It looked organic, like a cocoon, but it was metallic.

Deadly Robert's serious face slipped for a moment, and his usual composure was visibly shaken. He and the Professor exchanged a knowing glance.

"Can you open it?" the Professor asked.

Deadly Robert cautiously approached the strange metallic cocoon.

"I'm not sure."

He carefully felt around the edges of the cocoon. He concentrated, closed his eyes.

"Yes. I think I can," Robert said.

"Do it," the Professor said.

Everybody stepped back and formed a semicircle around Deadly Robert and the metallic cocoon. Robert put his hands on the cocoon and closed his eyes. He concentrated, slowly moving his hands. Minutes passed as Robert focused his energy and attention. He began to perspire in the cold air, and his face grew red and showed the strain of the effort. His arms began to tremble, and it seemed he had reached the physical limits of his exertions.

"Yarg!"

Deadly Robert cried out and fell back from the cocoon. The others stepped back. He crouched on the floor, watching the cocoon, and the Professor moved behind him and placed a firm hand on his shoulder.

There was a quiet click, and the cocoon began softly to hum. The humming grew louder, and then they heard the soft whirring of a dense mechanism in motion. There was a loud, solid thunk like the sound of a thrown bolt, and the cocoon became translucent and began to glow from within with a shimmering, golden light. It expelled steam from either side with a loud hiss. Then the cocoon split down the middle and peeled opened vertically in sections. Steam was billowing out of the inside of the open cocoon. Something was inside. They edged closer to see it more clearly.

Inside the cocoon was a human figure. As the steam cleared, they could see that the human figure was a tall man with a dark beard. He was wearing a coon-skin cap and a finely-tanned buckskin hunting frock.

The man in the cocoon was Kit Carson.

Kit Carson fell forward, unconscious, and the others rushed to catch him.

"Let's get him to an infirmary," the Professor said.

*   *   *

The invention of the quantum catapult had enabled faster-than-light space travel. An era of interstellar exploration had followed, but it was still a technical challenge to deliver an organic human brain to a destination light years away. For this reason, a valid space passport had to include a complete neural schema digitized from the bearer's organic brain. The quantum catapult technicians made a copy of the neural schema, and the schema was beamed to the target destination light years away as insurance in case of brain damage to the passenger. A complete neural schema held an immense amount of data, and neuroplastic nano-surgery was a long and challenging procedure. Reconstruction of an entire human brain was possible, but even on Earth, it could result in cognitive discrepancies, neural lacunae, phantom memories. To obtain a passport, a catapult jockey had to undergo psychological training to prepare for the possibility of organic brain damage. Despite the risks, hundreds of thousands of space pioneers had made the journey safely across distances of light years, and some had made dozens of tours.

Most humans, however, did not want to risk brain damage even for interstellar space travel. As an alternative, it had become easier and safer to digitize a partial neural schema and use a catapult to beam the partial schema into a waiting receptacle, usually a lifelike android. The android was often physically consistent, if not identical, in appearance to the human source code. The android twin usually had a constrained objective and time frame after which — not unlike Cinderella at the stroke of midnight in the ancient fairy tale — the neural schema was beamed back and used to reconfigure the neurochemical structure of the organic brain in the human source. Once the human source had recovered, which could take days, the new data integrated quickly into an existing set of memories, experiences, skills. The twinning facilitated integration of the new data. The procedure could be disorienting at first for the reconstructed source, but most subjects described it as remembering very clearly something they thought they had forgotten, like a memory from childhood. The procedure was far safer than real-time space travel. The only problems were ethical, but they applied to everything involving neuroplasticity, and the Drumhead monitored every procedure down to the nanometer. In all of human history, there had never been an instance of unauthorized neuroplastic reconstruction.

*   *   *

The boy held the flat, round disc carefully between the fingertips of his outstretched hands.

"What is it?" the girl asked.

"Music," the boy said.

The girl looked closer at the disc, her feline pupils shifting. The finely-grooved black vinyl gleamed in the sphere of light that shone from the june bug clinging to her shoulder. The june bug scissored its golden wings and made a barely-audible thrumming sound. Perched in the darkness, on the back of a nearby chair, the boy's parrot cocked its head, adjusting the intensity of its light. Its lenses silently refocused on the surface of the disc. The parrot's cooling system kicked on, humming quietly for a few seconds, then kicked off.

"But how?" the girl asked.

"It's analog. Inert. Raw data. Pure and non-degraded."

"How do you load it?"

"You don't. You have to use a physical interface. It's called a turntable. Wait till you see this."

The boy pivoted to the wall behind him and positioned the vinyl disk on the flat, round surface of the turntable.

"Feel this," he said, and guided her fingertip to the end of the stylus and the sharp point of the needle. The girl frowned.

"The disc spins and the needle bounces across the data. At least, I think that's what's supposed to happen," the boy explained.

"It's, like, medieval," the girl said, incredulous.

"Yeah," the boy laughed. "I hope my parrot can play it."

The boy plugged the turntable's power cord into the parrot's universal interface. Because the parrot used the same wireless networks as every other modern device, the boy was operating on guesswork and what he had studied in his history of technology classes. He could not find the parrot's audio jack and had to ask the parrot where it was located. The boy followed the parrot's instructions and found the jack at the bottom of the parrot's feathered breast. He plugged the turntable's audio output into the parrot. The parrot positioned its wings, spreading them half open, exposing its tiny speakers. The boy's hand trembled slightly as he depressed the turntable power switch.

When he spoke again, there was a nervous quaver in his voice.

"Listen," he said, and pressed the turntable's play button.

The boy and the girl leaned forward expectantly, and the silence in the basement of the old house seemed to deepen. The vinyl disc slowly began to spin. There was an abrupt thunk as the needle dropped onto the disc, and the parrot's speakers crackled and popped for loud, painful moments. Then the parrot's software swiftly filtered out most of the noise. The first few notes of music began to play. The june bug crawled forward on the girl's shoulder, alertly swiveling its tiny silver antennae to and fro. The parrot shifted its head slightly, its quantum processors clicking quietly somewhere within its feathered breast.

The music moved through the still, dead air. It filled the close spaces of the ancient basement. It was piano music, lyrical, a melody. A woman's voice began to sing. She sang with utter confidence. Her voice was sad, weary, oddly fragile. She sang of loneliness, of her absent lover. The song reached into their brains and subtly began to alter their neurochemistry. It summoned forth a bittersweet longing, the pain and pleasure of memory and time. The happy melody and her sad voice together seemed inevitable, doomed, tragic.

The song drifted up the darkened stairs of the basement. It filled the cavernous rooms of the first floor of the old house. It moved around the rotting furniture shrouded in mildewed linens, past the hand-cut masonry of the huge fireplace, the sepia-stained walls, the warped wainscoting, the twisted molding and sagging, irregular slats of broken wooden blinds, past the tarnished chandeliers and plaster ceiling crumbling piece by piece onto the gnawed remains of rugs lying in spiraled cylinders like fallen trees on the pock-marked mahogany and teakwood floors, on through the foyer and its shattered beveled glass, across the marbled threshold and its twin sculptures gilded with the excrement of gulls. The woman's sad song crept onto the massive granite porch overlooking an angry shore. It floated on the wind, mingled with the sounds of the beach and was lost finally amid the rhythmic pounding of the sea.

The ruins of the old house were on a point of land far from any inhabitable area. A helicopter landing pad had long ago been reclaimed by weeds and sand. The house had settled into the shoreline over the decades. Drifting sand had covered half of the monumental porch. One side of the second-floor dome had collapsed. Even so, the structure was still recognizable as what had once been an extravagant retreat, the sort of comfortable and secure pleasure dome only great wealth could afford. Farther down the beach were the familiar Glissade/Frappe signs warning of a restricted area, data contamination, prosecution, danger. The boy's and girl's sun bikes were parked on the shore near the front porch.

The boy had stumbled across the location of the old house while performing research in the Glissade/Frappe archives for his mentor. The shore was within the range of a fully-charged sun-bike, and the boy had a higher security clearance than most of the other apprentices. He discovered the vault in the basement by accident and told no one. He had invited the girl to come with him to explore the ruins and listen to the raw data he had discovered. He packed a lunch and an ambitious bottle of wine. The girl was in her third decade and had a thoughtful, enchanting presence. The boy and the girl both had access to the best cosmetic surgeons on the Glissade/Frappe campus, but the girl had also activated her chimera genes. She had selected for feline accents that manifested in inhuman green eyes, subtle whiskers, golden striped patterns in her short-cropped hair and in the shimmering suggestion of fur that covered most of her body. Both of them wore programmable skin wraps and had downloaded the latest in fashionable designs, a retro ebony zoot-suit for her, a rust-colored, Aztec-themed, psychedelic dream-robe for him.

The song ended, and they stood silently for a moment in the darkened basement.

"Who is it?" the girl asked, still entranced by the woman's sad song.

"I don't know," the boy said.

"She sounds a little like Kali,"

"Yes . . . but not the same."

"And that girl in that vert . . ."

"Yes . . ."

"For the new biologs . . ."

"Yes."

"But not the same."

"No. Not the same."

"Or that woman in that mod . . ."

"The one with the lounge singer?"

"Yes. The torch song."

"The femme fatale."

"Yes."

"But not the same."

"No," the boy said. "Not the same."

"No . . ." the girl said slowly. "Not the same at all."

The turntable had stopped turning. The parrot's speakers were silent.

The boy spoke casually to the parrot.

"Who was singing that song?" the boy asked.

They waited a moment. The parrot cocked its head, but did not respond.

"Play it again," the girl said quietly.

The boy positioned the stylus above the spinning disc, lowered the stylus, and the song began again.

The june bug shifted its silver antennae, scissored its golden wings. The music seemed to agitate it. The june bug's wings began to beat, becoming a golden blur, and the june bug took flight. A gold chain tethered the june bug to the girl's wrap. The june bug rose through the air until the thin chain was taut. It hovered there at the end of its tether, buzzing insistently near the girl's ear. The newer june bugs had a better chip and did not need a tether. They were like the boy's parrot, more autonomous, with better AI.

"What's with your bug?" the boy asked.

"I don't know," she said.

The song was playing again. On the top of the chair back, the parrot was intently processing, moving its beak, cocking its head from side to side. The parrot's cooling system quietly kicked on. The parrot ruffled its tail feathers. The air in the room subtly shifted. It was a mag lev passing overhead. A tremor rumbled through the house, and the turntable needle skipped. The boy and the girl looked at each other. Something big had just landed on the beach outside the house. The boy quickly lifted the stylus, but there was no more time. They heard the miners fanning throughout the first floor of the house. A voice over a loudspeaker was saying something about cease and desist. The boy's parrot squawked. The june bug froze in mid-fight and dropped to the girl's breast, dangling at the end of its tether. The parrot and the june bug began to broadcast the same message as the loudspeaker: "Cease and desist all activities. This is a restricted area. You are in violation of Glissade/Frappe law. Step away from any content delivery system and lie face down on the floor . . ." A military parrot swooped down into the basement. A blinding spotlight shone down the basement stairs, and the boy and the girl listened as the heavy footfalls of a dreadnought exoskeleton came ponderously down the steps. The boy and the girl stood stricken beside the turntable. The dreadnought stooped beneath the basement ceiling. Its spotlights lit up the entire sprawling basement. The boy and the girl held their hands up, squinting in the harsh light. A human voice came from somewhere within the dreadnought. "Cease and desist all activities. This is a restricted area. You are in violation of Glissade/Frappe law. Please step away from the turntable."

*   *   *

Kit Carson sat in the small white room with the narrow windows and looked at the faces of the people seated around the conference room table. Among them was a pale man in the gray uniform with the disquieting black eyes. Once he had been human, a man named Jeb Stuart from nineteenth-century Earth, a soldier in the army of the Confederate States of America, but that man, like the Confederacy, had ceased to exist many centuries earlier. Now Kit Carson knew the sepulchral man in the gray uniform as an intergalactic outlaw with a bounty on his head. Now he was known throughout the universe as the undead leader of the Confederate vampires. That was reason enough to make Kit Carson uneasy.

Jeb Stuart sat with two other Confederate vampires. Their faces were papery-pale ashes and looked as if they would crumble at the touch of a hand.

Beside the Confederate vampires, there were several men and women who appeared to be members of a technologically primitive culture from eighteenth-century Earth. Their presence he could not explain. Their appearance was far too deliberate, almost a parody of the indigenous people of North America. Kit had seen popular entertainments from the twentieth-century. His sharp eyes detected a computer-generated patina. He wondered if only he saw the Indians before him as costumed and theatrical. Whatever the Indians were, their outward appearance cloaked their true identity.

A woman at the table was speaking to him, and he was trying to pay attention. She spoke in a calm voice, soothing but firm, with an easy authority. She was small and wizened and appeared to be human. Her brown face was pock-marked and lined with age, and her dark eyes were spotted with cloudy gray cataracts. Kit knew there was no way of knowing how old she truly was and that her appearance, her complexion, the cataracts were almost certainly cosmetic affectation.

He was not sure anymore what it meant to grow old, not sure if the words still applied. Everything had gotten so confused in his mind. Humans, robots, avatars, fake memories, cosmetic surgery, chimera genes, artificial intelligence. It was often more than Kit could keep straight. He had a few fixed ideas he had come to rely on to keep his bearings, and one of those fixed ideas was that Jeb Stuart was as close to evil as a self-aware creature could come.

The cloudy-eyed woman wore a black, tatted shawl over her almost-white hair. Around her neck, she wore a necklace with a pendant that rested on the cloth across her sternum. The pendant was a figurine carved from alabaster in the shape of a serpent in a circle with its tail in its mouth. The serpent's eyes glinted at him with tiny red rubies.

"Normally we would have waited until after your debriefing," the cloudy-eyed woman was saying. "But, as I've said, we don't have the luxury of time. It is certainly understandable if you are experiencing some confusion or disorientation."

Behind the old woman on a raised wooden stand, a snow-colored owl perched. It was all but motionless, occasionally shifting its large, round, yellow eyes or subtly tilting its feathered head.

Kit looked around the table again.

Several other figures gathered around the table were dressed alike, with short hair, wearing plain, loose, black trousers and a black top tied with a crude belt.

Ninjas, Kit thought. Never a good sign.

Kit recognized the Professor with his bald head and spectacles. There was a woman with dark skin and coarse gray hair cropped close to her head. A young woman with white hair braided in cornrows. A man with a square jaw and a serious face. A raven-haired woman, almost hidden, watching from in the rear.

"Who is in charge here?" Kit said looking at the cloudy-eyed woman with the snake pendant.

She sat back and watched his face.

The dark-skinned woman with the short gray hair spoke to him.

"We don't typically adhere to a hierarchical organizational structure," she said and paused.

The Professor continued.

"Although sometimes we do," he said with a smile.

"When the circumstances require it," added one of the Indian women.

The black-skinned woman spoke.

"Much has changed while you were in the suspended animation pod."

Kit looked at Jeb Stuart and the Confederate vampires.

"That must be true if I am to sit peacefully at the same table with the undead," Kit said and nodded toward Jeb Stuart.

Jeb Stuart turned toward him. Kit looked away from the strange, dark eyes.

"We are no longer your enemy, Kit Carson," Jeb Stuart said.

His voice was soft, sibilant, almost a whisper. Kit had heard Jeb Stuart's voice before, but he still was not prepared. It reminded him of water, like a shallow stream, like gently flowing water that could carry you far, far away, if you let it. A chill ran down his back, and Kit shifted uncomfortably in his chair.

"The Confederate vampires have become agents of peace, ministers of mercy," the Professor said.

Kit Carson laughed.

"It is a ruse. Mass murderers should be imprisoned, treated, re-inculcated."

Jeb Stuart watched Kit with his black liquid eyes. He was stroking his beard.

"We could say the same of you, Kit Carson, could we not?"

Kit said nothing, and the silence in the room grew.

Jeb Stuart rose and walked to one of the narrow windows. Kit Carson tensed his body and watched him closely.

The others calmly listened.

Jeb Stuart looked through the window. Outside was the vastness of interstellar space. Jeb's bloodless face was reflected in the surface of the window.

"A thousand years is a long time to carry sorrow and regret and guilt, my friend. We seek now only peace and harmony. We seek now penance and the promise of rest."

Jeb Stuart turned from the window and addressed the figures gathered around the table.

"For a long time, we believed a voodoo spell had transformed us. The battlefield was still fresh, and our new-born hunger was strong. Perhaps you remember those days, Kit Carson."

The undead man paused. His voice had filled the room. Kit averted his gaze, stared at his hands on the table before him. Beneath his gray beard, Jeb Stuart may have been smiling.

"But it was not a voodoo spell that changed me. It was the Drumhead."

Kit Carson shook his head.

"Impossible," Kit said. He appealed to the others around the table. "Don't listen to his lies."

Jeb Stuart turned, and his liquid eyes focused on Kit.

"I thought it was a game, Kit Carson. Numbers on a piece of foolscap. Chalk on a piece of slate. When I thought I was playing the game, it was teaching me how to communicate, teaching me how to survive. I thought it was an augury at first, a ouija board, tarot cards, something supernatural. Slowly we all began to understand. It took us a long time to realize it was logic. A language. For a machine. That it was a fragment of computer code. A piece of shrapnel, caught in the past. It took us a long time to realize it was a part of the Drumhead."

Jeb Stuart returned to the table and sat down. His black-eyed gaze swept around the table and came to rest on Kit Carson's face.

"Something happened," Jeb continued. "To the Drumhead. Or will happen. In the future. Something that changes the Drumhead and will throw pieces of it across space and time. Slowly, for thousands of years, it has been putting itself back together."

Jeb Stuart sat back in his seat.

"We have learned to control our hunger and to survive without corruption, without violence, without death."

He placed one gloved hand on his breast.

"I am not a vampire. I am an agent of the Drumhead."

He gestured, sweeping his hand toward each figure gathered around the table.

"We are all agents of the Drumhead."

Kit Carson and the Professor sat alone at the table in the small white room with the narrow windows. The room was darkened, and the chairs around the table were empty. A pale blue glow outlined the closed doorway. Faint starlight from the narrow windows fell on one side of the Professor's round face. Kit's face was lost in shadow.

A soft, constant rumbling sound came from somewhere outside the room. It was the deep throbbing of the dense machinery around them, a sound almost below their level of awareness, but loud enough to remind them of the many and varied distances in which they had come to dwell.

Kit was thinking of things that had happened long ago, memories he was no longer sure were his, no longer sure were true.

"It's a lot to take in," the Professor said.

"That's the same thing the shrink said."

"Normally, you wouldn't have to acclimate so quickly."

"Normally?"

"Yes, well . . ."

They were silent for a moment.

"What about you?" Kit said.

The Professor sighed.

"I have my doubts."

"Such as?"

The Professor shifted in his chair and waved a dismissive hand to one side.

"The Drumhead deals in probabilities. It can predict the near future for small systems, but the Drumhead is not infallible. It does make mistakes. Or, rather, I should say, they appear to be mistakes. To us. To me. What the Drumhead is trying to do now is beyond human understanding. It is at a new order of magnitude. The outcome is unforeseeable . . . terra incognita."

"But it needs us, right? It can't do this alone. Otherwise it would just use bots."

"Perhaps. Up until now, the Drumhead has had something like a symbiotic relationship with humans and other carbon-based life. There is no reason for us to think that will change."

"What about the Indians?" Kit said.

The Professor blinked at him for a moment.

"What do you mean?"

"The people wearing the feathers and the deerskin. Are they human?"

"They didn't brief you?"

" 'Friendly observers.' "

The Professor frowned and looked to one side.

"We're not sure what they are," the Professor said.

Kit gave the Professor a long, cold stare. The Professor finally looked up.

"It's a lot to take in," the Professor said.

Kit blew out an incredulous puff of breath.

He was thinking of something he remembered dimly like a fragment of a dream. He was thinking of the fastnesses of the canyon and the last unconquered remnant and the stream of survivors and their faces as they passed.

"Why would there be fake Indians here now? Like something plucked out of a twentieth-century movie? Who would do that? What would do that?"

"I don't know, Kit. Some of us think they may be avatars. An unknown AI."

Kit clenched his fist.

"I don't like any of this. Jeb Stuart all but called me a mass murderer. The undead Jeb Stuart whose name strikes terror in the hearts of people on planets across the galaxy."

He turned toward the Professor, and the faint starlight shone on his face, his dark beard, his wide bright eyes.

"I was following orders, Professor. When the massacre. On Earth. When the slaughter . . . when I slaughtered my fellow human beings . . . I was following orders."

His deep voice wavered briefly with rising emotion.

"Tell me, Professor, was I an agent of the Drumhead, too?"

The Professor shook his head. His voice was heavy with a growing sadness.

"I don't know, Kit."

"I was brought here. You thawed me out."

The Professor said nothing and stared at the surface of the table.

"I feel like a game piece on a chessboard. A character in an old blood-and-thunder with no will of my own. I don't know which of my memories are mine and which are neuroplastic fantasy."

Kit sat back and looked toward the ceiling and grimaced. His face seemed to roil with his conflicted emotions.

"Good faith and fair dealing!" he exclaimed at last.

He crossed his arms across his chest and looked the Professor in the eye.

"I will help you, Professor, but I feel as I did long ago on nineteenth-century Earth. I am blindly following orders. I fear that we all are blindly following orders."

*   *   *

The wind came blasting around the buildings and whipped the cold rain into his face. In one hand, he grasped the handle of a square, box-shaped briefcase. In the other, he held his umbrella. He was struggling to keep the umbrella open in the wind. He hesitated, leaning forward, one sodden foot submerged in the water on the sidewalk.

There was a sudden incandescence, and the night-wet city leaped out of the darkness. Slick, dark surfaces lit up, alive for an instant, colored with silver and mercury and the darkest cobalt blue. He tensed his shoulders, and almost immediately, there was a crack of thunder that shook the ground. Lightning had been striking the area steadily for the last half hour.

A taxi slowed and rolled past, windshield wipers lashing. The man carrying the box-shaped briefcase shied away from the taxi's dark windows. In the wake of its tires, water sluiced over the curb and rolled towards his feet. He hurried around the corner, head down, shouldering into a sideways rain.

Glissade/Frappe had successfully contained the data breach at the beach ruin, and most of the remediation was complete. The two young researchers who found the vault hidden in the basement of the old mansion had been interrogated and were still being detained for employment-related observation at an unverifiable location. A cell of human analysts, working closely with Glissade/Frappe's proprietary AI, had concluded that there was an eighty-six percent probability that the data breach was accidental. Glissade/Frappe's AI estimated that less than one percent of the raw data was still extant on the open networks. The probability of unforeseen outcomes for the greater information ecosystem was approaching zero. The Glissade/Frappe AI had concluded that the leaching data presented an acceptable risk. Glissade/Frappe issued a public statement: Glissade/Frappe will continue to seek recovery of one hundred percent of the raw data and the elimination of all unforeseeable outcomes.

In the meantime, an anomalous storm system over the Pacific Ocean was wreaking havoc with global weather patterns. The jet stream had shifted drastically; satellite orbits were perturbed; and, the storm surge was hemispheric, bicoastal, among several other unprecedented phenomena. Though Glissade/Frappe had made no public comment about the chaotic weather, internally the Glissade/Frappe AI was quietly running several esoteric models testing whether the recent data breach could somehow be altering the Earth's atmosphere.

It took a while for the man with the box-shaped briefcase to find the townhouse. It was near the end of a dead-end alley under a darkened street light. It was a narrow building covered in a forgettable gray stucco. It was set back from the other townhouses, and the entrance was under an overhang, almost in the basement beneath the sidewalk. It was the kind of unremarkable building he would usually pass by without a second look. He stood under the overhang and fumbled for a moment looking for the ancient key. No pass codes or card swipes or biometrics on this night.

Inside the vestibule, he set the briefcase down and stood for a few minutes, dripping water onto the uneven tile floor. The vestibule was lit by a single led bulb in a dusty sconce on the wall. His raincoat was soaked through, and his feet were squelching in his shoes. He heard the slow drip of water and looked up. The rain was leaking from a stained section of the vestibule ceiling.

The townhouse had been subdivided long ago into apartments and offices. There were five floors and at least one door on each floor. The rain-soaked man seized the box-shaped briefcase with his free hand and started climbing the dimly-lit stairs.

The interior of the old townhouse stairwell had probably changed little over the decades. A large, oval window gave a cloudy view of the sky and the street. There were several small, red, cylindrical, fire-fighting foam-bots clinging to the walls, a glowing exit sign in the shadows near the roof and, near the top, bolted to the wall, a pre-millennium metal box with emergency lights that looked like headlights from an antique car.

On the fifth floor landing, there was a single wooden door with an old-fashioned peephole in the middle and a small, slotted metal frame below the peephole. In the metal frame, there was a card with printed letters on it. The rain-soaked man leaned close to the door and read the printed card in the frame.

Functional Desuetude, Inc.
Antiques & Ephemera

The man paused and took a few deep breaths. He propped the closed umbrella against the wall, shifted the briefcase from one hand to the other. He checked the time. His heart was thudding in his chest, and his hand was unsteady. He glanced directly into the peephole and quickly looked away. He squared his shoulders and lightly rapped with one knuckle against the door. He heard a soft rustling, and the door cracked open. A face peered out at him. He glimpsed an eye, half a nose, the corner of a mouth. Then the door swung open, and he was face to face with a vaguely-familiar woman.

They stood like statues for several seconds. They each searched unflinchingly the features of the face in front of them. He waited for recognition, waited for the past to come rising up out of the dark waters of his mind.

Who was she? Classmate? Neighbor? Co-worker? He did not immediately recognize her, but something about her tickled his memory. She looked to be about the same age as he, but he knew that meant nothing. Her face was round and full, with puffy dark circles under her brown eyes. She looked Asian, Japanese, maybe, but there was only a suggestion of ethnicity around her eyes, and, like the appearance of age or youth, he knew it could be deceptive. Her plump mouth had settled into a tired frown that she made no effort to hide. She had a neon blue streak in her spiky dark hair.

There was a flash of lightning from the oval window that illuminated the stairwell, followed closely by a crashing boom of thunder. The woman raised a cautionary index finger to her lips and looked him in the eyes. He nodded his head. She took him firmly by the arm and guided him inside and shut the door.

The room behind the door was darkened. Weak light was coming from a doorway in the back. The front room was filled with cheap office furniture. Old office parrots perched, sleeping, in the dark corners. There was an interactive surface on one wall. There was a single window and a potted fern in desperate need of water. A small, framed photograph of a nineteenth-century sailing vessel hung at a steep angle on one wall. As the sky outside thundered and flashed, the askew photograph of the ship seemed oddly appropriate and storm-tossed. She guided him across hardwood floors towards the smaller room in the rear.

In the smaller room, there was a crooked, mottled brass floor lamp with a tattered shade. In the middle of the room, there was a cheap nylon tent pitched on top of a neat pile of blankets. The room was windowless and otherwise empty, just plaintive hardwood floors and bare white walls. The woman stepped beside the tent and reached inside and pulled back the flap and beckoned for him to enter. He set the briefcase inside the tent and crawled inside and sat cross-legged on the floor. The woman turned the lamp off, and the room was completely dark. The woman followed him into the tent and sealed the flap.

He heard the faint, high-pitched sound of a wand powering up. He waited while she swept the inside of the tent. He could hear her moving in the dark. He rocked from side to side, and she swept the wand beneath him. He felt the wand brushing over his clothes, his head. It was probably a homemade wand, illegal, forbidden, contraband.

A box of matches rattled softly in the dark. There was the scratch of a match on the side of the box, bright sparks crackling blue and yellow-white around a red match head. A flame bloomed in the darkness. She held the wooden match for a moment, the steady flame creeping down towards two rose-shadowed fingertips. She lit a candle in a hurricane lamp and stubbed the match out in a large bowl made out of green translucent glass. She hung the lamp above their heads, and the light shone softly on their faces.

He looked at her face in the candlelight. She was waiting patiently. He still could not place her round face, her tired eyes, her stern mouth. He looked around inside the tent. The wand rested on the floor of the tent next to her knee. It looked innocuous, like a bulky, old-fashioned curling iron for styling hair. In addition to the large green bowl and the wand, there was a small hourglass filled with white sand and a neat stack of paper.

He placed the box-shaped briefcase in front of them and unlatched the top. She watched him intently. He swung the top open on its hinges and revealed the contents.

Inside was an antique manual typewriter, a rebuilt Underwood with a customized, unreadable black ribbon.

The woman was pleased. Silently, she clasped her hands together at her breast. She nodded at him, and the round surfaces of her face briefly lifted together in something like a smile. She powered up the wand and swept it over the Underwood and the inside of the briefcase. Then she swept the tent again. She reached behind her and found the stack of paper. She set the hourglass next to the typewriter on the floor between them and looked calmly into his eyes, waiting.

He was not ready, and he shook his head and held up his hand. He still could not remember how he knew her.

He looked steadily at her face and tried to find the place in his memory where she was hiding. She waited patiently while he gazed at her and furrowed his brow.

Could it be a mistake? No. The fault lay with him. If he could not remember, it would simply be human error, his error. He alone would be responsible for an unforeseeable outcome. He was prepared to abort, if necessary. There was too much at stake.

He took a sheet of paper off the top of the stack. He could feel its texture between his fingers. It was the real thing. Just twenty pound with only a hint of decay, but still, old-school paper fresh out of climate-controlled storage. He held it close to his nose and inhaled the faint aroma. He slid the page into the roller of the Underwood, locked the roller down and positioned the typewriter where they both could easily type. He paused, collecting himself. He looked one last time at the woman's face. She placed one hand on the hourglass and gave him a cool nod.

He closed his eyes and took a deep breath. His hands were poised above the keyboard. He opened his eyes and began to type, and as he began, the woman turned the hourglass over and the sand began to fall. They turned as one to the waiting blank page.

The sound of the typebars striking the paper seemed deafening. He stopped typing and gently but firmly slid the carriage back to the beginning. The roller turned, and the paper advanced. He pulled his hands back from the keyboard.

The woman silently read the typed words.

Zach Stone.

For long, excruciating moments, the sand trickled through the hourglass. In the dark empty room, inside the cheap nylon tent, the candle burned. In the other room, rain drummed against a window pane, and the sleeping parrots roosted. The woman's eyes were staring somewhere far beyond the name on the page. The man clenched his hands into fists and quietly coiled himself, ready to abort, ready to leave the Underwood and walk away.

Then the woman smoothly began to type on the next line. She returned the carriage and drew back her hands.

Camp Pendleton?

Zach felt a wave a relief. His father had been stationed at Camp Pendleton when he was a boy.

Yes, Zach typed and returned the carriage.

Sara Simpatico, the woman typed.

Zach allowed himself a tight smile. His family had lived at Camp Pendleton for several years. The family next door had a daughter his age named Sara. He saw her clearly, climbing in the eucalyptus tree, looking at him from across the yard.

He pivoted through a constellation of memories.

The eucalyptus tree.

Sara nodded, smiling.

My little koala bears.

His mind trembled like a touched mobile, turning slowly in and out of the sun.

My little koala bears. That was what his mother had called them. A botanist, she had been in the thick of her interplanetary transplantation research. She joked for years that it took an act of Congress to plant the eucalyptus tree on the military base. His father, out of uniform for once, had dug the hole himself with an old post-hole digger. He let Zach try to lift it. Had Sara been there?

The sand was trickling through the hourglass.

Sara and Zach had been playmates when their families had lived side by side. He would bring the little quantum cowboys with all their paraphernalia, the tiny helmets and boots and escape pods. She brought the classic jeep, olive green with white stencil and black plastic tires that left tracks in the sand. They spent several weeks one summer playing house, long sunny afternoons rolling the jeep and its dismayed passengers through freshly dug canyons, across the summit and down the metal slopes of playground slides. At some point, the quantum cowboys lost most of their accessories but acquired offspring, two pine cones that bounced around in the back of the jeep. He had forgotten how tenderly they tucked the pine cones away at the end of the day.

The pine cones.

Sara frowned for a moment, and then her eyes opened wide. She rocked back, stunned by the memories. She held her head up looking toward the top of the tent. She began slowly to shake her head. She leaned over the keyboard.

Yoshi and Hiro. My mother helped us name them.

Had she? Zach could not remember that. Or he wasn't there. Or it never happened. Either way, if she told her mother, then what Sara had typed was open, visible, on the record and easily fabricated by a talented AI.

They had not found the occlusion.

Zach looked at the hourglass, at the stream of white sand trickling down. A little, round declivity was growing, spreading at the center of the remaining sand.

The miners were probably already on their way.

Sara Simpatico.

The dark-haired girl in the eucalyptus tree. One hand on the limb over her head. The sun hot in a clear southern California sky. Bangs on her forehead. A stray lock of hair falling across her pudgy cheek. The way she was looking at him. Something sour and sad and angry. This was not a happy memory. He did not like the way she was looking at him. Was it regret? Was it regret he was feeling. Why? What had he done?

He looked at her face across from him in the candle light. Her brows were drawn together. Her mouth set firmly. She was calm, but her steady gaze had grown urgent.

He glanced at the hourglass. The white sand was quickly vanishing from the top chamber. He had practiced on his own with an hourglass many times, shuffling through his memories as the sand ran out, but there was almost no way to practice unobserved in real time with another person. Finding an occlusion was something of an art. It only happened in the field under the pressure of time.

Sara Simpatico. The dark-haired girl in the eucalyptus tree. My little koala bears. They had climbed in the limbs of the young tree. He could smell the leaves. The smell of the leaves and grass clippings.

And then it came to him.

The bicycle.

Sara's parents had given her a bicycle with training wheels. When she showed it to him, he stole it and hid it in the closet in their garage, stood in the hot darkness, in the faint odor of eucalyptus and grass clippings and old lithium ion batteries, grasping the little handlebar grips with their dangling plastic fringe. Sara knew he had taken the bike, but she said nothing. She gave him the silent treatment, climbing in the eucalyptus tree, wounding him from across the yard with a poisonous stare. After two days, he was so overwhelmed, he sneaked out at night and returned the bike, and they never spoke of it again.

Your bicycle?

Sara leaned forward and read the words. Her expression softened. She began to nod her head. She placed her fingertips on the typewriter keys and concentrated.

Zach glanced at the hourglass. The last of the white sand was draining relentlessly downward. It always seemed to go faster toward the end.

Hurry, Sara.

I knew it was you.

Zach squelched down a rising panic. She had not given him much to go on. But it was enough. He quickly typed his answer.

Did you tell anyone?

Not a soul.

Zach and Sara looked at each other for a few precious, silent seconds.

I'm sorry.

All is forgiven.

The bicycle was the occlusion.

Zach had never undergone neuroplastic reconstruction. The bicycle was the unspoken secret no AI could recreate, no android could mimic. It was the ultimate encryption key, the secret handshake, data locked away in the gray matter of the only two eyewitnesses on the scene.

Zach typed out the information he had been sent to convey.

Glissade/Frappe data breach caused a download cascade. There was a thermal induction near the Philippines. Additional capacity was amphibious and mobile. The Drumhead has lost contact with the server platform. There are echoes of a geosynchronous ribbon above the amphibious array. Our analysts believe they have discovered a new AI. Autonomous. Class Five.

Sara read what Zach had typed.

Acknowledged.

She nodded to Zach and pulled the page out of the Underwood. Zach checked the customized ribbon spools. The letters they had just typed on the ribbon were filling in with ink. The rest of the used ribbon was solid black, unreadable as if brand new.

Sara was reading the typed page one more time. She committed to her memory the message Zach had conveyed. Zach watched her profile as she leaned over the page.

Then she lit a match and held the flame to the corner of the typed page. Flames licked up the edges, and it began to burn. Sara held the burning page carefully with two fingers and put the last of it in the green glass bowl. Then she calmly ate the ashes and licked her fingertips.

Bon appétit.

Zach closed the briefcase top over the Underwood and fastened the clasps. Once they might have tried sign language, but it had become impossible to learn in secret, and those who remembered had died or were held quietly in isolation. A homemade stylus or brush or even a fingertip pressed to flesh was too slow and prone to be misread. The Underwood, an unregistered antique, was still allowed to circulate.

They both stopped and watched the last few grains of sand as they trickled out of the top chamber of the hourglass and disappeared through the channel at the bottom. They exchanged a quick glance, and they both got out of the tent.

Sara turned on the floor lamp. The rain was still falling outside the townhouse. Zach was thinking of the rooftop and the ladder to the emergency exit. The foam-bots would probably be checking for smoke outside the door.

Zach paused in the doorway of the small room and looked back at Sara. She was standing beside the tent. She raised an open hand.

Goodbye.

He strode back across the room. Her face was bewildered. He hugged her close and kissed her quickly on her cheek. For the quantum cowboys and their lost pine cones and his mother's eucalyptus tree. Her cheeks reddened, and she pointed urgently at the door. A grudging smile was twisting across her lips. He stopped at the door for one last look. The smile was gone. She stood with her open hand facing him. He nodded.

My little koala bears.

Goodbye, Sara Simpatico.

*   *   *

A veil of thin clouds passed across a sliver of a moon. A shadow was climbing steadily up the side of the museum. The museum was spun from white marble and granite like a huge, irregular honeycomb. Its rounded, ribbed exterior loomed over the older buildings and square city blocks like something that had grown there. It seemed to have oozed from between the older structures and appeared to be slowly encroaching on the rest of the city. The climbing shadow paused near one fibrous span. The shapes of a cowl and cape were briefly outlined against the shifting sky. Then the shadow was gone, and the thin clouds were racing again across the crescent moon.

The shadow climbed with unerring confidence. Bare fingertips quickly found the thin edges of the marble and granite surfaces. With a burst of strength and agility, the shadow leaped from a ledge and caught hold of an outcropping. The shadow's feet dangled over the city street, searching blindly for the next toehold.

The shadow vaulted onto a section of the roof and crouched down like a big cat. The shadow paused and surveyed where the roof came together, the pale flat surfaces and deep shadows, hidden paths floating above the city streets. The shadow turned and disappeared into a maze of darkness and light.

Inside the museum, there were unexpected variations in the monitoring data. There was a glitch in the video, a whisper of static in the audio, fluctuations in the thermals, a tremble in the motion detectors. The security AI sent a parrot to investigate. The parrot glided past the shadows in the corridors. Once the parrot had safely passed, one shadow separated from the wall and continued to move silently toward the interface with the security AI.

Not long after that, various digital permissions were authorized, certain data streams inexplicably ceased, and the security AI abruptly withdrew for an unscheduled self-diagnostic. At that opportune moment, the shadow silently crossed the threshold of the section of the museum devoted to antiquities from ancient Earth. The dimmed ceiling spotlights shone on the shadowy figure's cowl and cape. In a fortified alcove especially constructed for the preservation and study of certain rare and invaluable artifacts, the shadow approached a certain pedestal, but there was something wrong. The red velvet of the pedestal was empty. There was only an absence where an object had been. The shadow took a step back in confusion.

"Looking for this?" a voice said.

The shadowy figure spun around, and the cowl fell from her face. The woman beneath the cowl was none other than Marcel the Cat, notorious intergalactic jewel thief, queen of the quantum pirates, the most dangerous woman in that quarter of the cosmos.

Her sharp eyes were glaring at the man across from her until she realized who it was.

She allowed herself a brief, wry smile.

Standing across from Marcel the Cat was her annoying nemesis and occasional lover, Deadly Robert.

Deadly Robert, ninja assassin, vampire hunter.

Deadly Robert, insufferable square-toed fool.

In his hand, Robert held what Marcel had come for, the object that had so recently rested on the red velvet pedestal. In his hand, Deadly Robert casually held the obsidian blade.

Marcel brushed her hair from her face and deployed a broad smile so disingenuous, it was somehow sincere.

"Well, isn't this a pleasant surprise," she said, her voice purring with irony.

Robert held up the obsidian blade and turned it back and forth. He looked at it admiringly as the sharp black edge glinted in the dim light.

He smiled smugly at Marcel.

"How do you like my new paperweight?"

Marcel quit smiling.

So much for witty repartee, she thought.

Faster than he could react, she snatched the obsidian blade from his hand and kicked him hard in the chest.

Robert staggered back against the wall.

"Sorry I can't stay and chat," she said over her shoulder.

Marcel bounded towards the door, but stopped short when she saw another person standing in her way.

"Hello, Marcel," the Professor said calmly.

Robert lurched back next to her and tried to wrest the obsidian blade from her hand. She jerked it away, annoyed, and pushed his face away with the palm of her free hand.

"How did you find me?" she said.

"We had some help," the Professor said, and Kit Carson stepped out of the shadows.

Marcel the Cat was stunned. For once, her quick eyes and sharp features seemed unsure.

Deadly Robert pulled the obsidian blade from her slack fingers.

"So . . . so this is serious."

*　　*　　*

Several hours later, the museum's security AI investigated an irregularity in a routine inventory of the ancient Earth catalog. Human inspection verified that the obsidian blade was not on its pedestal, yet there was no evidence of a breach in museum security. Somehow, the fabled obsidian blade had vanished. The security AI called several investigatory functions, and the functions initialized additional semi-autonomous agents. The agents dispatched the relevant information to law enforcement and various interested third parties. The data disseminated immediately, and the global networks updated accordingly. There was a thirty-minute delay before the next catapult pulse beamed the data packets into the interstellar networks. By that time, Marcel the Cat and the obsidian blade were light years away, and the liability insurer had already initiated a legal proceeding. The insurer's lawyers began methodically to dismantle the museum's security AI. Within twenty-four hours, the resulting crisis had quickly toppled the city government and was threatening to create a geopolitical instability in the larger urban sprawl up and down the coast.

Marcel the Cat sipped her drink and scanned the faces of the creatures sitting around her. She was sitting in a dark corner of a dive bar with Deadly Robert, Kit Carson and the Professor. It was the sort of unruly place that sprang up overnight in the dead spots in the interstices of the interstellar networks. It was a refuge for those who were offline and wanted to stay that way. It might survive for a few days before the Drumhead noticed and the networks dispatched new nodes and updated their coverage.

"Make it quick, boys," Marcel said.

She was watching a Titan vapor-troll across the room. The troll had an oscillating chameleon on its shoulder valve, and the chameleon kept looking at her.

The Professor spoke in a low voice.

"What the vampires have sensed is a potentiality. The opening of a cosmic window, if you will. Our data are consistent, and the Drumhead agrees."

"I'm still not clear on why we'd want to do this," Marcel said, her restless eyes cutting between the Professor and the faces in the darkened room.

Was that damned chameleon winking at her?

"What's in it for us?" Marcel said.

"Peace," Robert said.

"I got peace," Marcel said and drained her drink. "Right here," she said showing them the bottom of her empty glass.

"It would be the end of violence as we know it," said Kit.

"For ten thousand years, perhaps longer," the Professor said. "Perhaps for as long as we might endure."

"Some of us think it may be . . . the end of human suffering."

There was an uncomfortable silence.

"Yeah, well, everybody wants to go to heaven, but no one wants to die," Marcel muttered.

"If the vampires can position themselves correctly in the space-time continuum, it will work. The Drumhead foresees a structural change in the fabric of space-time. It all comes down to timing and distance."

The sound of a glass shattering came from across the bar. Marcel stiffened in her seat. Two angry voices rose above the murmuring in the bar. A big guy with rhino enhancements was snorting in the receptors of a plasma-scarred tin man. The Professor placed a steady hand on Marcel's arm. The Titan vapor-troll stepped between the rhino and the tin man, and the tension evaporated. No one wants to deal with a vapor-troll. The chameleon had skittered to a shelf above the bar and was pulsing with a hypnotic pattern of scarlet and orange that cycled and slowed to a more pleasant sea green and pale blue. As the chameleon climbed down and crept back toward the vapor-troll, Marcel saw a familiar face sitting at the bar. It was the raven-haired woman. When she saw Marcel looking at her, she coolly turned away.

"The only way the vampires can be ready is with the help of creative hyper-cognitives," Kit said.

"Like the Professor's students," Marcel said.

"Like you and me," Robert said.

"And Zach," the Professor said.

Marcel shook her head.

"That's not going to happen," she said.

They were silent for a moment.

"Has anyone ever asked Zach why he renounced creative hyper-cognition?" Kit said.

"Seems pretty obvious to me," Marcel said. "He couldn't handle it."

"I don't believe that," Robert said.

"I don't either," Kit said.

"I blame myself," the Professor said.

"Why? What did you do?" Marcel said.

"He told me he wasn't ready, but I kept pushing."

"I think there's another reason," Kit said.

Kit caught the Pirate Queen's eye.

"I think he did it for Robert and Marcel. I think the two of you staying together was more important to Zach than being a creative hyper-cognitive."

Marcel and Robert exchanged glances.

"We need to find him."

"He doesn't want to be found."

"People change."

"Do they?"

6

MARCEL WALKED THROUGH HER OFFICE door and flipped the light switch and saw the little ninjas sitting in the upholstered chairs in front of her desk. It was early in the morning, and people had only just begun to trickle into the building and settle in behind their desks, to check their email, to savor a fresh cup of coffee. Marcel stared at the ninjas as she walked around behind her desk.

The little ninjas sat up straight and smiled at her brightly. They were wearing identical coats and ties. They each had their hair slicked back, one with the part on the right, the other on the left.

Marcel set her coffee on the desk. She slipped her satchel from her shoulder and dropped it to the floor. She was carrying cut flowers — irises — and she put them in the crystal vase.

She opened her mouth to speak.

Then she reconsidered.

She was halfway out of her black suede jacket and had one hand on the floral-print silk scarf draped around her neck.

She looked out the door into the hallway.

"Bernice . . ." she called.

In the hallway, the desk where Bernice sat was vacant. Bernice had not yet arrived.

Marcel turned back to the ninjas, looked back and forth from one little, expectant face to the other.

She frowned, puzzled.

"How did you get in here?" Marcel said.

They were wearing blue blazers with little gold buttons. Conservative, diagonally striped ties. Little cordovan loafers with tiny tassels.

"We need your help, Ms. Arrow," said one of the ninjas, the one with hair parted on the left.

"Zach Stone is missing," said the other, the one with the part on the right.

"We suspect the worst."

Marcel raised her eyebrows.

"The worst?" she said.

"Sabotage."

"Skullduggery."

"Honey-potted monkey-wrenchery."

Marcel narrowed her eyes.

"I think you're in the wrong office," Marcel said.

"You're Marcel Arrow?"

"Yes."

"The attorney?"

Marcel shook her head.

"I'm Marcel Arrow, the curator. This is a museum."

The little ninjas exchanged puzzled glances.

"And this is not a good time," she said.

Marcel gestured towards the door with her open hand.

"My assistant handles my schedule," Marcel said.

She smiled. A brisk apology. A valediction.

The ninjas were undeterred.

"Your assistant can be somewhat . . . inflexible," said the ninja with the part on the right.

"The woman is like a pit bull," said the other, softly, with admiration, and perhaps a little awe.

Marcel dropped her jacket and scarf on her chair and walked towards the door.

"Listen . . . gentlemen," Marcel said, bemused, stressing the word gentlemen, though she was not entirely sure of their gender.

"I've got a busy day ahead of me."

She stood next to the door and grasped the doorknob.

The little ninjas were bewildered. They sat on the edge of Marcel's upholstered chairs, their little hands on the armrests, little shoes dangling over the expensive rug. They looked up at her with pinched, flummoxed little faces.

Marcel sighed.

"Get out," Marcel said, looking at the ceiling.

There was an awkward silence.

"But —"

"Go," Marcel said firmly, nodding towards the door, resisting the urge to shoo them out.

The little ninjas filed out of the office with an icy composure, their noses in the air.

"Very unprofessional," one ninja sniffed.

"Such a discourtesy," the other huffed.

Marcel walked back behind her desk and sat down.

Zach Stone.

She had not thought of him in years.

Marcel saw Bernice pass by in the hallway, a flash of short brown frosted hair, bright rouge, blue sparkly eyeshadow. She was wearing a new jacket, some sort of leather thing with fringe. Marcel took a closer look.

Bernice's small, thick body was in steady motion behind

her desk. The jacket looked like something for a hunter or a pioneer, natural colored, finely tanned. Somehow, the jacket suited Bernice, like she was on her way to Woodstock or some righteous sit in.

Funny, Marcel thought, how things get commodified.

Bernice was busy with her morning rituals which were intricate. Marcel had only a vague understanding but knew they involved sugar and coffee, lumbar support, an emergency sweater, an antibacterial dispenser, a Derek Jeter bobble head and several troll figurines standing guard near the carefully positioned photographs of her children and grandchildren. Marcel wanted to ask Bernice about the little ninjas, but knew from past experience that it was unwise to interrupt her morning routine. Marcel plunged back into the details of the approaching day — the new Dysette-Zee was just so delightfully huge — and quickly forgot about the visitation from the little ninjas.

*　　*　　*

That evening, when Marcel arrived at her apartment, the little ninjas were waiting for her inside. They were wearing their matching black outfits, cinched at the waist with black cloth belts. Their faces were covered with black masks with only a slit for their eyes. They were seated on the couch, barefoot, each little leg crossed casually, one ninja with the ankle across the right knee, the other with the ankle across the left knee.

After she opened the door and saw them, Marcel dropped her dry cleaning, her keys and a soggy bag of take-out chinese. She backed up against the wall, whipped out her phone and sucked in a lungful of air preparing to scream at a decibel level loud enough to penetrate her neighbors' apartments, even old Mrs. Magellan in 3B who kept her television volume cranked up so loud, you could hear it before you got out of the elevator.

One of the little ninjas hopped up from the couch and smoothly grabbed a serving tray from the coffee table.

"Hors d'oeuvre?" the little ninja said, deftly offering the tray to Marcel.

The tray was lined with the little strawberry-kiwi prosciutto morsels she usually could not resist.

"Uh, no thank you," she said, dazed, unsteady, her stomach growling.

The other little ninja was at her elbow.

"Club soda?" the ninja said. "Scotch whisky?"

She was a second away from calling 911, her finger poised above the button on her sleek phone.

"Why are you little freaks in my apartment?"

"Please, Ms. Arrow. Don't be alarmed."

"Relax. Have a seat."

"It is extremely important that we speak with you."

A ninja had taken her gently by the arm and was guiding her towards the couch. Marcel was looking at the hors d'oeuvres.

Maybe I'm having a stroke, she thought.

A ninja set a cold drink on a coaster near her hand.

"Johnny Walker. Rocks."

Her favorite.

And on a coaster.

Is my face drooping, Marcel wondered. She was smiling mechanically and leaning to one side to look in the mirror across the room.

"It's about Zach Stone," said one of the ninjas.

"He's disappeared," said the other ninja.

Marcel could smell the aroma of the strawberry-kiwi prosciutto. They smelled delicious. The toothpicks with frilly colored cellophane on one end were hovering at the edge of her vision.

Maybe just one, she thought.

If I'm already having a stroke . . .

"And the interloper."

"The honey pot."

"The monkey wrench."

"Jolene."

"If that's her real name."

"She's invaded Terra Incognita."

Marcel was chewing. She had stacked the toothpicks in a neat little pile.

"She talked Zach into a mindfulness section."

"In the corner where the inflatable Cthulhu used to be."

"She canceled Thursday-night Magic: The Gathering."

"Now she teaches yoga."

"Yoga," the other ninja muttered, with a shudder.

Marcel set the empty glass of Johnny Walker back on the coaster.

Damn, she thought.

These guys should cater.

One of the little ninjas was waving something around.

"Have you read this?" the little ninja asked.

It was typed pages, a grimy-edged, dog-eared manuscript clasped at the corner with a big, black metal clip.

Marcel shook her head, swallowing.

"He's getting distracted with all this interpersonal stuff."

"The sentimental touchy-feely stuff."

The little ninja read from the manuscript, pointing, following the text with his tiny fingertip.

" 'I think he did it for Robert and Marcel. I think the two of you staying together was more important to Zach than being a creative hyper-cognitive.' "

The ninja tossed the manuscript on the coffee table. It spoiled the neat pile of toothpicks Marcel had arranged.

"I mean, come on!"

"Seriously."

"He needs to stay focused on the plot, right? The vampires. The Drumhead."

"It's because of the interloper."

"Jolene."

"If that's her real name."

"She's the problem."

"She knows where he is."

"But she's not saying."

"It's tortious interference, I tell you."

"Monkey-wrenched sabotage."

"Honey-potted skullduggery."

"Plus, she's an android."

The other ninja paused.

Marcel looked up at the sudden silence, dabbing at the corner of her mouth with a cocktail napkin.

The other ninja spoke with a belabored patience.

"I'm pretty sure she's not an android."

"But you don't know."

It appeared to be an old argument.

There was a quick sidebar.

"She's not an android," the other ninja said quietly.

"But she could be."

"So she's like, what . . . a sex bot?"

"Exactly. A super-human sex bot."

The other ninja was silent, thinking, fingers to chin.

"With her weird experiments."

"How far is Wolverine from Sailor Moon?"

"I know, right?"

"And her deconstruction."

"And her Derrida."

"So pretentious."

"And those tattoos?"

"And her boobs?"

"Zach never had a chance."

Marcel cleared her throat.

The little ninjas stopped talking and looked at her.

"Did you say . . . 'sex bot?' " Marcel said.

The little ninjas looked at her for a long moment.

"Oh, they were fornicating," the little ninja said.

The other ninja was nodding vigorously.

"Like crazed weasels."

"In heat."

Marcel was still holding her phone in one hand. She set it on the coffee table and handed her empty glass to the nearest ninja.

"Bring me another one of these," she said.

"And you . . ." she said, turning to the other little ninja. "Start at the beginning. And tell me everything."

*　　*　　*

Terra Incognita was a comic book store. It was near the colleges and the University, down a narrow, cobblestone alley, in the basement of an old townhouse. There was a small hand-painted sign near the door, blood-red letters on an unfurled here-be-dragons map, with compass points in one corner and a little sea serpent swimming near the opposite corner.

It was easy to miss Terra Incognita. There was a for-tune-teller in the space above with a neon palm blazing red and blue in the bay window. Next door, near the corner, was the steady drone and gurgle of a catacombed video-game arcade.

Before Zach arrived, Terra Incognita was in decline. It

had all the ambiance of an opium den. Near the front door, there were a few ragged cardboard boxes full of old comics in their plastic bags, but in the darkened rooms and dim aisles in the back, the slightly sweet smell of aging paper pulp and incense lingered in the air. Shelves lined the walls, sagging beneath the weight of paperbacks and comics and magazines, their edges beginning to yellow and flake. Shifting stacks spilled onto the floor, a Life magazine with a portrait of Liz Taylor or a Mad Magazine and Alfred E. Newman asking *What me worry* or Little Lotta or Richie Rich. Soft sounds within — the flutter of pages, the knock of a chair leg on the hardwood floor — came from a deceptive distance, someplace close and yet, somehow, very far away. A page would softly turn, and a pale face might glance up, a figure shifting now in the gloom, then gone, motes churning slowly in the dead air. It was easy to imagine getting lost in the close spaces and never finding your way back out.

Zach changed all that. It seemed folly to buy the comic book store at the time, but, as the little ninjas learned, Zach was an idiot savant, some kind of holy fool. (Marcel found herself nodding in agreement. Yeah, that sounds about right. That was the Zach she remembered. The slumbering, unshaven oaf in Winston Straw's seminar.) Zach cleaned out the sedimentary layers that had accumulated in the rooms in the back. He called it the cleaning of the Augean stables. The little ninjas helped him cull the valuable items from the dross, the collectible from the kitsch. The Frazetta Conans and the tijuana bibles, the R. Crumb comix and the Bakshi videos. Zach tore down the black light posters and the head shop tapestries. He replaced the ghastly, flickering florescent ceiling lights. Terra Incognita began to look like a place you might actually allow your children to visit rather than the place where you steered them by the shoulders firmly and quickly past.

Zach understood that the people, the fans, the different communities, knitted together with their shared beliefs and rituals, with their baroque, impenetrable argots, their obscure disputes and silly celebrations, they were more important than the merchandise. This was before social media and the really big conventions, the ComicCons and the cosplay, before the mmogs and the movies, before Confederate Vampires in Space.

Terra Incognita became a destination in the real world, not just a place to browse through pop culture, but a place to experience pop culture with your friends and like-minded consumers, a place to belong. The old comic-book compost heap had become a busy mecca with neat stacks of new comics, book signings and poetry slams, gaming tournaments on the weekends. Zach had mined an old vein of pop culture and counter-culture and found a profitable new seam.

But Zach grew restless at Terra Incognita. In the midst of a dice-throwing frenzy in the battle to end all battles with the fearsome lich king of Wyvern Hill, the little ninjas caught Zach staring off into space, his mind far from the intricacies of their Dungeons & Dragons worlds. He began to spend more and more time in the tiny office in the back at a broken down desk amid stacks of old movie merchandise and last summer's forgotten figurines. The ninjas noticed the dusty, old manual typewriter he sometimes left uncovered, waiting on the desk. When Zach was occupied elsewhere, sorting new comics into personal folders or explaining the continuity of that summer's crossover event to some neophyte, or searching for the origin issue with the limited-edition holographic cover, the ninjas were quietly inspecting the strange contraption on his desk. They noticed the dust was missing from most of the smooth, shiny lettered keys. Late at night, after the store was closed and the lights were off, the ninjas heard typing coming from behind the closed office door. During the day, the desk drawers were always locked.

The ninjas did not know what the ninjas did not know. And that gnawed at them. Zach left the key to the desk hanging from the antlers of the big female dryad. The ninjas, being ninjas, found the manuscript in the bottom drawer, on top of a cluttered heap of buckeyes and pine cones and sycamore bark and oak leaves and miniature race cars and bottle caps and match books and ticket stubs and a bottle of Tabasco and a turtle shell and a big multicolored superball.

The ninjas thought that what Zach had written so far had potential. They left a rough draft of their graphic novel on his chair, a subtle suggestion, a subliminal spark plug. To their surprise, Zach read the whole thing, and Confederate Vampires in Space was born. They began posting it online. In short order, the fans were arguing over who should play Kit Carson in the CVS movie.

*　　*　　*

The next morning was the day Marcel had scheduled for the hanging of the new Dysette-Zee. It was an extraordinary piece that had sat undiscovered in a barn in upstate New York for years. The resolution of an interminable probate battle had finally delivered the heroic canvas with its unquestionable provenance safely into the museum's permanent collection and into Marcel's waiting embrace. It had taken some time to make room and coherently rearrange the other members of what she thought of as the museum's family, but there was only one spot that made sense — the wall near the balcony at the top of the stairs overlooking the Calder.

As curator, Marcel supervised the hanging of the Dysette-Zee which meant for the most part staying out of the way and letting everyone else do their job. She held her breath as the crew carefully maneuvered the crane and the ladders and the scaffolding and eased the sections of the huge canvas into position against the expanse of empty white wall. For weeks, she had gazed at the empty space and imagined the sections of the huge blue canvas hanging there. To see it actually happen was like a deus ex machina moment from one of her most elaborate and fanciful dreams. Though the physical shape and size of the museum had not changed, the hanging of the Dysette-Zee had completely transformed everything around it.

Before she had decided on the location of the new canvas, Marcel had used her computer to reconfigure the collection and to visualize new combinations in the three-dimensional model of the museum on the screen in her office. She had fit and refit the museum's familiar pieces into the same unforgiving spaces until she found the one best arrangement, or, at least, the one that satisfied her and her sense of comparison and contrast, echo and quotation, history and character, movement and rest, silence and sound, beauty and desire.

Late in the day, when the last measurement had been taken, and the last of the scaffolding had been disassembled and removed, and the last piece of equipment had been hauled away, she sat alone in front of the huge canvas. She was tired, but it was that luxurious sort of tired when the exam is over, the deadline has passed, the job is finished, and all that is left is the almost pleasant buzz of your synapses and dendrites still gapping at full speed. There would be a formal unveiling for the new painting, later, of course, with a reception and all the usual trappings, but for a brief while, Marcel could relax.

Marcel gazed at the Dysette-Zee as if for the first time. She let her mind wander away from the details, the schedules, the facts, the history, from all the mundane parts of her job the painting embodied.

The Dysette-Zee went on and on in a glorious swath of

cerulean blue. She got pleasantly lost in the serene, abstracted space, the particles of color, hazy, indistinct, drifting.

Marcel had spent many hours of her life up to that point in close proximity to extraordinary works of art. For as long as she could remember, each time she had engaged with art and with everything the experience engendered, even with the most challenging material, she had also felt a simple sense of wonder and awe and gratitude. She had felt it at the beginning when she first knew she wanted to be a curator, and she felt it at that moment looking at the new Dysette-Zee. She thought she might eventually lose that first feeling, that sense of wonder and awe and gratitude, but that day had not yet come, and she hoped it never would.

While Marcel was enjoying the Dysette-Zee, Bernice came up the staircase behind her. The stairs swept up from the first floor in a small atrium that opened out from the front entrance. A Calder sculpture hung from the ceiling of the atrium and gracefully dominated the space. The balcony was at the same level as the Calder, and the many arms of the huge sculpture gently moved, sweeping close and drifting slowly farther away from the edge of the balcony.

Bernice joined Marcel on the bench in front of the Dysette-Zee. She sat and gazed up at the huge blue canvas.

Bernice thought the new painting was okay, but abstract expression was not really her cup of tea. It had been a long day, her back hurt, and she was ready to go home. After what seemed a respectful amount of time, she looked out of the side of her eyes at Marcel's face.

"I left your messages on your desk."

Marcel nodded.

"See you tomorrow," Marcel said.

They sat in silence for a moment. Behind them, the Calder gently swept past.

"It's like it was made for this spot," Bernice said.

Marcel turned and looked at her.

"Thank you, Bernice."

Marcel noticed that she was wearing the leather jacket with the fringe.

"So, I love this, by the way," Marcel said waving a hand around the jacket. Bernice looked down at the jacket and her face brightened.

"Really?"

She stood up and stepped into the cerulean blue.

"I made it," Bernice said, beaming, hands on her hips, turning from side to side. "Inspired by Kit Carson and that online novel. You know the one I'm talking about? Confederate Vampires in Space?"

Marcel watched as Bernice walked an imaginary catwalk. Behind her, the field of cerulean blue floated at some wavering, unknowable distance.

"Yeah . . . I haven't read that yet," Marcel said slowly, her head swimming, feeling a little disoriented.

"I'm making one for my cousin Louisa. It's faux leather. My neighbors want one, too. They're a big hit."

Bernice was speaking in her flat, gravelly monotone. She walked on her sturdy legs, with one hand on her broad hip. She circled behind Marcel to the top of the stairs. She posed beside the balcony, the Calder drifting behind her.

"I can make you one, too, if you want. Gratis. You're worth the free advertising."

She laughed her short, abrupt laugh.

"Hah."

Marcel was not sure if she was serious.

"I don't know, Bee. Sounds like it might be a conflict of interest."

"Okay then. Full price. But you drive a hard bargain."

Bernice barked out another laugh, and Marcel chuckled, wondering if she had just obligated herself to buy one of Bernice's creations.

Bernice paused and looked at Marcel, sitting on the bench, turned at the waist, facing her. The Dysette-Zee loomed huge behind Marcel. Bernice thought Marcel was especially beautiful at that moment, composed like another piece of art, her short brown hair swept over one shoulder, her limbs perfect in repose, her back and shoulders effortlessly poised, a striking figure made small by the scale of the mural-sized canvas behind her.

"So the girl that does my nails has this son who went to Pratt. He's got a studio in her garage. She thought you might want to meet him. For coffee or something. Talk about art, see what you might have in common, that sort of thing."

There was a brief silence. Marcel inclined her head and stared at the floor beside the bench.

She was quietly seething.

"Bernice, what did I say about that?"

"Okay, okay. I was just saying."

"I know what you were doing, and I know you mean well, but, as we've discussed, I find it demeaning and totally inappropriate."

Bernice gave her a look full of pity.

"Don't look at me like that," Marcel said.

Bernice shook her head and turned to go.

"See you tomorrow, dear."

"And don't call me dear," Marcel said, trying not to raise her voice as Bernice descended the stairs.

*   *   *

That evening, when Marcel returned home, the little ninjas were waiting for her again. They had grilled scallops and pancetta on fresh rosemary skewers, asparagus with lemon butter, a dry chardonnay. Marcel thawed out a cheesecake, fetched three forks from her kitchen.

"So what comes next?" Marcel said, kicking off her shoes, curling her legs beneath her on the couch.

The little ninjas continued with their tale of Terra Incognita.

After they started posting Zach's novel online, Confederate Vampires in Space began to grow in popularity. It became a viral phenomenon. Curious readers were coming into Terra Incognita in search of the author. Zach even combed his hair and posed for a few pictures. The increase in foot traffic brought an increase in customers, and Zach was busy ringing up new sales of graphic novels or playing-card expansion packs or the odd back issue. When he could, he would steal away and hole up in the office in the back with his manual typewriter and churn out a few more paragraphs.

"You mean he didn't try to burn it all?" Marcel said, spearing a crisp bite of asparagus with her fork.

"Not on my watch," the little ninja said.

The other ninja was refilling Marcel's wine glass, tilting the bottle of chilled chardonnay with both hands, smoothly rolling the bottle away when the glass was full.

Zach decided he wanted to spend more time working on CVS, so he hired the little ninjas full time at Terra Incognita. The ninjas were ecstatic. They were already there all the time anyway. It was their dream job.

The first thing the ninjas decided to do was to upgrade the surveillance.

"Loss prevention is basic," a little ninja explained.

"No telling how many sticky fingers were cutting into the profits," the other ninja chimed in, nodding.

The ninjas added better video and audio surveillance and

integrated it into the displays around the store. The cameras and mikes were so small, nobody suspected a thing.

"That little red light in the Terminator's eye?" said one ninja.

"Fish-eye view of the whole floor," said the other.

The little ninjas set up a command center in the back. They had multiple views of the entire store and the front and back doors. They could see and hear everything 24/7.

"It was awesome," the ninjas said together, clenching their little fists, practically levitating at the thought.

"But that was before . . . the interloper," Marcel murmured, licking cheesecake from her knife.

"Yes. The honey pot."

"The monkey wrench."

"Jolene."

"If that's her real name," Marcel said.

There was something about Jolene. The ninjas noticed her immediately. Not because of the bleach-blond corn rows or the delicate arabesque tattoo inked over one shoulder or the stud in her navel or her annoying perfect posture. There was something else. Most adults, when they came through the door, were not prepared for the small flight of steps. They usually had an off-balance moment on the first step, peering into the store while they got their bearings. The adults who were regulars had learned to stop and navigate the three steps. As for young people, the steps did not seem to faze them. They simply tumbled down or bounded over them on their way into the store.

When Jolene came through the door, however, she came down the steps gracefully, without hesitation. She sailed into the swirling center of Terra Incognita, planted her feet wide and stood there, with her hands on her hips and a half-smile on her face.

The little ninja nearest Marcel leaned over and spoke with a confidential tone.

"That's when I first suspected she was an android."

The other ninja paused and heaved a tremendous little sigh.

The silence grew uncomfortable, and Marcel looked back and forth from one little face to the other.

The little ninja nearest Marcel responded with a tiny tectonic shrug.

The other ninja scowled a moment longer and then soldiered on.

Females were welcome in Terra Incognita, but they tended to be a rarity. The ninjas expected that Jolene would browse for a brief while, and then beat a hasty retreat back out the door. To their surprise, Jolene waded deeper into the welter of comics and merchandise and super-human swag, completely at ease in the otherwise empty store.

Dragon-headed kites peered at her from the ceilings. X-wings and a death star floated past her head. A gleaming katana and its carved jade-and-ivory sheath hung on one wall. Beneath it, on a shelf, was a shiny brass djinni lamp and silk pillows the color of Tyrian purple. On another wall, crossed harpoons and below them, a coiled bullwhip. A western saddle with dangling stirrups rested on a small tripod. A suit of samurai armor stood guard by the front door. There was an elaborate gold armillary sphere near the cash register. A gnarled wizard's staff in the corner. Zach called the pearly-colored credit-card reader the philosopher's stone.

Life-size characters stood frozen in dynamic poses at various stations around the rooms. The characters were cardboard or inflatable or mannequins. You moved past them, through the rooms, down the aisles, round the corners, like Perseus in Medusa's lair. One frozen figure — say, Bella Lugosi's Dracula

— would disappear from your line of sight, and, across the room, another — the robot from Lost in Space, perhaps — would come into view.

Jolene spotted the Alien behind the counter against one wall, and immediately she walked straight towards it. She walked past a cardboard Lynda Carter clad in red white and blue with arms akimbo and her golden lasso on one spangled hip. She walked past the Terminator and his gleaming red eye.

Above the Alien was a prominent hand-lettered sign. The sign read: "Ask The Alien."

The Alien had been Zach's idea. When he was a boy, his mother took him to get new shoes at a shoe store with a talking tree. The tree was positioned near the front door and had what appeared to be a human face carved into the trunk. As you entered, the tree would speak to you and welcome you to the store, and as you exited, the tree would call your name and ask you a riddle and say goodbye. It was just an old, twisted tree trunk with a speaker behind the carved mouth and someone in the back of the store speaking into a clunky microphone. For small children, though, it was a potent illusion, one Zach never forgot.

The Alien, of course, was an iconic monster from the 1979 film, a nightmare born from the imagination of surrealist artist H. R. Giger and brought to the big screen by director Ridley Scott. Zach had purchased the life-size bust of the Alien at a comic book convention. The bust was made of polyurethane and vinyl and was a very accurate reproduction of the monster from the movie. It had a second set of jaws that could extend from the inside of the mouth, not as impressive without all the fake, drooling saliva, but still, pretty darn creepy.

The Alien was positioned behind a glass counter, as if it were a seated employee. Beneath the locked glass counter were rare comic books sealed in clear plastic bags with the prices written on colorful round stickers fastened to the corners. There were bowls heaped with pristine twenty-sided dice. There were tiny, detailed, hand-painted figurines from Middle Earth. Harry Potter's wand. Iron Man's glove. A bulky communicator from Star Trek. The Eye of Agamotto.

Jolene stepped directly in front of the Alien and stood facing the smooth, eyeless, elongated carapace.

She read the sign: Ask The Alien.

Jolene peered into the Alien's mouth. Her face was inches from the jaws and teeth.

The little ninjas in their command center, watching on their closed-circuit monitors, jumped back when Jolene peered into the jaws of the Alien, her face looming large on their small screens.

"It's Ripley," one of them said with mock reverence.

"Or a Predator," said the other.

Jolene took a step back from the counter.

"I'm looking for Zach Stone," she said in a firm voice.

There was a brief pause.

The Alien and Jolene quietly regarded one another.

There was a soft electric click and some static.

"He'll be right out . . . earthling female."

Zach was in his office working on CVS. When he emerged from the back of the store, his mind was in a daze, still focused on quantum catapults and the obsidian blade. He appeared much as he did when he was in college — rumpled but solid, thick, broad-shouldered, with messy brown hair and an open, earnest face.

"Hi, I'm Zach," he said. "How can I help you?"

Jolene turned, and they stood facing each other across the long, neat boxes of comic books, near the cardboard Wonder Woman, the Terminator, the Alien. Over Jolene's tattooed shoulder, a large, ornate dragon kite was hanging from the ceiling. The head of the dragon was sewn from green and yellow fabric, and its long rainbow-colored tail spiraled around the ceiling in loops of draped fabric.

"Quick, how far is it to the door?" Jolene said, watching him intently.

"Um, how far?" Zach said, unsure.

"From where you're standing. How far is it to the door? Quick! Don't think about it."

Zach looked toward the door. At his elbow was a large figurine of Doctor Tempus and his winged steed, Tachyon, rampant, the feathered tips of ivory-colored wings sweeping wide on either side. Zach leaned to one side to get a better view of the door. Near the ceiling, a model of the Enterprise from Star Trek was descending from the folds of the dragon's tail. Next to the door, the empty suit of samurai armor stood guard.

"I don't know," Zach shrugged. "Not that far."

Jolene nodded her head.

"Okay, but how would you describe it, the distance from here . . . to there?"

The Terminator's eye was blinking at him. Zach rubbed the back of his neck. His hair was sticking up, and he smoothed it down. He wiped his hand over his face. Sometimes when he fell asleep at his desk, there would be stuff stuck to his face when he woke up, like a paper clip or a rubber band, and nobody would tell him, and it might be hours before it fell off.

"Who's asking?" Zach said.

"Just me. Jolene. Just me Jolene," she said.

She had a knowing, half-smile and brown eyes, an intense gaze, but Zach kind of liked it. Thin braids of bleached hair fell across her face and she pulled them back and fixed them with her fingers behind one ear. She wore rings on almost every finger, bangles and bracelets around her wrist, a pale lime-colored polish on her nails. There was a seriously huge silver ring through the piercing in her nose.

"Well, Jolene. I'd say it depends."

Her brown eyes opened even wider. She blinked a few times.

"On what?" she said.

He put his hands deep in the pockets of his cargo shorts and rocked back and forth on the heels of his high-top tennis shoes.

"On what's in here . . . and what's outside the door."

For a moment, something inchoate seemed to pass across her face, an unsettled mixture that Zach could not recognize, a veil of sadness and confusion and anger maybe, but then Jolene smiled, a quick, blinding flash of big, white teeth behind her silvery, mint-green lips.

"I think I'm going to like you, Zach Stone."

Marcel snorted derisively.

"Oh, please . . ." Marcel protested, pouring herself another glass of wine.

"Indeed," the little ninja said.

"In retrospect, we should have known," the other little ninja said.

"Should have seen it coming."

"Should have nipped it . . ."

"We underestimated her at every juncture."

"Should have nipped it in the bud."

*   *   *

The ninjas began to see more of Jolene on their closed-circuit screens. She would visit after her yoga class in the evening. She left the front tire of her bicycle and her rolled yoga mat propped next to the samurai armor at the front door. She browsed through the back issues, leaning with her hips against the table, flipping through a box of bagged comics. Her braids hung down to her shoulders on either side of her bowed head. She crossed one leg lazily at the ankle behind the other. The little ninjas glimpsed, beneath the hem of her faded pale-green half-tee, the large ornate tattoo on her bare lower back.

At first the ninjas were alarmed because she would untape the plastic bags and remove the comics and page through, her eyes scrolling quickly down the pages, but she was careful and slid the comics back in and taped the bags shut and put them back in the right spot in the box. Zach did not seem to mind, so the ninjas let it slide.

Jolene would linger until closing time, and Zach began to come out of his office earlier each day. Jolene and Zach began to have long, meandering, comic-book-tinged conversations.

In their command center, the ninjas listened.

"But *why* is the Hulk so angry?"

"Well, I think it has something to do with being irradiated with a massive blast of gamma particles."

"And that affected his impulse control?"

"Umm . . . maybe."

"Has anyone suggested anger management? Meditation? Acupuncture? Aromatherapy?"

"For the Hulk?"

"Maybe a few days at a spa?"

Jolene was a student at the University. One of her teachers was Zach's old college classmate, Robert Hitch. She had been discussing her ideas for research with Doctor Hitch and Zach's name had come up.

"Really?" Zach said, surprised. "Robert Hitch? Steady Robert?"

If being a college student was Jolene's cover, as the ninjas suspected, it was hard to believe Robert Hitch was not also part of the conspiracy.

"Conspiracy?" Marcel said.

"The skullduggery."

"The sabotage."

Jolene wanted to use Terra Incognita as one of the settings for her research about how humans perceive and describe distance.

"The epistemology . . . of distance," Jolene whispered, heavy lidded, a beaded blond braid twisted around one ringed finger.

She was fixated on distance. Obsessed with getting from here to there. She could talk for an hour about a flock of birds she had seen flying in the park and the way they spaced themselves out. It had something to do with her childhood, but the ninjas never understood why exactly.

She would challenge Zach and the occasional unsuspecting customer to spontaneous, improvised contests that always involved guessing the distance to various objects in the comic book store. She had the unerring ability to guess the distance down to the millimeter or fractional inch. It was her superpower.

Zach bought her a little laser device that would find a distance and display it on the screen. She loved it and carried it with her everywhere attached at her hip. She wore it there with things like her phone and keys. It was her utility belt.

She bought him a yoga mat, and in the mornings the ninjas watched him on their closed-circuit screens as he inhaled and exhaled, alone on his office floor, stretching in clumsy, awkward jerks and starts through the asanas of a sunrise salutation.

She was a dancer and always seemed to move with a heightened awareness of her body, but occasionally she would bust out some wicked en pointe pirouette that seemed inhuman and left everyone momentarily speechless.

"Do that again," Zach would say, and she would just smile her knowing, half smile and walk out the door.

Despite her obvious physical coordination, Jolene was serenely uninterested in sports. This was almost ironic or even anachronistic given that many of the young women her age were, if anything, more conversant in the lingua franca of sports talk than the young men. She said she was reserving that section of her brain for future use.

Perhaps related to her sports allergy and her infallible distance-measuring radar, she had the uncanny ability to bat down any object thrown at her. It became a recurring source of amusement as they tried to catch her unaware. She would walk through Terra Incognita and bat away a volley of Nerf balls, tennis balls, beach balls, Frisbees, pillows, stuffed animals, without blinking. If you tried to sneak up on her and throw something at her head, she would bat it down without even looking up. The ninjas never tired of that.

And that was how it happened.

Smoothly, so smoothly the ninjas were not fully aware of it, Jolene had insinuated herself into Terra Incognita. Zach and Jolene had become inseparable. Zach would watch her with dazed, blissful eyes as she and the ninjas were busily sorting their Pokemon cards. The ninjas noted on their closed-circuit screens the way she touched him when she thought they were alone. This in itself was not objectionable, but there were other unforeseen strategic consequences. Most ominous, Confederate Vampires in Space began to change. Zach was spending more time writing about feelings and relationships. Melodrama was creeping into his prose. This offended the ninjas' delicate artistic sensibilities. They wanted a more spare and unforgiving narrative. They were losing editorial control.

So they began subtly to try to keep them apart. But this Jolene creature was diabolical, foiling them at every turn. Zach's judgment was clouded. He was defenseless against her French theory and her downward facing dogs. She began to make suggestions about the displays in Terra Incognita. There was casual mention that sales from the Cthulhu section were not exactly robust. A tattoo appeared on the inside of Zach's forearm, a snake in a circle with its tail in its mouth.

She had become an interloper. A monkey wrench. The honey pot in black yoga pants. A hostile in a sports bra on their closed-circuit screens. Suddenly, the whole enterprise seemed in jeopardy. The ninjas did not like where things were headed. They needed more information, better intelligence.

The ninjas did not know what the ninjas did not know.

So they decided to be proactive.

* * *

Marcel was sitting at her desk in her office in the museum. She was staring off into space thinking about the days when she and Zach and Robert had been inseparable, the way the three of them sat so close side by side on the steps in the sun on those autumn afternoons after the Professor's class. It was early in the morning, and she heard Bernice stirring in the hall. Marcel shook off the past, swept away the fog of old memories, and walked out into the hall.

Bernice was wearing something on her head. Marcel had to look at it closely before she was sure what she was seeing. It was a hat made out of fur, imitation fur knowing Bernice. There was a ringed tail hanging down the back. It looked like it was made from a raccoon pelt. Marcel blinked several times.

It was a coon-skin cap.

Bernice took the hat off and put it in a drawer.

"Uh, what was that?" Marcel asked.

"Fashion experiment. I wanted to see what people on the street thought."

"And?"

"Cumsi cumsa," Bernice said, pivoting the palm of one hand in the air beside her shoulder. "The jury is still out."

Marcel was slack jawed and realized she was staring at Bernice.

"What's wrong?"

"I'm not sure," Marcel said slowly.

Bernice was busy positioning her Derek Jeter bobble head.

"I'm going out for a while," Marcel said and turned on her heel.

The date scheduled for the unveiling of the Dysette-Zee was approaching, but Marcel found herself unfocused. She was planning the reception, choosing music for the string quartet, writing commentary to put the piece in context, preparing remarks for her introduction of the historians from the University, but she kept thinking about the little ninjas and Terra Incognita, and her mind wandered.

She had been slipping away in the middle of the day and would find herself an hour later sitting in front of the Dysette-Zee lost in thought. When she was out in the museum working in some other area, she found a reason to walk up to the balcony and spend a few minutes gazing into the cerulean blue.

The epistemology of distance.

Marcel thought she knew more than a little about distance.

Marcel left the museum in her car, a black Mustang convertible. She was driving aimlessly at first, but really she knew all along where she was going.

Before her parents divorced, her mother was often home alone, and she would take Marcel and her sister on long drives through the city. Her mother drove this enormous Buick Electra 225, maybe the longest car ever made. Before that, she had driven a Corvair, and the Buick seemed to be some sort of concession from her father for ever having let them drive around cooped up in the Corvair. Her mother would take Marcel and her sister out in the Buick and just drive through the city, through the darkening neighborhoods, down empty streets past the quiet homes with their big cars parked in the driveways, and the girls would sit in the enormous back seat, quietly playing or softly singing or sometimes just sleeping. It was winter, near Christmas, and there was snow on the ground. Her father was spending a lot of time away from home, and her mother always told Marcel that his work was very important. It was before she understood about adults and office Christmas parties.

On that snowy winter night, her mother drove into a neighborhood where the yards were large and well-tended, and the Christmas lights were serene, and the snow looked peaceful the way it always does in photographs and paintings, and there were cars parked end to end along the street in front of one house, and her mother parked the Buick in the dark off the side of the quiet street, and somehow she persuaded Marcel and her sister to play a game, to sneak towards the brightly lit house, and they crept like spies through the snow and peered like spies through the windows, and they saw that there were many adults in the home, and the adults were standing amid the Christmas decorations and a beautiful tree, and it was a party, and the adults were laughing and smiling, and there among them was their father sitting on a couch with a woman who was not their mother.

Marcel and her sister crouched down in the snow. They looked at each other, quiet as the midnight hour, the Pirate Queen and her loyal confrere. They peered over the top of the bushes and watched their father and this strange woman with red lipstick and big hair, watched the way they were looking at each other, the way they were drinking and smiling and laughing.

When Marcel and her sister snuck back to the car, their mother was waiting, her small hands tight on the big steering wheel. She asked them if they had seen their father, and they told her, like spies, what they had seen.

Marcel never forgot the game her mother tricked her into playing, and years later after her parents had divorced and she understood better what she and her sister had seen that night, she felt pity for her mother, not just because of what had happened to their family, but perhaps most of all because of the memory of that night, the night when her mother had led her daughters to that window outside the bright house in the quiet neighborhood in the Christmas snow.

Marcel parked her Mustang across the street where she could see the front of the apartment building. She did not have to wait long. Robert Hitch came pedaling down the street on his bicycle. He was wearing a neon green vest and a huge helmet with a flashing light and several mirrors sticking in several directions. His pant legs were carefully fastened around his ankles. His bike had mirrors and horns and bells and bottles and a pump and a basket and a bulky black saddle bag with an orange flag flying high over the rear tire. Marcel could not help but smile at the sight of him.

She watched him lock up his bike and slowly climb the rusty metal stairs and open the apartment door. She got out of her Mustang and walked across the street. It was a modest apartment building, no trees in the yard, dirt at the edges against the brick walls. A skinny white dog with a furry muzzle paused to watch her, and then continued on its way, trotting around the corner.

She had to knock on the door several times. She could sense him standing behind the door, watching her.

"What do you want?" he said behind the door.

"Open up, Robert," Marcel said. "We need to talk."

He cracked the door open.

"Marcel Arrow," he said.

He looked tired, with a scruffy beard. He needed a haircut.

She smiled with the side of her mouth.

"Steady Robert," she said.

"How did you find me?"

"Ninjas."

He began slowly to shake his head

"Those little bastards," he said, matter-of-fact.

He swung the door open.

"Come on in."

*　*　*

Robert and Marcel had managed to live and work in the same metropolitan area for years without any awkward unanticipated encounters. Robert did not stray far from the University, and Marcel spent most of her time at the museum. On a few occasions, she had been at the same social function as Robert and his wife, Tilda, but they had not exchanged more than the most perfunctory of pleasantries.

Marcel was aware of Tilda. She was petite, friendly, self-assured. She wore her blond hair in a pixie cut, but pixie was not a word anyone would ever associate with Tilda. She radiated a focused energy and a polite insistence. She, like Marcel, was part of the civic glue. They had volunteered together on several committees and boards for projects connected with the city and the University and the museum. Lately, she had been increasingly involved in local politics.

Marcel had passed Tilda a few times in the grocery. They each felt the other's gravitational pull, but an actual conversation seemed too fraught. They would pivot around each other, smiling politely, gathering momentum, and sling-shot their way back into the middle distances and the safety of the city.

When they both were serving on the committee for the city's annual Festival of the Bird, there had been a display of public art with dozens of small drawings in colored pencil. Marcel drew an insouciant pink flamingo. Tilda drew a tidy little bluebird with a thought bubble over its head. Inside the thought bubble, the words were clearly written: "I am the harbinger of happiness."

Robert closed the door and followed Marcel as she walked into the apartment. It was a small apartment with a single bedroom. Marcel walked past a brand-new easy chair and a flat-screen television propped unsteadily on a milk crate against one bare wall. Next to the easy chair on the tan carpeting, she saw a desiccated brown apple core, an almost empty jar of peanuts, a bottle opener, bottle caps, and a few empty bottles.

Through the bedroom door, Marcel could see a mattress on the floor and a dark green nylon sleeping bag wadded up in the corner. It looked like the same sleeping bag Robert had in college. She was intimately acquainted with that old green sleeping bag. Her disheveled college self raised her head and peered out from beneath the musky green bedding. Marcel cringed inwardly and quickly looked away.

Marcel casually inspected the kitchen table. Robert silently trailed behind her. The kitchen table was covered with pads of lined paper with blocks of handwriting marching down the middle of the pages. There was an open laptop computer on the table in front of an empty chair. A collection of half-empty coffee cups and an open package of oatmeal cookies were clustered beside the laptop. Above the table, there was a weak light. Inside the yellowed, round light fixture, the dark shadows of dead bugs.

Robert followed her into the small kitchen. Her heels clicked softly on the tile. The trash receptacle was full of take-out food containers. She opened the refrigerator. There was an impressive variety of bottled craft beers and a large, fresh bunch of something green and leafy.

Marcel picked up the leafy greens.

It appeared to be kale.

"Seriously?"

"Don't judge me," he said.

She tossed the kale back in the fridge.

"May I?" she asked, nodding toward the beer.

He shrugged.

She found a bottle of hoppy pale ale she had read about in a magazine. There was a cloudy, spotted glass in the cupboard. She looked at him evenly as she wiped clean the rim of the glass with the hem of her Armani suit. He began searching for the bottle opener.

"It's beside the easy chair," Marcel said.

He retrieved the opener and poured the beer into her glass.

As he poured the beer, she noted duly the wedding ring on his finger.

She took a sip of the beer, leaned against the kitchen counter.

"So, Robert . . ."

She knitted her brow, looked in his eyes.

"What's going on here?"

"The little ninjas didn't tell you?" he said, sardonic.

She took another sip of beer.

"How's Tilda?"

Robert crossed his arms across his chest.

"Tilda's fine. Tilda's great."

Marcel walked out of the kitchen. Robert followed her. She slid sideways into the easy chair. She crossed her legs and dangled them over one armrest and leaned back against the other side of the chair. Her Chanel No. 5 was subtle.

"Not much of a man cave," she said, watching his face over the rim of her glass as she drank from her beer.

"You seem comfortable."

She smiled with the side of her mouth.

"Old habits."

Robert smiled, and she saw, beneath his scruffy, college-professor beard, the Robert she remembered. She caught a glimpse of his familiar square jaw, the old square toes.

He sat down on the carpet against a bare wall with his knees raised and his arms draped across them, his fingers laced together loosely in front of his long, skinny legs.

Marcel could see him across the room. Time seemed to be moving in a strange, diagonal way. She saw his younger face in the late-afternoon sun, his profile outlined in the glow of a stereo console display. How would she describe it now, the distance across the room?

"Do you know about Professor Straw?" he said.

"No," Marcel said, shaking her head. "What happened?"

"He's been ill."

"With what?"

"They're not sure. You should go see him."

"Me? Why?"

"He talks about you. All the time."

Marcel turned away.

"I haven't seen him in years."

Winston Straw.

That name once meant so much to her. His name alone still set off a complicated cascade of feelings and memories.

Marcel took a sip from her beer.

She was thinking of the small white room and the narrow windows and their faces gathered around the long oak table, the way the light would reflect off the lenses of the Professor's glasses, the way he would gesture with his little finger.

"Ironic, isn't it?" she said. "Confederate vampires."

"In space."

"Is that what all this is about?" she said, waving a hand at the empty apartment around her.

"I don't know. Maybe."

He paused for a moment.

"I'm trying to write a screenplay."

Marcel rolled her eyes.

"I know . . ." he said. "What a cliché, right?"

"I didn't say that."

"The condo, our condo . . . Tilda and I . . . it's been . . . noisy . . . crowded. She's running for city council."

"I like Tilda."

"Everyone likes Tilda."

He sighed.

"It's like being married to Joan of Arc."

Marcel tilted her head slightly to one side.

They were silent for a while.

Marcel's disheveled college self was peeking at them from the bedroom. She wore a mischievous grin.

"I like Tilda," Marcel said, again, quietly.

"Yeah," he said, quietly. "Me, too."

Marcel finished her beer. She held the glass with the top against her palm and rested its bottom at an angle on the chair. She leaned her head back and looked at the ceiling.

"So . . . this Jolene person . . ."

"Yeah," Robert said. "About that."

"The ninjas think she might be a super-human sex bot."

Robert laughed.

"It's not outside the realm of possibility."

"And, if I'm not mistaken, Doctor Hitch, I do believe she's one of your students," Marcel said with a certain prosecutorial lilt in her voice.

Robert ignored her tone.

"Jolene has some interesting ideas. She's kind of an inspiring story. She's overcome a lot. Foster care. A disability. She doesn't talk much about it, but she grew up on a reservation."

"She's Native American?"

"Her mother was."

"The little ninjas think you sent her to Terra Incognita to interfere with Zach's writing."

"Marcel, the little ninjas are like a biblical plague."

Marcel shrugged.

"They do good work. . . . I highly recommend their shrimp dijon."

"Those little bastards cut the cables to the brakes on my bike. I know it was them. I couldn't get off the road on the hill near the water tower. I had to steer into the lake. There was this ramp. I . . . I was airborne. I had to walk back to the condo covered in algae and mud. You should have seen their faces — the campaign volunteers, Tilda, the Mayor — when I opened the front door."

"I saw it, actually. The ninjas have that on video."

They were silent.

"It's pretty funny."

"Those little bastards," Robert muttered.

"The ninjas think Zach has disappeared and that Jolene had something to do with it. I checked around. No one has seen him in weeks."

"What about Jolene?"

"The ninjas say she's still coming into Terra Incognita. She's been teaching classes in yoga and meditation. The ninjas say she's avoiding them."

"Do you want me to talk with her?"

"Maybe. There's something else, though. Zach was last seen in Terra Incognita near the Emily Dickinson action figures. The ninjas have it on video."

"Of course they do."

"Here's the thing, Square-Toes. The ninjas say he disappears. On the video. I've seen it. He's there, and then — shazam — he's gone. And that's the last anyone's seen of him."

"That sounds like a ninja mind fuck. Did they edit the video?"

"I don't know. But why would they? They said they wanted to keep CVS on schedule."

"Maybe they're the ones invading Terra Incognita. Maybe the little ninjas want you to get rid of Jolene."

They were silent for a moment.

"Fucking ninjas."

"Those little bastards."

They looked at each other for the briefest of moments. The expressions on their faces were so familiar, even after all the time that had passed. There was an instant of recognition, of sympathy, of wordless understanding.

They burst out in laughter, and their laughter blew through the room like a gale. Their laughing eyes met across the room, and, for a moment, they both felt a great sense of comfort, of safety, of all the old shared pleasures.

"Look," Robert said, struggling to find his usual sober voice. "The ninjas are right. I did send Jolene to Terra Incognita. And maybe I am a little jealous of Confederate vampires."

"In space," Marcel said, still a little giddy.

"In space. But I thought Jolene would be good for him. I thought they would be good for each other. I thought they might . . . be happy together."

"Oh, you silly, silly boy."

"You don't believe me."

She looked at him carefully.

"I wanted Zach to keep writing," Robert said. "I've always felt that way. I was as disappointed as anyone when he quit."

Marcel sighed.

"Yeah," she said. "That sucked."

She rocked up from the easy chair and took several long strides toward the kitchen.

"Have you read CVS?" she said, over one shoulder.

"No," Robert said.

He listened as Marcel's heels clicked on the kitchen tile.

She set the glass in the sink.

"Well . . . I may have skimmed it," Robert said.

She walked back into the room and stood looking down at him with her hands on her hips.

"Okay," he admitted, "I read the whole thing. Twice."

Marcel nodded.

"I've got to go," she said.

He stood up, and they faced each other.

Marcel took him by the arm, and they walked to the door.

"Do you think what Kit Carson said about us is true?" she asked him.

"That Zach renounced writing because he thought it would keep us together?"

"Yes."

They were standing at the door facing each other. Marcel had her hand on his arm.

"I don't know," Robert said.

Marcel looked into his eyes.

He opened the door.

"It was good to see you, Robert."

"Yes. You need to come over to the condo for dinner sometime. After all this election sturm un drang has passed."

"The museum keeps me pretty busy."

"Let us know, then."

"I will."

She paused, searching his face one last time.

"If I go to see the Professor . . ." Marcel said.

"He'd love to see you."

"Would you . . . would you come with me?"

"Sure. Of course."

She smiled.

"Steady Robert."

He felt her hand on his arm.

"Good luck with your screenplay."

She turned to go, and Robert watched as she walked across the street and got in her car and drove away.

*   *   *

That night, Marcel dreamed:

The nib of a fountain pen. The faint scratching sound as it moves across the surface of thick, cream-colored paper. Black ink glistening, bleeding at the edges into the dense fibers of the paper. Blotting paper, stained and spotted, carefully applied. Graceful, spidery cursive arcs smooth on the surface of the page.

Red wax dripping on the back of a closed envelope. A large bead of wax that covers the bottom edge of the flap. The wax smooth against the thick, cream-colored paper. A metal seal pressed gently into the circle of red wax. An impression, embossed, two intertwined cursive letters, a W and an S. The red wax cools.

The sealed letter.

The Professor sets the sealed letter aside. Lamp light catches the fine honeyed grain of polished cherry wood. An antique desk, a blotter, an ink well, the fountain pen, an open gold pocket watch.

The Professor has grown frail with age and illness. His blunt features, so vigorous in his youth, have sharpened. The bones of his bald head are prominent beneath his thin skin. He is hollow cheeked, and his skull at his temples is a delicate, milky shade of violet and blue. Behind his round, rimless spectacles, his eyes are sharp and clear, dark like a bird's. His eyes give him a strange sort of agelessness, a quality of intellect that seems to swing somewhere between imperious king and mischievous child.

He is seated behind his desk in his darkened study. The light from a brass lamp with a dark green shade just reaches the walls of the small, windowless room. From floor to ceiling, books line the entirety of each wall, arranged neatly on uniform black shelves. There are several small stacks of books on the floor beside the chair. Books surround him like a womb.

The Professor hears a rustle and a hush. He looks up from his desk. The raven-haired woman is standing in the doorway. She regards him without expression. She is, as always, dressed in the most tasteful and appropriate fashion. She wears ebony brocade and a black veil of needled lace with a simple but striking pattern. Behind the lace, her lips are wine dark. Her raven hair is swept up, arranged with black silk roses, tortoise-shell combs and pearly-headed pins. She wears a demi-parure of teardrop rubies and jet and silver. The white pendant, the snake in a circle, the ouroboros, rests on her chest. She moves to the Professor's side and takes the sealed letter. Her fingers are tipped with scarlet. She quietly departs, and the Professor is alone.

* * *

The arms of the Calder sculpture swept gracefully around the vaulted spaces of the museum's atrium. Marcel leaned against the railing of the balcony and watched as the crowd began to gather below her. The evening of the formal unveiling of the new Dysette-Zee had finally arrived.

Let the schmooze-fest begin, Marcel thought.

Trevor the intern was standing next to her. Thin and pale, usually seen gnawing on a fingernail, Trevor had cleaned up for the unveiling. He wore a tan linen blazer and a solid pink silk tie. Marcel had seen too many similar transformations to be surprised or impressed, but she did take notice of the stylistic effort, of the wavy brown hair. Trevor was a not unattractive man.

Marcel had kept it simple, a strapless little black dress with a pale blue cashmere shawl over her bare shoulders. She wore pale blue studs in her earlobes, a matching clasp in her hair at the back of her neck and a string of dark pearls.

Earlier, she and Trevor had been alone in the elevator.

"I like your shawl," Trevor had said, blithe, fearless. "It looks like part of the painting."

Riding a wave of caffeine and adrenalin, she had seized his lapel, backed him into a corner and stared into his eyes.

"Very good, Trevor. Tell me, does it seem as if hazy islands of color are floating beyond the edges of the canvas?"

Her eyes had a maniacal glint.

Trevor nervously glanced down at the shawl.

"I'm going to say yes," he said.

"Does it seem as if you and I are standing at a secret,

magical place beyond time and memory where the borders between life and art have grown thin, and the dimensionless particles of two realities have begun to shift and mingle?"

He was afraid to answer.

He was fairly certain they were standing in an elevator.

"Yes. All that. And more," Trevor said, beginning to regret his foray into fashion commentary.

Marcel released his lapel from her clenched fingers.

"You're very perceptive, Trevor," she said, smoothing his lapel, straightening his pink tie, patting him on the arm.

Trevor loosened his collar with one finger.

The elevator doors parted. They heard music. Vivaldi. It was the string quartet.

"I may have misjudged you," Marcel said serenely as the sharp edge of her attention swept away from the relieved young intern.

Safely ensconced in the balcony, Marcel and Trevor were sipping their drinks and watching each new group of guests as they came through the front entrance. A few other members of the museum staff were on the balcony with them, but the balcony and the area around the blue expanse of the Dysette-Zee behind them were mostly empty. The wet bar and the food were downstairs. Rows of folding chairs were arrayed before a small podium. The string quartet was unobtrusive in one rounded corner. Marcel hoped that at least a few people might climb the stairs or take the elevator to actually look at the painting before everyone sat down and began to slice it up into little academic morsels.

The museum's executive director was known professionally as Doctor Elliot Jean-Marie Pitts-Popper. His staff knew him simply as the Popper or Doctor P. He was a nervous, rotund man with a beard and a bow tie. The Popper was standing in a cluster of silver hair and frosted highlights that included Dagmar von Geldingham and Eschoat Glissade, two of the largest contributors to the museum's endowment. The Popper kept looking up at Marcel, silently importuning her to join him. He was trying to be subtle, rolling his eyes and moving his head and shoulders in a series of increasingly spasmodic shrugs and nods.

Marcel and Trevor smiled and waved each time he looked up at them.

"I think he's getting a facial tic."

"He might throw his back out."

Marcel usually enjoyed socializing with the museum crowd. A carousel of eccentrics had come whirling through her office door, dilettantes and academics and artists and philanthropists. It was often hard to tell one from the other, which Marcel found both amusing and fascinating. That was one part of her job that Marcel loved. Lately, though, what had seemed a happy mix of the personal and the professional had begun to seem more like an expected social duty, and she was beginning to resent it. The Popper generally deferred to her judgment and opinions with regard to art, but, as executive director, the Popper dealt with the governing boards and had the final say regarding financial decisions. Marcel wanted to make the museum's collection more easily accessible to everyone. The Popper did not. Marcel wanted to acquire more contemporary pieces. The Popper did not.

Marcel looked toward the entrance just as Robert and Tilda arrived. She watched as they threaded their way through the crowd. Tilda had long been active at the fringes of the museum, but she and Robert had not attended any events or exhibits that Marcel could remember.

Marcel stared at the top of Steady Robert's head as he filled his plate with a little pyramid of crab rangoon. His hair was thinning at the crown. She dared him to look up at the balcony, to find her eyes across the room.

Was this your idea, Square-Toes? Hey, Hon, let's go to that art thing at the museum?

Marcel measured them with her scalpel-sharp eyes. Tilda was in campaign mode and was effusive. She smiled with her blond face at the world. Robert was dutiful and supportive over her shoulder, ever ready with a well-timed joke or laugh. They appeared to be a smoothly-functioning social machine. There were no visible cracks in their marital façade.

Marcel watched as Tilda and Robert breached the invisible outer membrane surrounding the nucleus of silver hair and frosted highlights.

Tilda was skillfully working the room.

"I really like her," Trevor said, following Marcel's gaze.

Marcel gave him a sideways glance.

Yeah," she said, her voice fading ever so slightly. "Me, too."

Trevor looked at her.

"What?" Marcel said.

"Nothing," Trevor said.

"No, what is it?"

"You rolled your eyes."

"I did not."

"Verbally. I heard your eyes roll."

"You're insane."

Tilda was nodding agreeably as she listened to Dagmar von Geldingham. The Popper looked up to the balcony with a frozen smile. His face was glistening. His pleading eyes found Marcel. He rolled his head several times toward the crowd, emoting like a chubby, desperate mime.

Marcel and Trevor waved and smiled.

He scowled back at them.

"Aww, he looks like a grumpy teddy bear."

"Don't laugh," Marcel warned Trevor. "I think he's getting angry."

She and Trevor looked at each other.

Marcel sighed.

"I guess I better get down there," Marcel said.

But before she could descend, something amazing happened.

A figure was moving quickly through the crowd toward the tight circle around the Popper and Tilda and Robert and the museum's major benefactors.

"Is that Bernice?" Trevor said.

She was wearing her finely-tanned leather jacket with the fringe. On her head, she wore the coon-skin cap with its ringed tail.

Marcel and Trevor watched, transfixed, horrified.

"Somebody do something," Trevor said.

For an instant, Marcel considered sweeping down the stairs and barreling into the crowd and physically throwing her body between Bernice and Dagmar von Geldingham.

She watched as Bernice pierced the silver-haired inner circle and began vigorously shaking hands with a visibly startled Eschoat Glissade.

Marcel mentally rifled through alternative diversions. If she pushed Trevor over the railing, would he survive the fall?

But it was too late.

Tilda had tried on the coon-skin cap.

And it looked good.

"I can't look away," Trevor said.

Marcel was confounded. People kept putting a so-called article of clothing that looked like a damned dead animal on the top of their heads, and the result was not hilarity and mortification and ridicule and the searing pain of a fashion Chernobyl, but rather each time someone put one of those unspeakable abominations on their head, it became weirdly and increasingly more appropriate. How could this be? How could so many people be comfortable wearing a simulated raccoon pelt perched on the top of their head like a clotted clump of decomposing road kill?

Tilda's face lit up with the hat on. She had a pleasing smile with brilliant, white teeth. She seemed even more charismatic with the hat resting on the crown of her head.

Bernice was beaming triumphantly.

Dagmar von Geldingham seemed intrigued.

The Popper was sweating through his suit jacket.

"What just happened?" Trevor said.

"I . . . I'm not sure," Marcel said, astonished.

"Are we overdressed?"

"Apparently so."

Trevor held up his phone to take a photo of the atrium and the gathered crowd and Tilda in the coon-skin cap.

"It's like a picnic at Manassas," he said.

"Manassas?"

"The Civil War. Didn't Mathew Brady make war porn at Manassas?"

"I think it was Antietam," Marcel said, distracted.

Her mind was drifting back to the days when she and Robert and Zach were sitting around the long oak table and the Professor was reading *The Iliad* and the autumn leaves were spiraling down.

She was looking at Robert's face as he watched Tilda modeling the coon-skin cap at the center of the silver-haired circle.

"I feel like Athena," Marcel said.

"What? Why?"

"In The Iliad, the gods watched the battles from the ramparts."

Trevor thought about that for a moment.

"So who am I?"

"You? A centaur. No, a satyr. No, a frolicking woodland nymph."

Trevor raised an eyebrow.

"Maybe I'm Hermes in disguise."

She turned and gave him a skeptical look down the length of her nose.

"That would be one very effective disguise." she said dryly.

"I'll take that as a complement," Trevor said, with a grin.

She handed Trevor her empty glass. The cerulean blue was dancing and shimmering over his shoulder.

"Dysette-Zee was a pacifist, by the way," she said and turned to go down the stairs and walk among the mortals.

* * *

After Doctor Elliot Jean-Marie Pitts-Popper finished speaking and sat down, Marcel took her turn behind the podium and faced the seated and expectant crowd.

"Thank you, Elliot, for those kind words," she said into the microphone. She looked over at the Popper, who was busy toweling off with a handkerchief.

"I want to echo Doctor Pitts-Popper and express my gratitude and appreciation to the many kind and generous people who have nurtured and supported this museum, this great institutional treasure, here in the heart of our diverse and thriving city.

"I have the best job in the world, and I'm thankful for people like Doctor P and the good people gathered here this evening who have made it possible for me to work every day doing what I love. Thank you all.

"I also want to recognize the generosity of Declan Croghan. Without his wise foresight, we would not be here tonight. Though sadly he is no longer with us, I would be remiss if I did not mention the importance of individual private patrons and collectors and the essential role their donations play in the preservation, exhibition and study of fine art at this institution and others like it around the world.

"Tonight we unveil a beautiful work of art by Richard Dysette-Zee and welcome it into our permanent collection. We don't know what Dysette-Zee would have titled this mural-sized painting, but we have the correspondence between the artist and Declan Croghan to guide us. In those letters, the artist referred to the project as his Untitled Blue. After consultation with the Dysette-Zee family and my esteemed colleagues at the University, the museum has decided to name the new painting Untitled Blue.

"One of my favorite professors in college often told us that people love a good story. They will always want to know what happens next. With that in mind, I hope you will indulge me and let me briefly tell the story of how I first saw Untitled Blue.

"The story begins with a letter. Each morning, I go through a stack of mail on my desk, and on that morning, the stack included an unexpected and somewhat ominous letter from a law firm. I opened the letter with a not inconsiderable amount of trepidation, but I was relieved to learn that it was only to notify me that the museum had been named as a beneficiary in Declan Croghan's will. Who, I wondered, was Declan Croghan? As I discovered, Mister Croghan was a real-estate developer with an old-fashioned sense of probate and very keen eye for modern art.

"I was not expecting much when I dutifully attended the reading of Declan Croghan's will. The conference room was crowded. I sat in the back and listened quietly. Mister Croghan's lawyers were thorough. Very thorough. I confess as the morning progressed I may have started scrolling discreetly through the messages on my phone. It was a shock, frankly, when I heard the lawyer dryly inform us that Mister Croghan had bequeathed a heretofore unknown work of art by a leading abstract expressionist to the safety and care of our humble institution.

"I managed to wait a day and a sleepless night before I drove myself to Declan Croghan's farm in upstate New York. I don't remember much of the drive, but I will say some speed limits may have been exceeded. The farm's caretaker was a lovely man named Adian Clabby. He spoke with the most charming Irish brogue and lit a pipe he smoked the entire time I was there. I'll never forget the intoxicating aroma of his tobacco smoke — sweet with a tinge of cherry.

"I was wearing heels when Mister Clabby led me to the barn, and I was barefoot when we climbed the ladder to the loft. There, piled against one wall, was a stack of objects that looked like rolled-up rugs. Each one was long and cylindrical and wrapped in a tarp and covered in burlap. Mister Clabby helped me lift one off the top of the pile. We untied it and pulled away the coverings and unfurled it all at once across the floor of the loft.

"Imagine, if you will, standing beneath a bare incandescent light bulb and more than a few fluttering moths, high in the straw-scattered loft of that ramshackle barn on a farm, breathing in the tobacco-sweet air, in the still, quiet hours of a darkening summer night in an obscure little corner of upstate New York. Imagine drawing back the burlap and the tarp and unfurling a section of a canvas and seeing before you for the first time the sudden and remarkable colors of the painting that now hangs on the wall in the balcony above us.

"Ladies and gentlemen, it was an extraordinary moment. It still takes my breath away.

"Untitled Blue is comprised of fifteen sections of canvas. Each section is four feet by six feet. As now assembled, the painting is twelve feet in height and thirty feet in length. Pablo Picasso's Guernica is 349 centimeters by 776 centimeters. Jackson Pollock's Number One or Lavender Mist is 221 centimeters by 299 centimeters. Henri Matisse's The Dance II is fifteen feet by forty-five feet.

"Untitled Blue appears to have been commissioned for the lobby of a skyscraper in New York City that was never completed. It is not clear whether it was intended as a mural or as a heroic painting. We have decided to exhibit Untitled Blue as a free-standing heroic painting.

"We believe Dysette-Zee painted Untitled Blue in the summer and fall of 19--. It is not clear where he painted it, but the correspondence between Dysette-Zee and Declan Croghan unequivocally identifies the barn on Declan Croghan's farm as a place of temporary storage. My friend, the pipe-smoking caretaker, Adian Clabby, recalls the day he helped the artist and others move the rolled canvases into the loft of Mister Croghan's barn.

"I think it is clear that Untitled Blue is consistent with Dysette-Zee's later work, but it also offers a new perspective and insight, especially with regard to his monumental canvases and those of other abstract expressionists. I'll let my esteemed colleagues from the University talk more about how Untitled Blue fits into our understanding of abstract expression and the New York School.

"I would, however, like to offer, if I may, some brief personal comments.

"Many observers have remarked on the spiritual qualities of Dysette-Zee's heroic canvases, and Untitled Blue certainly elicits similar responses in me. In this sense, I would liken it to Rothko's multiforms. It is peaceful. It is serene. Untitled Blue evokes a sense of gradual movement on a monumental scale, but without any clear demarcation of distance or space. It implies a location, a fixed point somewhere, but it is perceptually unconstrained, constantly changing, unmoored. We cannot locate the serene space that is Untitled Blue, but we know it exists. This to me is one of the great strengths of abstract expression. It confronts me clearly with the paradox of what the philosophers call dualism. Untitled Blue is an inanimate composition of color and line in the material world, but in my mind its image evokes something that seems universal, timeless and eternal. I'm left to wonder if there is some hidden, unseen essence that Dysette-Zee has revealed, or if it is only a moment of texture and color and line, another layer in a glorious, endless palimpsest.

"But don't take my word for it. I encourage you to spend some time with Untitled Blue and see for yourself. It is a stunning work of art. Beautiful. Mysterious. Challenging. And we are thrilled beyond measure to unveil it to you this evening.

"And now I'd like to introduce an old friend from the University. Doctor Carmen Delacroix. Doctor Delacroix is an expert in the area of abstract expressionism and modern American art. . . ."

*   *   *

Marcel was alone when she came to visit the Professor.

He was sitting in his wheelchair in the small garden behind his townhouse. He was in shadow, the late-day sun bright in the green garden behind him. She saw him from behind, a frail figure with sharp shoulders and a smooth, round head. Marcel remembered his face from her dreams, the prominent bones of his skull, the milky-blue skin at his temples. When he turned, his eyes were like a bird's, as bright as ever behind the round lenses of his glasses.

"Marcel Arrow."

He raised his thin, bony hands from the afghan across his lap and held them out to her, open, waiting. His short, delicate fingers began to tremble.

"What a vision you are," he said.

Her heart was beating wildly in her chest.

She quickly took his hands in hers.

"Professor Straw—"

"Please. Winston."

"Winston. It's been too long."

"Indeed it has."

They went for a walk in the park.

Marcel guided his wheelchair along the paved paths.

The sun was setting, and the shadows had grown long.

Their conversation was awkward at first, but it quickly settled into something familiar and comfortable.

The Professor had been writing haikus.

One every day.

"You become much more aware of the seasons," he said. "Of the passing of time. And finally, in the end, I think, less aware. It is a paradox. One of the pleasant ones. The season is not as important in the end. It is just a convention. A conceit, really. Part of a cycle, a revolution, a turning. Just . . . turning."

A diffuse light lingered in the sky.

Fireflies were rising from the long grass.

Beneath the trees, in the darkening shadows, a few cicadas had begun their evening song.

"Perhaps our Buddhist friends have the right idea," Marcel said.

"Yes, perhaps so. . . ."

Runners came on with steady steps, grim-faced, earbudded, swiftly past, gone.

"The strange things we desire. . . ."

The passing couples nodded and smiled.

"When I was a boy working on my father's farm, I couldn't wait to leave, and now that I am an old man on the downward slope, I find myself missing the fields, the labor, the spent feeling at the end of the day. . . ."

The sky was changing.

His voice lingered, an incantation.

"Some things haunt you for a lifetime. . . ."

A runner came from behind and passed them.

"When I was a politician . . . in another lifetime . . . many, many years ago . . . I told myself I was doing it for other people. Because I wanted to do good works, to leave a legacy. Even when I was breaking the law. Even then, that's what I was telling myself. That it was for . . . the greater good."

He turned and looked up at her.

"But it was all still ego, Marcel."

He tapped his fingertips against his fallen chest.

"A yearning," he said. "Inside."

The path began to follow the edge of a still pond.

Across the water, the lights atop the lampposts had begun gently to glow.

"Do you think you could have written a novel without it?" Marcel said. "Without the ego? Without that . . . yearning?"

"I think I could have. I think I would have had the same tools. The memory. The words. But would I have wanted to?"

He shrugged.

"I think you would have," she said.

"Why do any of us strive, Marcel?" the Professor said. "Fame? Praise? Good works? A legacy? . . . Enlightenment? Inner peace? . . . Love? . . . Or the absence . . . of love?"

He bowed his head.

Marcel guided the wheelchair along the path.

The rubber wheels rolled silently across the pavement.

"Where does any of it come from?" he said. "The frayed threads . . . the raveled yarn . . . the old garments . . . the wet clay . . . the fallow ground—"

The Professor stopped speaking.

He shook his head slowly and steadily.

"Forgive me," he said. "I'm rambling."

"Not at all," Marcel said.

Marcel was thinking of Zach and Jolene. The younger woman had made Marcel begin to question herself. She had not regretted her choices in life. She was confident about that. She had always been in control. Always. She had briefly wanted children, but had not thought about it for years. She had not finished her novel, but she had fashioned a comfortable, secure life on her own terms. She was not ashamed of that. She had worked hard for that. She had fought for that. And yet. And yet . . .

"It's never enough," she said. "The world of getting and spending."

"Yes. . . . Who is that? Keats? Shelly?"

"I don't remember," she said.

She sighed.

"I used to know."

They fell silent and followed the path as it curved back towards the city.

The cicadas' song was all around them. It waxed and waned in the darkness, like something substantial, like a texture, vast and unseen, moving, just beyond the edges of their perception.

The fireflies were myriad, silently flashing in the gathering darkness.

"When I was a girl, I thought the fireflies were trying to speak to me. In code."

"You don't speak firefly?" he said, coy, sly.

Marcel smiled.

"Well . . . I'm not fluent."

"Just that one summer abroad."

She laughed.

"I used a little flashlight to send them messages," she said.

"What did you say?"

"I can't recall. Probably something like what the Voyager satellite was saying. Name, rank, serial number. My favorite pop song."

"So they never responded?"

"I don't think so. But if they had, I think it would have probably been something along the lines of . . . 'Please stop anthropomorphizing us you strange little girl.' "

The Professor smiled.

"They do keep their secrets."

The Professor reached over his shoulder and laid his hand on Marcel's where she was guiding the wheelchair.

"I want you to tell you something. Something I've been thinking about for a long time."

She stopped pushing, and they came to a stop.

"I didn't appreciate it as much when I was in the thick of it," the Professor said, "but I was most alive with you in that classroom. With you and Zach and Robert. More so than any other time in my life. I thought it was all drudgery and routine at the time, but now . . . looking back . . . it is precious to me."

She could see the downward profile of his face. He was watching her hand beside him on the wheelchair.

"I feel the same way, Professor Straw. The time we spent together around that oak table is very special to me. I know Robert feels the same way."

He pressed her hand and patted it gently, gratefully.

They were silent, listening to the cicadas.

The fireflies were blinking quietly and insistently.

A bat angled across the sky.

"Marcel, tell me what happened with Zach. Back then."

Marcel sighed.

"Was it something I did?"

"No," Marcel said. "It wasn't your fault. We were . . . young. It just happened."

"I shouldn't have pitted you against one another. You all were splendid writers. Each of you. In your own unique way."

"I doubt you could have stopped it. We were . . . pretty full of ourselves."

"I could have done more. I could have given more. To you especially. I didn't teach you in the same way as I taught the boys. I see that now. I'm not sure why. It may have been good old-fashioned sexism. It may have been my brothers and . . . and . . . the War. . . ."

His head turned as he looked at her hand on the wheel-chair.

"I may have just loved Zach and Robert more. . . ."

He touched her hand again.

"I'm sorry, Marcel."

Marcel was watching his face, the smooth top of his head, the bony shoulders beneath his shirt, the blue veins and dark spots on his hand, his small pale fingers.

She was thinking of the cool tile on the floor in the empty hallway outside the closed door, sitting on the floor waiting for the door to open. She was thinking of her manuscript before him resting on the long oak table in the small white room with the narrow windows.

She gently laid her other hand on his.

It was Wordsworth, she recalled.

The world of getting and spending.

"You were a wonderful teacher, Winston."

* * *

The blue and red neon light in the shape of an open palm was burning brightly in the bay window of the fortuneteller's shop. Darkness had fallen, and the yoga class was emerging from the doorway to the basement of the old townhouse. They carried their rolled up mats and walked, for a while at least, with a centered mind, a renewed body, a different energy. Marcel watched from her parked Mustang across the street as the last of them dispersed on bicycle and foot into the night.

When the alley was empty, Marcel got out of the Mustang. A streetlight threw her long shadow across the cobblestones as she walked toward the townhouse. She heard the steady drone of the video-game arcade near the corner. At the door to the basement, she paused and looked at the sign. Its blood-red letters were scrawled across what appeared to be an old map with compass points in one corner and a little sea serpent in another. Terra Incognita. Marcel took a deep breath and prepared to cross the threshold.

She walked through the door and paused before the three steps down. The interior was not what she was expecting. Terra Incognita had changed considerably from what she had seen on the little ninjas' videos.

The samurai armor next to the door was gone. In its place was a tripod with a blackboard. In colored chalks, written in a careful artistic hand, the blackboard listed the dates and times for classes in meditation and various types of yoga.

The starship models and dragon kites that had been hanging from the ceiling had decamped to a new galaxy. Now Marcel saw only warped foam ceiling panels, smoky spider webs and a few dangling strings.

The old comic-book-store super-nova had collapsed into a single, dense, crowded corner, a nascent commercial black hole. It seemed to be shrinking and receding before her eyes.

The fantastic figures from the old labyrinth had been reduced to a loitering, dispirited huddle. The Terminator, Wonder Woman, the Alien. They stood idled like a sullen line-up of unemployed super-humans and washed-up movie monsters. Darth Vader had toppled over and was leaning against Marvin the Martian and Fallout Boy.

On the floor of Terra Incognita, new displays and shelves neatly beckoned. Where Doctor Tempus and his winged steed, Tachyon, once held sway, now pylons and kiosks guarded an open space and plain, bare aisles. The shelves were stocked with meager rows of organic beauty products, bottles of dietary supplements, thin stacks of self-help books and pamphlets.

Against the wall devoted to the latest comics, the shelves had been replaced with paperback books about meditation, cleanses, chakras, the pineal gland. The locked glass case displayed handmade jewelry. The sign on the wall above remained. Ask The Alien, now just a cryptic non sequitur.

"Watch your step," Jolene said.

Marcel swayed above the steps, searching the interior of the store. At first, she could not locate Jolene. She thought her voice might have come from the league of cardboard heroes that had been herded into the corner with all the other comic book paraphernalia.

"I thought this place was a comic book store," Marcel said, squinting into the depths of the room.

"It still is."

Jolene stepped away from the cardboard figures and man-nequins.

She looked for a moment, with her braided white hair and tattoos, like another one of the displaced characters, as if she had come to life and had stepped from the pages of a comic book.

Jolene was dressed for yoga, barefoot, holding a towel in one hand. Marcel was surprised and perhaps slightly disappointed when Jolene proved to be physically a rather ordinary young woman. The images of her from the ninjas' videos were recorded from odd angles and were flickering and indistinct. Marcel had listened to the ninjas' descriptions of Jolene, their careful scrutiny of her tattoos, her piercings, her yoga pants, her sports bras. In her mind, Marcel had built Jolene up into a ninja-flavored fantasy. A hyper-sexualized Native-American amazon. Tall, lean and cut, with muscles and six-pack abs.

Jolene was indeed hard to ignore. She was poised with striking bleached corn rows and the physical presence and posture of a dancer, but she was hardly the superhuman erotic enchantrix the little ninjas had conjured up in Marcel's mind.

Marcel slowly came down the steps.

Jolene was staring intently at Marcel, but Marcel suspected that she always looked at people that way because of how her brain perceived depth. She had to concentrate to keep herself oriented properly, and the staring was an unavoidable part of her adaptive routine.

Jolene set the towel aside.

"I know you," Jolene said.

"Do you?" Marcel said lightly, a whiffle ball of badinage.

Jolene reached into the ranks of cardboard heroes and pulled one out from the back. It was the colorful image of a character from Confederate Vampires in Space, a woman in a cowl and a cape. In the character's hand was the obsidian blade.

"You're the Cat. Queen of the Quantum Pirates."

Marcel walked over slowly and stood next to the cardboard figure. She looked it up and down with casual disdain.

"Please. Call me Marcel."

As she looked at her considerably more buxom comic-book incarnation, Marcel was also trying to locate the exact spot where Zach Stone had disappeared. She was trying to align the new interior of Terra Incognita with the one she remembered seeing in the ninjas' videos. Marcel had watched the video in which Zach disappeared many times. The instant before he blinked off the screen had replayed in her mind again and again. In her mind, she could see the overhead view of that section of the store, the display of Emily Dickinson action figures, Zach, his head turned, his face glimpsed from above in profile, stepping forward, then not there, vanished, erased, gone.

"Zach said you might come looking for him," Jolene said.

Marcel was looking at the jumbled piles of comic-book merchandise.

"I thought Confederate Vampires in Space might be . . . a cry for help."

She smiled with the side of her mouth.

Jolene's voice grew cool.

"You don't need to worry about Zach," Jolene said.

Marcel had found a coon-skin cap among the super-heroic flotsam. She was inspecting it as she spoke.

"That's good to know," Marcel said.

She threw the cap back on the pile and turned to look Jolene in the eye.

"Can I see him?" Marcel asked. "Is he here?"

Marcel watched Jolene closely, trying to be intimidating. Marcel was older, successful, more confident. She had known Zach longer than Jolene. She thought that might unsettle the younger woman, but if Jolene was intimidated, she did not let it show. She paused only for an instant before answering. Her voice was high-pitched and singsong, but when she spoke, she was calm and assured.

"He's not here. He wanted to get away from all the distractions. The attention has been . . . a little surreal."

"I'm sure . . ." Marcel murmured and turned away.

She picked up a dietary supplement from a nearby shelf and began to read the label.

"Seems like a good business opportunity, though . . . if you care about that sort of thing," Marcel said.

"Zach told me about you."

Marcel continued reading the label on the bottle.

"Really?" Marcel said. "What did he say?"

Jolene ignored the question.

"I'll tell him you stopped by," she said coolly.

She stepped toward the door.

"I, um, need to finish closing."

Marcel glanced over her shoulder.

Guess we're going to have to do this the hard way, Marcel thought.

Marcel set the dietary supplement back on the shelf. There was a Nerf ball among the comic-book clutter. Marcel picked it up and turned around.

The two women stood facing each other.

"The little ninjas told me about you, too," Marcel said.

"Ninjas?" Jolene said. "What are you talking about?"

Marcel tossed the Nerf ball at Jolene's head, and Jolene smoothly spiked it to the ground.

Marcel crossed her arms and smiled smugly.

Jolene frowned, annoyed. She was staring at Marcel. Her eyes were enormous.

"You know . . ." Marcel said. "The ninjas. There's two of them. They look like twins. They wear these little black outfits. With a mask. They're . . . little. About this tall. They think they're spies. Or caterers. Or something."

Jolene looked confused.

"That's a comic book. Sara Simpatico. It has two little ninjas. Yoshi and Hiro. There's an issue around here somewhere."

Jolene flipped through a box of comics and plucked out one bagged comic. She handed it to Marcel.

Sara Simpatico was the title of the comic. The cover depicted a scene noir in which the two little ninjas were creeping past a gargoyle on a rooftop with a full moon in the sky behind them.

"No," Marcel said, less certain. "They're real. They've got cameras and microphones everywhere."

She looked around the room. She gestured at the cardboard figures near Jolene.

"The Terminator," Marcel said. "Look at his eye. It's a camera. It's a fish-eye view of the whole room."

Jolene looked at the Terminator's eye.

"It's just a little red bulb," she said.

Marcel stepped over to the Terminator. She looked at the little red bulb in the Terminator's eye.

It did not appear to be a camera.

Marcel turned and looked around the room. She saw in her mind the way the comic book store had appeared in the ninjas' videos. It seemed to hover in the air before her, like a ghostly afterimage. She saw the profile of Zach's face, saw him step forward just before he blinked off the screen. The room was swimming before her eyes. She suddenly felt dizzy and disoriented. The bright lights, the quiet street, the Christmas snow. At the far fringes, a tincture of cerulean blue. The ninjas were creeping across the roof. The silver ring in Jolene's nose was huge.

"I think I need to sit down," Marcel said.

Jolene quickly grabbed the western saddle on its little tripod. As she bent over, Marcel saw, on Jolene's lower back, beneath the bottom edge of her shirt, the large tattoo of the circled snake with its tail in its mouth. The snake seemed to be undulating across her back.

Jolene slid the saddle over beside Marcel, and Marcel carefully sat on one side of the saddle.

"Do you want some water?" Jolene asked.

"No. I just need a moment."

Marcel put her hand on the pommel of the saddle. She looked to the side. The Alien was watching her, its fangs sharp in its mouth. Behind the Alien, the Queen of the Quantum Pirates brandished the obsidian blade.

Jolene walked across the room and locked the front door. The sound of the bolt made a loud thunking sound.

Jolene turned back towards Marcel.

"Sounds like it's all in your mind," Jolene said.

She and Marcel were looking at each other across the room.

What is happening, Marcel thought.

For a yawning moment, Marcel was afraid that she was somehow in danger, that she was about to step off a high ledge, that she was about to vanish from the room.

Is she real? Is any of it?

Jolene was staring at her with that weird gaze, with those huge, intense eyes.

Marcel felt as if the room were dissolving, as if everything were slipping away. She knew she had to do something.

"Quick," Marcel said, desperate. "How far apart are we?"

Jolene laughed, staccato, high-pitched.

"Doctor Hitch told you about that."

"Not just that, Jolene. I know about your brother, too."

Jolene's face stiffened.

Finally, Marcel thought.

The little ninjas had dug deeper into Jolene's past. They had discovered the circumstances of her brother's death, an innocent boy in the wrong place at the wrong time, shot dead by police officers who thought the boy was reaching for a phantom gun in his waistband. Jolene had witnessed the entire incident, had watched it with the unblinking eyes of a credulous child.

"You don't know anything," Jolene said.

"Maybe not," Marcel said. "But here's my best guess. Your brother was a good kid. Mischievous, but not a criminal, not a user. He hung out with the other kids on the reservation, and some of them made mistakes, and your brother got caught up in some minor crime, throwing rocks at a vacant building, shoplifting, disturbing the peace, something like that, and he got a juvenile record, but he would have been okay, he would have grown up and left it behind, but he got caught off the reservation in town with city cops, and they only knew he was an Indian, not that he and his friends had gone to a movie that day or that he had brought his little sister with him, just that he matched the description, and it was more important to the city cops that they get a suspect, a perpetrator, a warm body, and there was a pretty good chance that an Indian boy already had a record anyway, had some warrants out, that his father was probably dead or in prison or long gone, that his mother was a drunk or an addict, so even if it was the wrong guy, no one on the reservation would care . . ."

Jolene slowly sank down and sat on the steps facing Marcel.

"And when the cops tried to detain your brother, he tried to run because he was scared, because he panicked, because he was just a kid in an adult's body, and he fell down or he tripped or maybe he gave up, and that was when the cop thought he saw your brother reaching for something in his waistband, and maybe your brother didn't follow the cop's orders, or maybe he didn't hear them, and they shot him . . ."

Jolene stared with cold, unblinking eyes.

"And in the newspaper they said your brother was a criminal, and people thought it didn't matter, that he was just another dead thug who got what he deserved, but he was your big brother, and you saw the whole thing, and you knew exactly where your brother was and where the cop was. You knew the distance. You knew it down to the millimeter because that's how your brain works, but you were just a girl, and you didn't know what to say."

"Thirty-three feet, nine inches and three fifths of an inch," Jolene said in a flat voice.

"The use-of-force report said it was five feet."

Jolene laughed a tired, bitter laugh.

"I asked everyone who was there," Jolene said. "Everyone remembered it differently. White folks on the street said it was point blank, said my brother was turning to charge at the officer. Other kids from the reservation said it was ten feet, twenty feet, a long way down the street . . . No. I was there. I saw it. It was thirty-three feet, nine inches and three fifths of an inch. There was no gun. He was afraid of guns. He was running away, and they shot him. They shot him in the back. From thirty-three feet, nine inches and three fifths of an inch."

"I'm sorry, Jolene."

"Yeah, well . . ."

Her voice trailed off, and they were silent for long moments.

"I think I know what you're trying to do here," Marcel said.

"Tell me then, white girl."

"You want to save the little boys like your brother. You want to save the little girls of color. You want to stop the violence, stop the killing, stop the rape. You want to change the world."

Jolene looked at her with a cool arrogance.

"Maybe I do."

"Fine," Marcel said. "Maybe I do, too."

Jolene looked at the floor and started shaking her head.

"What?" Marcel said.

"That's bullshit," Jolene said without emotion.

"No, it's not —"

"Let me ask you a question, Marcel. Whenever people talk about racist cops, the thing I hear over and over is white people saying that it's just a few bad apples, like there's nothing they can do about it. Why aren't people like you outraged that the police can't even get rid of the bad apples?"

"I am outraged."

"What have you done about it?"

What have I done about it, Marcel asked herself.

Marcel smiled.

Jolene was tough. She could see why Zach liked her.

"Change takes time," Marcel said. "Hearts and minds change generation by generation. I believe it has to come peacefully, not at the point of a bayonet. People have to want to change."

"The arc of history . . ."

"Yeah, the arc of history."

"Good luck with that," Jolene said, disgusted, dismissive, ironic.

"You don't mean that," Marcel said. "You don't mean that, or you wouldn't be here in Terra Incognita trying to write a different ending to Confederate Vampires in Space."

Jolene was silent.

"You know I'm right," Marcel said.

"Zach writes what he wants," Jolene said. "You should know that better than anyone."

Marcel looked down.

She was still holding the Sara Simpatico comic book in her hand. The little ninjas were creeping across the roof with the full moon behind them. Their sharp little eyes were cut to the side looking off the side of the page.

It was time for Marcel to go.

She set the comic book down and got up from the saddle where she had been sitting.

"Zach's not as tough as you, Jolene. He's got this self-destructive streak. You should . . . be careful with him. Just be careful."

She walked to one corner on the far side of the room. She turned and looked around her. There were new shelves with Jolene's merchandise on them. She looked up at the ceiling. She was standing in the same spot as Zach in the video. At the intersection. The obtuse angle. Ground zero. She was sure of it now. It was the spot where Zach had disappeared.

"What are you doing?" Jolene said.

Marcel looked up at the ceiling where the camera should have been. Then she closed her eyes and took a step forward onto the section of the floor next to where she had seen the display of Emily Dickinson action figures. She stepped forward the same way Zach had. She stood still for a moment, not breathing, her heart pounding in her chest.

What happens next?

Then she opened her eyes. She turned and looked around. She was still in Terra Incognita. Nothing appeared to have changed. Jolene was looking at her with a puzzled expression from across the room.

"Are you okay?" Jolene said.

7

To: Marcel Arrow, Bernice Gristle
From: Trevor R. Marq
Re: Glissade / Ring Tail Roar Due Diligence
Date:

INTRODUCTION

Glissade Fabrications & Confections Limited. ["Glissade"] has initiated exploratory discussions with Ring Tail Roar Incorporated ["RTR"] regarding merger or acquisition. This memorandum is pursuant to the due diligence audit RTR has requested in anticipation of further negotiations with Glissade. This memorandum is supplemental to ongoing legal audits and compatibility audits and is consistent with the contemplated integration of RTR into FCPA protocols. Accordingly, this memorandum summarizes the protection afforded RTR fashion designs under United States intellectual property law with an emphasis on the Kit Carson Coon-Skin Cap. The Kit

Carson Coon-Skin Cap is currently the subject matter of litigation in federal court between RTR and Little Ninja Publishing.

(Remember to get bulgur for Nanna.)

CONCLUSION

This memorandum reaffirms the litigation strategy in this matter and recommends no change to the ongoing legal audit or compatibility audit. The claims of Little Ninja Publishing against RTR are meritless. A motion to dismiss is pending.

(Remember: <u>Coarse</u> bulgur. Nanna says the fine doesn't stick right.)

FACTUAL BACKGROUND

RTR is a publicly-traded for-profit entity incorporated under Delaware law. RTR is engaged in the design, manufacture, production and sale of fashion apparel and accessories. RTR operates online and at retail locations in the United States and in major metropolitan areas around the world.

RTR began when Bernice Gristle created her first line of "pioneer couture" inspired in part by Kit Carson the Quantum Cowboy, a fictional character in *Confederate Vampires in Space*, a series of online novels published independently by Zach Stone and Jolene Walker.

Working out of her home on evenings and weekends, Ms. Gristle began selling individual custom-designed items, such as the Kit Carson Frock and the Kit Carson Jerkin, to family and friends. As the demand for her hand-made items grew, Ms. Gristle began to design and sew garments full time as a sole proprietor and later hired employees and moved to larger facilities. Ms. Gristle created her first line of pioneer couture under the RTR label in 20—.

(Bernice used to eat tuna fish and onions and Melba toast for lunch every day. She smoked a pack a day, and her breath could melt your face.)

RTR incorporated under Delaware law and came to market in an initial public offering in 20--. RTR reported over three billion dollars in revenue last fiscal year, and the Kit Carson Coon-Skin Cap has generated over seven billion dollars in sales to date worldwide. The Kit Carson Coon-Skin Cap is perhaps the single ugliest article of clothing in all of human history. Bernice still eats tuna fish for lunch every day.

(I think I'm going to quit tomorrow.)

Glissade is a privately-held international conglomerate engaged in a variety of commercial activities including, but not limited to, microcircuit fabrication, cloud data analytics, applied artificial intelligence, drone manufacture and confection. It is estimated that Glissade has assets worldwide in excess of 400 billion dollars with annual revenues in excess of 10 billion dollars.

(I'd quit today, but I think Marcel would have a nervous breakdown and eviscerate one of the paralegals.)

Glissade is governed de facto by the Glissade family which owns a controlling percentage of Glissade stock and holds a permanent majority of the seats on Glissade's board of directors. Glissade began as a small candy emporium in 18th—century Geneva. The Glissade family still maintains a candy shop on the site where Anton Glissade first made and sold toffee and hard candies.

(Autumn loves Glissade chocolate.)

Confederate Vampires in Space ["CVS"] began as a series of online science-fiction novels written and created by Zach Stone and Jolene Walker. Stone and Walker have retained all intellectual property rights in CVS, but have licensed derivative rights in some CVS characters, such as Kit Carson the Quantum Cowboy, to various licensees including RTR and Little Ninja Publishing.

(Autumn tells this great story about Marcel. Autumn was working on a brief for Marcel, and she had been avoiding her all morning, and Autumn was sitting at her desk and dropped her pen. The pen rolled under her desk, and she had to get on her hands and knees to find it. It was at that moment that Marcel came through the office door, which was totally unexpected. Marcel's office is on the other side of the building. Marcel couldn't see Autumn under the desk, and she made this exasperated sound, like a little gasp, like, I can't believe she's not here. Autumn could see Marcel's Jimmy Choos digging into the carpet in front of the desk. Autumn thought about jumping out from under the desk and saying "Surprise!" — which I think would have been hilarious — but then she heard Marcel make this sound, like grrr, under her breath, like she was growling, and Autumn decided she felt better staying under the desk. She watched Marcel's shoes as she turned and stalked out of the office. Autumn said she literally peeked over the top of her desk to make sure it was safe to come out.)

Kit Carson is an historical figure who lived during the mid–19th century in the United States. Carson was a scout in the southwestern frontier between St. Louis and the Pacific Ocean. He was also a trapper and merchant in Taos and Santa Fe, New Mexico. Carson was a soldier in the U.S. Army, fought for the Union during the Civil War, and often acted as a liaison with Native Americans in the southwest territories. Carson has been the subject of a variety of works of art, scholarship and biography.

(I'm afraid Marcel has buried her hopes and dreams beneath a mountain of middle-aged cynicism and regret and soulless professional ambition. She drives us like a team of dray animals. I worry about Marcel.)

Stone and Walker acknowledge that the character in the CVS novels, Kit Carson the Quantum Cowboy, is unambiguously based on the historical Kit Carson. The CVS novels were the first to portray Carson as a flawed hero redeemed somewhat by his stubborn adherence to ancient ethical axioms summed up in the legal doctrines of good faith and fair dealing, a phrase Carson utters repeatedly throughout the fictional works.

("Good faith and fair dealing!")

Little Ninja Publishing ["Little Ninja"] is an unincorporated association or partnership engaged in the for-profit business of publishing magazines, books, calendars and playing cards. Little Ninja is closely held and appears to have little or no formal organizational structure or governance. Little Ninja has sued RTR, asserting in various claims under state and federal law that the Kit Carson Coon-Skin Cap violates Little Ninja's trademarks, design patents and other intellectual property rights. Little Ninja claims it created the CVS character Kit Carson the Quantum Cowboy.

(The last time I saw Autumn:

When I arrived that morning, there was a single card-board file box sitting on the conference room table, sunlight gleaming on the polished wood. Later, on my way to get some coffee, there she was, seated at the table, her coppery hair —

she calls it her clown hair — bristling on either side of her head. The top was off the file box, and she was paging through a small stack of papers on the table in front of her. I rapped a knuckle on the conference room window. She looked up and saw me. She pushed her big, black, I'm-so-serious glasses up on her nose and rolled her eyes. She turned back to reviewing the documents. Why they didn't use digital scanners and electronic discovery, I'll never know.

The next morning there were three more boxes and two paralegals. Autumn had moved to the head of the table, and the stacks of paper in front of her had climbed several inches. She turned a page and began reading the next page in the stack. As I watched, a guy in a cap and a green jump suit arrived pushing a dolly with a fresh stack of boxes. I had seen his kind before. Couriers from off-site storage. It was not a good sign.

The courier wheeled the dolly into the conference room and began to drop the boxes one by one against the wall. Standing in the hallway, I heard the thud each box made as it hit the floor. Autumn looked up, and I caught her eye. She gave me a weak smile and did that little wave thing she does, like the Queen of England or maybe the Queen Mum. When I came back from lunch, there was a line of boxes along the conference room wall.

The next day, there were a few more harried attorneys, several more dazed paralegals. They sat at the table, hunched over stacks of paper, arm-deep in the boxes from off-site storage. They were there when I came in the morning. They were there when I left in the evening. They began to wear a path in the carpeting at the door. A blizzard of paper settled on every flat surface. Fast-food containers and pizza boxes collected on the floor. Someone brought a small fridge and microwave. Someone plugged in a coffee pot.

The off-site courier kept coming. The file boxes climbed the conference room walls. They edged down the length of the table like freight cars in a long, slow train. They tumbled out onto the floor, a field of boulders from a high mountain peak. They closed over the windows. They shut out the sun. I caught glimpses of Autumn behind the rising columns of boxes, the growing stacks of paper. Her serious face. Her black-rimmed glasses. Her bristling copper hair.

Still the off-site courier came. I passed him in the hallways. I stood next to him in the elevator. Silently, I eyed the grim cargo stacked on the dolly between us. In my office, I could almost hear the boxes as he dropped them to the floor. The conference room seemed to be straining to contain it all. I feared the walls might burst like a dam. I sat at my desk and imagined, as if in a dream, a flood of boxes and paper and lawyers and paralegals spilling out into the hallways, sweeping through my office and the rest of the firm, carrying us all to some distant land far, far away, a place unsullied by interrogatories and requests for admission, a place where the federal rules of civil procedure no longer applied, where the lawyers and judges ran wild and free, where the paralegals and assistants dozed in the shade.

And then, one morning, it was gone.

The boxes, the paper, the lawyers, the paralegals. All of it. I turned the corner, lurched to a stop in the hallway and stared at the empty room, at the sunlight in the windows, the scuff marks on the bare walls, the sudden expanse of conference room table. Nothing remained but yellow post-it notes and empty coffee cups, an unplugged coffee maker abandoned in the corner on the floor. That night, when I walked past on my way home, the cleaning people were vacuuming and dusting.

Someone said Autumn is in Texas now.

Another big document review.

There's talk of a settlement.

There's always talk of settlement.

She hasn't answered my messages for a while.)

In its Complaint, Little Ninja relies almost exclusively on a manuscript and affidavit as the basis for its claims. [See attached manuscript.] For example, Little Ninja relies on the following passage:

"They left a rough draft of their graphic novel on his chair, a subtle suggestion, a subliminal spark plug. To their surprise, Zach read the whole thing, and Confederate Vampires in Space was born. They began posting it online. In short order, the fans were arguing over who should play Kit Carson in the CVS movie."

Little Ninja cites other similar passages.

As discussed in more detail below, the manuscript defies description. It appears to be a pastiche of loosely-associated fictional fragments linked together in an awkward telescoping narrative structure. It is not at all clear who wrote any of the manuscript, and Little Ninja offers little in the way of proof of authorship for any of it. Little Ninja may offer a better evidentiary foundation during discovery, if the Complaint survives a motion to dismiss. For now, the manuscript appears to have little, if any, probative value.

(It's not entirely unprecedented for Autumn to not reply to my messages. She's not exactly an early adopter when it comes to new technology. Which is not to say she's a Luddite or anything like that. She just prefers face-to-face conversations. Or that's what she says. I occasionally wonder if she might not be avoiding me. Then I remember what she always says: "Buck up, Marq. Don't be so sensitive." Which is funny, because Autumn is the most sensitive person I know. She tries to present this icy façade, but she fools no one. Autumn seems to believe that you can't be a good litigator unless you're tough and cynical and flinty and merciless. I think she gets a lot of that from Marcel, but that's a whole nother story. Autumn says I'm turning into a neurotic basket-case, which is the sort of affectionate, witty banter we exchange face to face. She also says I have the attention span of a mosquito, which is her endearing way of saying I have trouble staying on task, which is also patently absurd because, well, my point being, my point being . . . (what *was* my point?) That's right: Nobody talks face to face anymore. I'm starting to believe people don't even have real conversations anymore. No one has the time. With email and voice mail and text messaging, everything seems rehearsed, targeted, focused-grouped. I got a six-month assignment by email from a west-coast partner I've never met. Just popped up on my computer screen one morning. I almost had a coronary. Even Autumn's spontaneous jokes seem automatic. She's still funny, but there's something missing. Some substance. Some essence. I can't quite put my finger on it. I try to think of the last meaningful conversation I had with anyone, and I have to go back years. Even with my parents on the phone. At least there's Nanna. That's one of the reasons I love having Nanna so close by. It's easy to visit, and it always feels like I'm having a real conversation, not just repeating something I heard, saying the expected thing, rushing on to the next page, the next screen, whatever comes next.

Remember: Coarse bulgur. The fine doesn't stick right.)

Pursuant to the Little Ninja/RTR litigation, this firm is engaged in an ongoing effort to discover information relevant to the authentication of the various sections of the attached manuscript. The attached manuscript makes reference to a number of acquaintances of Zach Stone. It is possible that Mr. Stone's friends and former acquaintances have personal knowledge relevant to the determination of the authorship of various sections of the attached manuscript. For example, the attached manuscript refers in several sections to a character known usually as the Professor or as Winston Straw. Winston Straw is currently incarcerated at the federal penitentiary at New Elysium. In an effort to authenticate the attached manuscript, I accompanied Ms. Arrow and Robert Hitch on a fact-finding interview with Winston Straw at New Elysium. [See attached transcript and video file.] Straw was not able to verify the authorship of any sections of the attached manuscript, and the interview was, in general, not helpful.

(He had the saddest eyes I've ever seen.

Slate-gray. Like overcast winter skies. Drifting behind those round lenses. Drifting like he didn't see you. Like you weren't even there.

We drove to New Elysium in Marcel's car. She, Robert Hitch, Autumn and I. Across the rivers and into the hills, all the way into the hinterland of West Virginia. "The boondocks," Autumn said, her voice low with a fake portentousness.

Normally, Marcel wouldn't have made the trip herself. Her time is simply too valuable, but she wanted to see Winston Straw face to face. I could tell it was important to her personally.

I told Marcel I could drive separately, but she insisted, in that non-negotiable tone, that we take one car. Autumn made the same objection and got the same curt response. It occurred to me that maybe Marcel didn't want to be alone with Robert Hitch. And that made me all the more curious to meet him.

Robert Hitch was naturally reserved, quiet. He listened closely and spoke with care. His voice was steady, calm, reassuring. He seemed bland and unremarkable, a sober adult. I wanted to let him do my taxes. He wore tailored trousers, a navy-blue cashmere blazer with an open collar, cufflinks, an expensive wristwatch, leather loafers that looked bespoke. It was an obvious display of wealth, but not ostentatious. If he was trying to impress his old college acquaintance, it was subtle. As always, Marcel looked like she had stepped out of a fashion magazine. It was impossible to know her intentions. I had given up on that long ago.

Hitch met us at the office. He and Marcel seemed genuinely happy to see each other. They shook hands, as awkward as I've ever seen Marcel. She wavered for a moment, dropped her guard and gave him a kiss on the cheek. Then, incredibly, she blushed. A little, unmistakable red burst of color on her cheek. Only for a second, then gone. When she turned toward Autumn and me, her face had resolved back into her usual opaque mask, nothing but sharp, cutting eyes and the occasional skeptical grin. I wondered what Marcel must have been like in college. It was hard to think of either of them as the sort of person who would ever take a creative writing class.

Hitch is an actuary for one of the big reinsurers. He lives in Connecticut with his wife, Satu, and kids. Marcel kept calling his wife Pippi, which Hitch seemed to accept amiably. He showed us pictures of the kids on his phone. They were cute, with freckles and red hair and their father's serious square jaw. I could see the echo of their mother's features in their faces. I imagined a petite woman with strawberry-blond bangs, a black hair band, tennis racket, a patient smile. A woman decidedly not like Marcel.

Hitch also objected to riding in one car, and I was amused

but not surprised when he realized there was no point in arguing with Marcel. Autumn and I exchanged a brief, knowing glance when he politely acceded.

Hitch had a dry sense of humor, and by the time we left the office, he was cracking jokes under his breath, almost to himself, then waiting with sparkling, shifting eyes, to see if anyone else shared his amusement. Marcel's replies were brief, wry, cryptic. Her smiles, quick and tight.

And their awkward familiarity spread to Autumn and me. As we loaded our briefcases into the trunk, the sum of all the old road trips and family vacations was scrolling through my mind. It was the old feeling of anticipation, the pre-dawn edge, the crisp-creased road map, the travel brochures, a distant, unspoiled destination. We had become a pseudo-nuclear family with Marcel and Hitch in the parental roles.

When Autumn and I climbed into the back seat, I couldn't help myself and said, joking sheepishly, "Are we there yet?"

Marcel was behind the wheel. She and Hitch exchanged a quiet look. Marcel gave me an angry glare in the rear view mirror, which made me feel even more like I was caught in some sort of weird workplace/summer vacation time warp. I could almost hear the sound of her gritting her teeth.

"I think we forgot Trevor's Gameboy," Autumn said.

Hitch chuckled quietly in the front seat.

We left the city behind and plunged into the countryside. We ascended steadily on interstate highways. They unspooled before us like huge gray ribbons falling smoothly across ochre and saffron hills, disappearing into hazy blue-gray horizons.

We drove through a brief storm, and the wipers sloshed back and forth on the front window. The rain snaked across the side windows, and then the storm was past, and we emerged into sunshine.

We stopped at a gas station perched awkwardly on a hillside, and I watched the interstate and the vehicles below as they passed. Highway travel makes me nostalgic. Or something like that. I'm not sure I know how to describe the feeling. It stirs something in me. Some residue of a safe, middle-class childhood and conventional small-town yearnings. The unbidden memory of my father neatly recording his mileage in a notepad he kept in the glove compartment. The lonely gas stations, the garish fast-food joints, the mile markers, the pay phones with their swollen, water-logged pages, the distant sound of traffic, the beef jerky, the stale chocolate bars. All of it speaks to me. It is an embarrassing sort of picaresque longing, I suppose. A sad, pathetic poetry from my not-so-distant childhood.

At the gas station, Autumn stepped next to me, and we watched the traffic passing in silence for a few moments. Behind us, Hitch and Marcel stood together speaking quietly beside the car.

Marcel took the New Elysium exit beneath the inevitable green sign with the white border. We climbed nearly-empty two-lane roads. They were recently paved with dark asphalt and freshly-painted clean white strips down the middle. Marcel passed the trucks on the hills, and we went sweeping through the shadows in the corridors cut by man through the ancient limestone. As we went higher, it got colder, and there were white icicles hanging from the face of the sheer rock. As we flew past, I watched the layers of limestone and shale as they blurred together. A thin seam of coal was like a black thread rising and falling beside my window.

For most of the latter part of the trip into West Virginia, Hitch and Marcel were holding forth on the subject of coonskin caps. We all had some knowledge of the history: The beneficent confluence of Walt Disney and broadcast television and mass-market merchandising in the 1950s that resulted, for a while, in just about every kid in America wearing a coon-skin cap.

But where Autumn and I knew only the basic mythology, Marcel's coon-skin-cap knowledge was granular. She knew coon-skin caps the way some baseball fans know box-score statistics. I'd lost count of how many believe-it-or-not tales Marcel had recounted during the course of our employment. Tales of frontier derring-do. Tales of Hollywood backlot romance. Tales of musket balls. Battlefield amputations. Baseball hitting streaks. Freakish sexual fertility. And all of them featuring the inevitable, redoubtable coon-skin cap.

Marcel had discovered, for example, that one coon-skin cap maker in the 1950s had offered a cap for girls made from pure white fur, including the tail. Marcel started collecting them. She has one in her office suite.

So Autumn and I were prepared for a long car ride with Marcel and the potential for spontaneous unabridged recitations. We knew that Marcel, with but the slightest of provocations, could effortlessly reel off yet another obscure example of coon-skin-cap lore.

What was surprising was Hitch. He immediately grasped the extent of Marcel's coon-skin-cappery, and he seemed to take a perverse satisfaction in egging her on. If anything, Hitch knew as much about coon-skin caps as the rest of us.

Autumn and I listened as he and Marcel went back and forth for a while about some politician from Tennessee, Estes Kefauver. Hitch explained that Kefauver had run for President in a coon-skin cap and made it central to his campaign. Kefauver was actually winning the Democratic primary in 1952, but the party nominated Adlai Stevenson instead. The party put Kefauver on the ticket as the vice-presidential candidate four years later in 1956, but the Stevenson-Kefauver ticket lost to the incumbents, Dwight Eisenhower and Richard Nixon, in one of the worst defeats in modern American politics.

Kefauver had led a congressional investigation into organized crime, but less well known was his investigation into obscenity and deviance in comic books.

Hitch sounded playful and arch as he reminded Marcel that the inspiration for Bernice Gristle's coon-skin cap design had come from *Confederate Vampires in Space* — a pop-culture entertainment that was not so very far removed from the Tales-From-The-Crypt comic books Kefauver's committee had investigated.

"Oh, please," Marcel said. "Spare me."

And those comic books were direct lineal descendants of the penny dreadfuls and blood-and-thunders that had made Kit Carson a household name in the 19th century.

"Because everyone knows coon-skin caps are like a gateway drug."

Her voice was dripping with sarcasm.

"It's a slippery slope," Hitch said.

"Riiiight . . ."

Autumn and I were laughing.

"Ascots . . . Cummerbunds . . . Lederhosen . . ."

Hitch was pointing at her with his little finger.

"Who knows where it ends?"

It was Kefauver's congressional investigation that introduced Frederic Wertham and his book *Seduction of the Innocent* to the public.

Marcel was relentless in her mockery of *Seduction of the Innocent*. She actually quoted passages from memory, much to our amusement.

And so the time passed.

Hitch had been mostly quiet in the flatland outside the city, with his dry asides, but by the time we had reached the mountains, he and Marcel had us convulsed with laughter. Listening to their thrust-and-parry about coon-skin caps and the Comics Code Authority and de facto prior restraints, it was impossible not to get caught up in their enthusiasm, their positive energy, their passion. But it was not just a passion for coon-skin caps and the freedom of expression. Rather, it was a passion for conversation, for words, and, as I think back now, a quiet passion for each other. They pulled us in and made us laugh. They were the sort of people who inspired and motivated everyone around them. Proud geeks, in the best sense of the word. It felt as if, for a brief while, we were all climbing toward the same summit, swimming for the same shore. And I wondered later how much a part of each other's lives they had been, how much time they had lost over the years. I wondered if they were even aware of it themselves. Marcel had never spoken of Robert Hitch, despite the legal work she had done involving Ring Tail Roar and Zach Stone. It was clear how much they enjoyed each other, how well-suited they seemed, the way her eyes sparkled and cut when they were together.

We crossed a long, high bridge. Far below us, the sun caught the surface of a river at the bottom of a gorge. We skirted cataracts plunging down rocky palisades.

We rounded the last bend in the road, and the New Elysium prison complex came into view. We could see it in the distance as Marcel took the final exit. Our conversation ceased, and we watched in silence as the prison loomed like a fortress against the ridges of blue mountains and the hazy gray sky. It was hard to believe a penal institution could be so striking, beautiful even. It looked like a monastery in the Himalayan mountains. Or a castle in the Alps. As we drew closer, I almost expected to see turrets and parapets and crenellations and spires.

The parking area overlooked the river gorge. Marcel and Hitch stood together at the edge while Autumn and I unloaded the trunk of the car. I was still thinking about how well-suited they seemed, almost like an old married couple. Marcel was saying something to him, had put her hand on his forearm. I wondered about the way people find each other, the way we randomly cross paths and rub elbows, the chance that any two people might find each other in the brief blink of a lifetime.

"They're in love with each other, you know."

Autumn was behind me, looking over my shoulder.

I turned and looked at her. Her big, black glasses were sliding toward the tip of her nose. She looked at me with her dark eyes. She was quietly eating a Glissade chocolate bar. She offered me a piece of chocolate.

"Should we tell them?" I joked, and popped the chocolate into my mouth.

Autumn smiled, pushed her glasses up on her nose.

"I don't think so," she said, precise, wry. It was a sly admonition.

I turned back to Marcel and Hitch and the river gorge spread out below them. Marcel was touching his arm, and he was listening to her, leaning close, a smile playing across the solemn features of his face.

I was happy for Marcel, happy to see her out of the office, happy to see two people so in tune.

And yet.

I could not help but feel a peculiar sadness.

The way her hand was resting against his arm.

The distance still between them.

Autumn's chocolate grew soft and thick against my tongue. The gorge was speaking silent sentences. Unknowable. Uncharted. Undiscovered. For a moment, I felt it, too.

That strange distance.

Or perhaps it was only a sugar rush.

New Elysium was a sprawling prison complex. The maximum security building was surrounded by barbed-wire fences and a high wall. That was what you first saw as you approached from the road, but the bulk of the prison was minimum security. Beyond the check points and the chain-link fences, the roads had sidewalks. White clapboard buildings with chimneys that looked like homes were interspersed among the more institutional, red-brick structures. With open fields, picnic tables, footpaths crossing on the diagonal and a flagpole flying the American flag, it had the disconcerting appearance of a high school or a small college campus.

Winston Straw was incarcerated in the minimum security facility. New Elysium had visitor's hours scheduled in designated areas, but Marcel had corresponded with Straw, and the prison had agreed to let us meet with Straw in a commons area at our convenience.

Even with this dispensation, we still had to be processed and credentialed, as it were. It reminded me of waiting on the tarmac before boarding a jet airplane.

The closed-circuit video cameras mounted on the walls near the ceiling. The uniformed attendants that, no matter how polite or helpful, remained faceless and impersonal. And the air. The strange, invisible texture of the air.

"We're here to see Winston Straw," Marcel said, leaning close to a speaker by one of the doors.

It felt like we were entering a huge, alien apparatus

designed for some unknown purpose. It drew us in one by one through metal detectors and fire doors, guided us into the unseen, unexpected spaces. My mind wandered down a crooked path into a thicket of memories. Empty grade-school hallways, the gymnasium after practice, hushed sanctuaries, lit candles, empty pews.

I had visited prisons and jails before, mostly when I took a clinical course in law school and for some pro bono work I had done fresh out of law school, so I was not unprepared, but I knew I also harbored a stubborn prejudice towards prisons and the inmates. Entering a prison still felt like walking into a different weather, a sort of miasma, even in minimum security, where the air was fresh and clean. I felt the intangible weight of surveillance and the sense of time arrested, of waiting, of an unseen process, like rust or mold, working quietly in the dark places, drifting through the air, settling on your clothes, your face, sinking into your skin. There was something irrational about it, and I did not know if it was something within the prison or something within me. It seemed there was an ancient cruelty at work, something perpetuated within, silently, invisibly. Something vast, unyielding, ineffective, primitive, vicious. In my mind, I struggled to push it all away.

One of the uniformed guards took us to Straw. The guard was a woman. She wore her hair in a large, tight bun at the back of her head. It was lustrous hair, black, raven dark. Her narrow face was expressionless as she led us through the empty hallways. She never spoke. She just stood to one side, at a distance, watching us the whole time with a steady, impassive gaze. Beneath the blouse of her uniform, I glimpsed, visible at the base of her slender neck, a large pendant. It was a strange figurine carved from a milky-white stone. A snake in the shape of a circle with its tail in its mouth.

The commons area was a large room in a building that looked out toward the river gorge. There were windows along one side, but they were covered with a metal mesh. The sunlight shone through, filtered and diffuse. There were plastic chairs gathered around an old television, a large vacuum-tube model in a wooden cabinet that looked like it came from my Nanna's old living room. There were several card tables. An upright piano against one wall.

Winston Straw was sitting in a wheelchair alone at one of the card tables arranging chess pieces on a board. It was one of those cheap chess sets with hollow plastic pieces and little, round pads of green felt glued to the bottom of the pieces. Many of the round pads of felt had come loose and rested unevenly beneath the chess pieces. The checkered board folded in half at the middle, but had come apart and separated at the crease. The two checkered sections rested flat next to each other, slightly out of alignment. There were several pawns missing, and someone had replaced them with bottle caps and a smooth, flat stone. Beside the board was a shoe box. The word "chess" was written in black magic marker on the lid. Scraps of the original cardboard game box were inside the shoe box.

The guard with the raven-dark hair touched him on the shoulder, and he looked up at her. He looked at her face for a long moment. The raven-haired woman stepped away and stood against one wall, watching us from across the room.

I knew Winston Straw from the photographs on the dust jackets of his books. A vital man with a bald head and strong features and a compelling gaze. The man in the wheelchair bore little resemblance to the man in his dust jacket cover photos.

The Winston Straw who met us that day in New Elysium was frail and hesitant, his head lolling slightly above one shoulder. His body had collapsed, and his face was sunken and drawn. He looked at us, his wrinkled lips set firmly, his eyes searching our faces.

Marcel stepped forward and held out her open hands.

"Professor Straw . . ." she said, hesitant, hopeful, with a tentative smile.

His eyes were slate gray, like overcast winter skies. Drifting behind those round lenses. Drifting like he didn't see her. Like she wasn't even there.

Marcel slowly withdrew her hands and the smile faded from her face.

Hitch stepped next to Marcel and put a hand gently against her back.

He spoke to Straw in his soft, steady voice.

"Professor Straw . . . Winston . . . it's Marcel Arrow and Robert Hitch. You taught us creative writing. At the University."

"You answered my letter," Marcel said faintly.

Straw's gaze drifted across our faces. There was a tremor in his hand. He was looking closely at Autumn, at me.

"So young . . ."

His voice was raspy and thin.

"You never age," he said.

"No, Professor Straw," I said and gestured at Autumn and myself. "We weren't your students, sir."

But he had drifted away.

If he had heard me, he gave no outward sign.

Marcel marched us through the rest of the interview. She methodically worked through the manuscript with Straw, patiently refreshing his memory again and again. Autumn and I set up the video camera and the tripod, centering his ruined face in the center of the tiny screen. As he hesitantly answered Marcel's questions and the red record light on the camera was silently blinking, I looked around the grim commons area.

The woman with raven-dark hair stood silently against the wall. There were closed-circuit video cameras mounted conspicuously in the corners near the ceiling. I looked steadily for a moment into the dark, unblinking lens of one of the cameras.

"I can't recall," Straw was saying.

"I don't know. . . ."

"That was a long time ago. . . ."

"I taught so many young people. . . ."

"It's hard to remember. . . ."

"I don't mean to be rude. . . ."

"I'm sorry . . . ."

"I'm sorry . . . ."

"I'm sorry . . . ."

I had watched Marcel many times in different settings, both social and professional. I had seen her in tense depositions, delicate negotiations, the crucible of court. I had watched her calmly sparring with testy panels of intimidating federal judges. She had an unshakable game face. Nothing rattled Marcel Arrow.

But this was different. We all stole glimpses of her face as she asked the next question and the next, as she gently probed the remnants of the old man's memory. She was professional and polite, graceful even, smiling often, deftly joking, to put Straw at ease. But when she finally stood aside with Hitch afterwards and we were packing up the equipment, her face was as drained and tired as I've ever seen.

It was at that moment that I felt someone tugging on my sleeve. I turned and found Straw next to me in his wheelchair. He had grabbed my sleeve with one gnarled hand.

"Robert," he croaked.

"No, sir. I'm Trevor. Trevor Marq."

Autumn was next to me, and I heard the startled breath

she took when Straw materialized next to us and began speaking.

He was looking up at me with those spooky, slate-gray eyes.

"I remember one story from back then," Straw said, speaking slowly and deliberately.

Marcel and Hitch stopped talking.

"It was about a quarry," Straw said. "I can remember it so clearly. The emerald surface of the water. The boy and his father. The white blossoms so far below. . . ."

Straw's voice trailed off.

There was a faint squeaking sound in the hallway. Someone was pushing something down the hall. It rolled past and began to recede.

"It was lovely and sad," Straw said. "The way time fills the absent spaces. The deepest wounds. The way love gets twisted around the truth. How we know. In the end."

I looked at Hitch and Marcel across the room. Their faces were stony and frozen. The circles had grown dark under Marcel's eyes.

"Who wrote it?" I said.

"Zach," he said. "Zach Stone."

Before we left, Marcel and Hitch had stilted, halting conversations with Straw, laughing awkwardly at the confusing things he said. Hitch and Marcel were scrupulously gracious, remembering Straw and their days at the University with respect and affection.

As we were leaving, he spoke to me again in a firm voice.

"It's never too late, Zach. You still might have a book or two in you."

The car ride back to the office was a quiet one. The light-hearted mood of that morning's journey had dissipated. Hitch was driving. Marcel sat next to him with her head against the head rest, her eyes closed. Autumn was scrolling through the messages on her phone. Every so often, Hitch and Marcel would exchange brief, quiet comments.

"It's a stupid law," Marcel said at one point.

"It seemed like a good idea at the time," Hitch said.

"It's vague. It's overbroad. It's . . . it's a stupid law."

" 'Active material translation?' What does that mean?"

"Exactly."

"Words!"

"Yes. Exactly. Words."

"So what was it? With Straw?"

"The Iliad."

"Really?"

Marcel nodded silently.

Hitch shook his head and sighed.

"It's a stupid law," Marcel said again.

Outside my office window, far below me, the traffic moves in starts and stops. Tiny pedestrians are crawling up and down the sidewalks. If a busy stranger stopped and looked up toward this building, would they see me in this one little window, my pale face inches from the glass? Would we exchange a knowing glance, a subtle nod, a meaningful moment amid the chaos of the city?

The pedestrians hurry on, oblivious to me above them.

I find my phone and check my messages.

Nothing.

Someone said she is in Texas now. Another big document review. There's talk of a settlement.

There's always talk of settlement.

I think I'm going to quit tomorrow.)

Zach Stone and Jolene Walker have neither confirmed nor denied that either of them wrote any portion of the attached manuscript. They have made no formal statements regarding the Little Ninja lawsuit, and neither Stone nor Walker has sought to intervene. To avoid any appearance of a conflict of interest, Stone and Walker have retained outside counsel in this matter. While an interview or deposition of Stone or Walker might be helpful at this point, it is not necessary and could create unneeded complexity, confusing counter-narratives and unintended consequences. Stone and Walker will almost certainly continue to rely on their existing intellectual property rights under US law.

As discussed in more detail below, US intellectual property law affords little protection for fashion designs such as the one at issue in this matter. Little Ninja may very well be able to offer a competing coon-skin cap in the US markets without infringing RTR trademarks. With regard to the due diligence audits for merger or acquisition in this matter, the relevant inquiry is whether Glissade might assume a significant, unforeseen liability in those new foreign markets in which a competitor, such as Little Ninja, might assert pre-existing intellectual property rights under foreign law to the Kit Carson Coon-Skin Cap.

(A couple places nearby sell coarse bulgur. The Oasis is closer, but the traffic near the embassies is always crazy this time of day. There's a gourmet grocer near P Street, but the lines are too long. My best bet is the World Bazaar near Georgetown. The World Bazaar is practically hidden in the basement of an old townhouse. It's always deserted. I've never had to wait. I'm not sure exactly how it stays in business. Sometimes it's sold out of coarse bulgur, but it's a nice trip on my bike.

I decide to go to lunch early. Kit Carson and his coon-skin caps can wait.

I hesitate near the doorway to my office, making sure the coast is clear.

In the hallway, I pass that heavy guy with the bow tie and the florid face.

What was his name?

"Marq," he says to me, in a smug basso profundo, drawing out the vowel in my surname.

Maaarq.

Look at you, you dog!

Maaaarq.

You're crushing it!

Maaaaarq.

Stevens.

That's right. His name is Stevens.

"Stevens," I say, trying to match his tone, mocking him, I suppose, in friendly, collegial way.

Steveeens.

"Get back to work," he says over his shoulder.

I turn the corner and press the button for the elevator. While I'm waiting, I find my phone in my pocket and begin to swipe through the screens. The elevator doors open, and I step inside.

If information technology has made real conversations obsolete, it has also made every other kind of communication incessant. I send my assistant a text message. OOTO for lunch. I download a copy of my memo and drop my phone in my pocket.

In the elevator, I'm thinking about Zach Stone, Jolene Walker and Tilda Frappe.

*   *   *

Not long after the trip to New Elysium, Marcel summoned me late one afternoon to her corner-office suite. She was sitting in her leather chair behind the shimmering black surface of her elegant desk.

She glanced up as I walked into the office.

"Let's go for a walk," she said.

We went outside the building to a coffee shop around the corner. I let her buy me a big cup of coffee I didn't really want. We sat beside each other facing the window. Outside, in front of the window, a steady procession of strangers was coming and going. The big cup was warm against my hand.

"I want you to do something for me," Marcel said. "Something that will take some finesse. It's not illegal. It's not unethical. . . . But we're not going to pay you. And you won't report your time."

Marcel was a partner in our law firm. A rainmaker. Ring Tail Roar had been her client from the beginning. As Ring Tail Roar had grown into a global fashion label, Marcel had ascended the ranks in the firm. I had been working with Marcel for only a few years, but we both, to an almost embarrassing extent, were at the beck and call of Bernice Gristle and her demented, quasi-human entourage. So I was not unfamiliar with the full panoply of unreasonable work-related tasks, the kind that started on a Thursday with the routine tweaking of a seemingly insignificant inter-office memo only to culminate somehow days later in a weekend-devouring test of loyalty, sanity, endurance and will.

"What did you have in mind?" I said.

"I want you to sound out Zach Stone."

She paused, watching me.

"For me," she said.

Her eyes were sharp and steady.

It felt as if she were confiding in me.

It felt as if we were suddenly intimate in a way we had never been before.

It was kind of intoxicating.

What Marcel proposed was that I volunteer for Tilda Frappe's senatorial campaign and use it as a way to approach Zach Stone without going through any official channels or legal counsel. She wanted me to give him a copy of the manuscript and ask him to read it and let her know what he said.

I thought about it for a few moments. He wasn't a party to the Little Ninja lawsuit. I couldn't think of any ethical reason not to contact him.

"Why the cloak and dagger?"

"They don't know you," Marcel said. "I want to hear what he says without Jolene and her lawyers looking over his shoulder."

She smiled at me.

"You've got an honest face, Marq."

I was thinking what I usually think when presented with a new assignment: I don't have time for this.

But it was Marcel.

I couldn't say no.

Zach Stone is not easy to approach, but he's not the hermit everyone says he is. Compared to Jolene Walker, however, he looks like a recluse. Jolene obviously enjoys the attention, and I think Zach is content to let her feed the beast. A lot of it is just tabloid churn and click bait. It's when they're together in public that Zach seems exposed. Everyone is used to watching Jolene's every move, her latest hair style, her newest tattoo, the slightest change in the shade of her lipstick. When the paparazzi ambush Jolene, Zach is the guy in the shadows behind her, squinting, his open hand raised, hair in his eyes, frozen in the glare of the camera flash.

There's a lot of frothy talk about Zach and Jolene and Tilda Frappe. I don't pay attention to most of it. I don't think there's any question that Zach and Jolene and Tilda share a lot of the same views about policy and technology. Her positions regarding space exploration and space tourism, for instance. Have Zach and Jolene influenced her? Maybe. But who can say for sure?

Tilda Frappe was an unknown public servant when she first met Jolene and Zach. Zach and Jolene were just beginning to enjoy the financial success of *Confederate Vampires in Space*. Tilda was taking a yoga class from Jolene, and the two women became fast friends. As Zach and Jolene parlayed their science-fiction novels into a thriving commercial enterprise, the friendship between Tilda and Jolene deepened. Tilda was idealistic, but she was also disciplined and quietly ambitious. Tilda won an upset election to Congress as a representative, and the three of them — Zach, Jolene, Tilda — began to occupy that uncanny space where celebrity and politics and wealth intersect. The chattering folk tried to brand them with Zildene, Zolda, Tajo, and the like, but I don't think any of the nicknames ever really caught on.

The nerve center of Tilda Frappe's senatorial campaign is in a Kalorama townhouse on a quiet, narrow residential street, one I have passed many times on my bike. It has two huge windows on the first floor and is always lit from within with a militantly convivial light. Inside, you can glimpse bookshelves, a fireplace, red-and-black textiles hanging like quilts on the pale walls, feathery gold sculptures that seem to float around the couches and armchairs. I had always wondered who lived there and was apparently the last person in the firm to learn it was Frappe's unofficial campaign office. It had become a salon of sorts for her Capitol Hill staff and volunteers, some of whom had migrated to and from our law firm. Stone and

Walker were often seen coming and going at the Kalorama townhouse. Marcel told me they both were involved in the day-to-day management of Frappe's campaign.

So Marcel's secret mission was well conceived. This was a world I could navigate with ease. I had spent my first year after college living on the edge of Rock Creek Park in a drafty, old mansion with a ragged assortment of students, interns, musicians and artists. We had formed a surrogate family the way twenty-somethings will when you have a good mix in a group house. For a few hopeful months, we shared the almost magical belief that our wildest dreams and aspirations might all come true. I never worked on a political campaign, but some of the others in our house did, and politics always seemed to be hovering in the background.

So, yes, I assured myself, you're well acquainted with the young professionals and aspiring dreamers drawn to Frappe's Kalorama townhouse.

Yes, Trevor, you can do this.

And that's what I kept telling myself right up to the moment when I locked up my bike and walked the last few yards along the sidewalk and began to climb the steps to the front of Frappe's townhouse. I carried the Little Ninja manuscript in a leather satchel slung over my shoulder. In my mind, the manuscript was glowing like something radioactive, like some trans-dimensional relic, a backscatter shape floating visibly under my arm. It was only when I paused before the heavy, wooden door that I began to feel the first flutter of nerves.

Was this really such a good idea?

I remembered Marcel's sharp, steady eyes in the coffee shop.

"For me," she had said.

Marcel's gratitude was a valuable commodity, no doubt.

But was this what I went to law school for?

My thoughts were racing as I stood on the landing before the door.

I felt a panic rising within me.

Maybe I should be doing more pro bono.

Maybe I should give more to charity.

Am I a good person?

Did I walk the dog?

I was well on my way to a full-blown existential crisis.

But then, with a loud sigh of air, the heavy, wooden door before me came ajar and cracked open. I could hear the buzz of activity coming from within. I took a step closer and could make out the sounds of many voices talking simultaneously. It sounded like a big cocktail party, but different. It was a buzzing, droning sound, like a hive of bees, maybe, or a roosting flock of birds. I'd never heard anything quite like it.

I carefully pushed the door open and peered inside. There were maybe two dozen people, mostly my age, mostly women. They were sitting on couches and armchairs, sitting cross-legged on the floor, pacing slowly through the rooms. Each one was talking, tethered to a computer tablet or a big smart phone with a delicate headset tucked behind one ear.

Just as I was going to step farther into the room, someone grabbed me by the arm and pulled me inside.

It was a small, slender woman, stylish in dark pleated pants and a vest with a white linen blouse and a neat bow tie. She was very pale with cherry-red lips. Her short, black hair was wispy and curly, and seemed to be boiling off the top of her head.

She handed me her tablet and slipped the headset behind my ear.

"Cover for me," she whispered in my ear. Her breath smelled like peppermint. She turned and hurried away, and I was standing there, bewildered, holding the tablet in one hand and listening to the sounds coming from the earpiece. There was a click in my ear and then a stranger's voice.

"Hello . . ." the stranger said.

It sounded like an older woman. Startled and rheumy. Her voice conjured the aroma of Vicks Vapo-rub and menthol cigarettes. I imagined her in an armchair, phone pressed to her ear, ashtray at one elbow, a muted soap opera playing on a television screen nearby.

I looked at the tablet screen in my hand. There was an app running. Across the top of the screen there was an empty window. Large text began to appear in the empty window.

Hello, Edith!

Below the window with the big text was another smaller window filled with what appeared to be a very detailed profile of a woman named Edith Miracle. I touched various crawling, highlighted fields and menus dropped down.

Edith attended the First Christian Church. Her daughter was named Gloria. She had a Pomeranian named CoCo.

"Hello . . ." Edith Miracle said again in my ear.

I wasn't sure what to do. I considered just hanging up, but short of turning the tablet's power off, I wasn't sure exactly how to hang up. I considered explaining the situation to Edith, arranging for a call back. I looked around the room, but everyone was intent on their own tablet or smart phone, busy with their own conversation.

More big text was appearing, scrolling down the lengthening window on the top of the screen:

Hello, Edith!

I'm calling on behalf of Tilda Frappe's campaign for the US Senate.

My name is Terri Cloud.

I spoke with you last time when you contributed to Tilda's campaign, and I wanted to take just a few minutes of

*your valuable time to update you on how your contribution
has been helping us . . .*

There was a little blinking red arrow next to the text that
read "Hello, Edith."

And then I heard it.

A second voice in my ear.

"Hello, Edith," the second voice said, gentle, persistent.

The second voice was also a woman's voice. It was a rich,
smooth, contralto. A seductive, professional voice with no
trace of obvious accent. I could imagine her reading the news
on the radio. The daily lilting of market volatility. Another
record high for the Nasdaq.

I wasn't sure if the voice was human.

"Hello . . . is anyone there?" Edith Miracle said.

Could Edith hear the other woman's voice?

"Hello, Edith," the contralto said again.

The second woman's contralto voice was oddly, precisely
evocative. It carried me back to grade school field trips to the
planetarium. I felt as if I were sitting in the dark again with my
classmates, rapt, our heads back, our unblinking eyes fixed on
the darkened dome above us, listening to a confident female
voice guiding us through the solar system, traveling through
space and time, navigating the constellations, the life cycle of a
star, the slow spiral of the Milky Way.

It was a pleasant feeling, a comfortable feeling, all tangled
up somehow with pulsing fiber-optic toys and ruby-quartz
lasers and magnets and dry ice and vinegar and baking soda
and the carefully crafted cardboard displays of half-remem-
bered science-fair projects.

Igneous. Metamorphic. Sedimentary.

The red arrow was blinking beside the big text at the top
of the tablet screen.

"Hello, Edith," the contralto voice said.

The voice was confident, persistent.

She was prompting me.

"Um. Hello. Edith," I said.

Almost at the instant I spoke, the app on the tablet screen froze. The red arrow quit blinking. The bristling, scrolling details of Edith Miracle's profile locked into place.

The big text in the top window vanished, and then, almost instantly, it began to reappear:

Hello, Edith!

I'm calling on behalf of Tilda Frappe's campaign for the US Senate.

My name is Trevor Marq.

Trevor Marq.

A sensation not unlike a chill went prickling down my spine.

The app had replaced Terri Cloud's name with my name.

It didn't seem possible.

I looked at the young people scattered in various locations throughout the rooms of the townhouse, each holding a tablet or a smart phone, each busily chatting away on their headsets tucked behind one ear.

The smooth female contralto was speaking in my ear again.

"I'm calling on behalf of Tilda Frappe's campaign for the US Senate. My name is Trevor Marq."

Now I knew.

It definitely wasn't a human voice.

It was a computer mimicking skillfully the spontaneity of a woman's voice. It was far better than the voices of the digital assistants on our smart phones and in our homes and in our cars, but it was still missing something, still false somehow to the human ear.

"Yes," Edith Miracle said in my ear, slightly annoyed. "Who is this? Delmar? Is that you?"

The contralto voice of the digital assistant was calmly whispering in my ear.

The blinking red arrow had moved down a line in the window with the big text.

With reluctance, I spoke.

"Hi, Edith," I said. "I'm, uh, calling on behalf of Tilda Frappe's campaign for the US Senate. My name is . . . Trevor Marq."

It was strange at first to hear the words as I spoke them, but as the call went on, it became easier and easier to follow the digital assistant's lead. As the big text scrolled down the screen, I often found myself speaking almost in unison with the digital assistant.

When Edith was wavering and wanted specific information or asked a question the assistant had not anticipated, the assistant gave me a menu of options. The big text window offered different forks in the conversational tree. I was amazed at how easy it became, how intuitive. I could ad lib and stick to the script without too much trouble.

"Edith, remember the street lights at the park on Elm Street?"

"I know that park. It's right down the street."

"Remember how dark it used to be? Before the street lights? Tilda was responsible for those street lights. Back when she was on the city council. She was the one who organized the neighborhood and introduced the resolution. Remember?"

"That's right. The street lights. I do remember. Yes indeed I most certainly do. At night, that park was black as pitch. Just black as pitch. It sure was. Dark and dangerous. A nuisance. And an eyesore, too. Law me. The trash and the weeds. Law me. Just a terrible, terrible eyesore."

Edith paused.

I heard the quiet hiss as she drew from a cigarette.

"But then Tilda got us those streetlights. Bless her heart. Cleaned that park right up. She sure did. I'd just about completely forgot all about that. Why, bless her heart."

By the end of the telephone call, Edith had agreed to make another small donation to Frappe's campaign. Our conversation concluded smoothly, and, after a brief pause, a new profile appeared on the screen. The assistant directed me to details in the profile, and, after another brief pause, the assistant placed a new call. I heard the click as a new donor answered the phone. The big text began scrolling down the window at the top of the tablet screen.

Hello, Madge!

I'm not sure how long I sat there or how many calls the assistant dialed. It may have been fifteen minutes. It may have been two hours. As one voice segued into the next, I began to lose track of time.

It was interesting to meet each new donor, to briefly browse through the precise details of their varied lives. I began to anticipate each new screen, each new objective. There was a running tally of the donations. I was vaguely aware that it all felt like a video game, like a high-tech telethon. I stole several more glimpses at the other people around me immersed in their conversations.

If there was an artificial intelligence out there somewhere, monitoring all the calls, customizing our responses, guiding dozens of simultaneous conversations, it was impressive to say the least. It was also more than a little disconcerting if I tried to stop and think about it. How could it know my name? At the same time, it also struck me as seductive and cool, the avant-garde, so cutting edge. How many people, I wondered, have experienced something like this?

The smooth contralto voice was whispering in my ear. I

made a mental note to revisit the experience later when there wasn't another call queued up on Terri Cloud's tablet.

At some point, a woman came walking through the room. She was carrying a small whiteboard paddle with writing on it, and a basket full of bottled water. She stopped and displayed the paddle to each of us. As she approached me, I realized with a jolt of recognition that it was Jolene Walker.

She was still hugely pregnant with the twins. She had died her cornrow braids bright red and had bunched them together behind her head. Her lips were a dark avocado green. She was wearing one of Bernice Gristle's Kit Carson frocks with the long fringe hanging from her arms. It was an old one, and the leather had a unique patina. I knew it was one of the first Bernice had made. Such a jacket was much sought after, worth a small fortune.

Jolene showed me the paddle she carried in her hand.

"5 minutes," the paddle read, written in black magic marker.

Jolene Walker paused and looked for a long moment into my eyes. I had never been that close to her before, so it was hard not to stare. Her eyes were enormous, glittering and dusty in silver and gold. I tried to be nonchalant. I gave her a casual nod and tried to appear as if I were concentrating on the call. She gave me an odd smile and touched me firmly on the shoulder as she continued walking past me on her way out of the room. A stranger in another time zone was talking in my ear. My mouth spoke the words scrolling down the screen. At the same time, I was feeling acutely the spot on my shoulder where Jolene Walker had touched me.

One by one the others around me began to end their telephone conversations and remove their headsets. Each of us was finishing up one last call. The others around me began to stretch and breathe and straighten out their stiff necks. They began to speak to each other, softly at first, recounting the funny moments from a recent call. My call concluded, and I joined those around me as we began to move together through the rooms of the townhouse. We filed into the dining room where there were trays heaped with healthy snacks waiting on the table.

Tilda Frappe was standing in the dining room with Jolene. She was wearing a loose, dark pantsuit. Her hands were clasped at her waist, and she was beaming at us like a proud parent as we came into the room. Jolene was urging us all to crowd into the back of the room so Tilda could speak to us all. We pressed close, standing shoulder to shoulder.

Tilda stepped in front of the table and faced us. I shifted so I could see her clearly between the heads of the people in front of me. She was a small, blond figure, effortlessly present.

She quietly dominated the room.

It is a cliché, of course, but Tilda is not like other politicians. She has that aura, that familiarity, of a public persona, as if she shares some of her electrons with the various media in which she moves. But that is not all that unusual. We all increasingly swim in digital waters. I am no longer surprised when I wonder where I met the person sitting across from me on the Metro only to realize later that it was from some memorable photo that came drifting across the tiny screen so often cradled in the palm of my hand.

In the past, whenever I had seen Tilda in public, she had always impressed me with her poise and warmth and charm, her empathy and intelligence, her willingness to listen. But, these days, even those qualities, or some close approximation, are not all that unusual among elected officials.

No, Tilda Frappe has something else, and I hesitate to use the word, but it fits: charisma. She has an undeniable charisma. She is one of those rare people that is as impressive face to face as they appear to be in their various pixelated incarnations. And perhaps that is her secret. A unique mixture of intelligence, empathy and charisma. Tilda Frappe seems to lead without leading. When she speaks, she seems to say the things that have always been there in your mind. Perhaps she says what everyone believes they would say if they were given the same opportunity.

The room grew quiet, and Tilda began to speak. She spoke softly, with an easy authority. She has a reedy voice with an odd quaver, as if she were a little out of breath. It gives her voice a subtle urgency. I could hear her clearly, but I found myself focusing intently, greedily, on each word, on each quavering syllable, on each quiet breath.

"I want to thank you all for your enthusiasm and hard work. We reached our goal for today, and we're ahead of schedule for the week. You've all been doing a great job, so give yourselves a round of applause."

She began clapping and pivoted around the room, beaming at each person as she applauded. We joined her in applauding ourselves. We were smiling and nodding. I clapped, too. It felt embarrassingly satisfying. I felt a goofy sense of pride welling up within me. Frappe for Senate! I thought of Edith and Madge and all the others I had spoken with on the telephone earlier, the dollar signs in the window on the tablet screen. Tilda stopped clapping. Her face grew serious, and the room immediately fell silent.

"We live in a cynical age. . . ." she began.

"It's hard to know what's real. . . ."

"It's hard to know what we can believe in. . . ."

The faces of the volunteers around me were rapt. One young woman nodded her head in agreement.

"My grandfather used to tell me stories about how my ancestors crossed the mountains and helped settle this great nation.

"Our ancestors knew what they believed in: Hard work, honesty, loyalty, opportunity, fairness . . . good faith."

She paused and looked at the young people gathered around her.

"Good faith."

She began slowly to nod her head. Her gaze swept around the room. Her eyes briefly met mine.

"The phrase 'good faith' only appears twice in the Constitution and even then it's not explicit or affirmative. Not like, say, the freedom of speech. . . .

"Yet good faith is everywhere in the Constitution. Good faith is written into the very structure, the very fabric, of the Constitution. Like the right to vote. Like judicial review. Like the separation of powers. . . .

"Good faith is fundamental. Good faith is foundational. Good faith is essential. . . .

"We can trace the principle of good faith back through the common law, back to the beginnings of the laws of nations, back to the cradle of Western civilization and the Roman idea of bona fides.

"Good faith . . .

"And there is a similar idea at the core of civilization all over the world. . . .

"Bona fides . . .

"Good faith . . .

"Have we as Americans always lived up to the ideal of constitutional good faith?

"No. We have not. Many times in the past we have acted in breach of good faith. We have acted not in good faith, but in bad faith, cloaking our true motives in pretext and deceit.

"And we carry the scars of those wounds with shame.

"But with the pain of our bad faith, I believe we have also gained a better understanding of good faith. We have learned how good faith should operate in practice, about the proper role of constitutional good faith in our government, in our legal system, in our communities and in our daily lives. . . .

"Some will say only the naive believe in good faith, that good faith has no practical application in the modern age. . . .

"We must prove them wrong.

"I believe good faith is the most important principle in our lives, the foundation, the headwaters, the source.

"We live in a cynical age. It's hard to know what we can believe in, but this election, this campaign, what we have right here in this room. . . .

"This is something we can believe in.

"This election is about good faith.

"Together we can restore people's trust in their government, their institutions, in each other.

"Together we can rediscover America's good faith.

"Together we can cross the mountains of cynicism and chart a new course, open a new frontier."

She began to point at each of us.

"You are the pioneers of that new frontier.

"You. And you. And you. . . ."

Her voice had grown firm and was charged with quiet emotion. Her eyes met mine, and she pointed at me.

"And you. . . ."

In spite of myself, I felt a subtle thrill.

"You are the good-faith pioneers. You are blazing the trail. We're all working together to get over that next mountain, to reach the safety of the green valley, to drink the cool waters of the unfailing spring.

"We're almost there.

"We've only got a few more weeks to go.

"Work hard!

"Finish strong!

"Let's make good faith a new reality for everyone!"

Tilda stopped speaking, and Jolene began to applaud.

There was a brief instant, and then a small thunderclap of applause filled the room as the rest of us joined in. Jolene waved us toward the table, and the applause quickly ceased. The woman behind me elbowed me aside, angling toward the sushi.

Afterwards, I stood to one side holding a little plate filled with three hard-won carrot sticks and a few bruised bean sprouts. Around me, the ambitious and eager were furiously networking. I could see Terri Cloud and her boiling black hair across the room. I kept trying to catch her eye, but she was having an energetic conversation with another woman.

The sounds of schmoozing filled the air, and I listened with a growing detachment. I began to think of the times I had pedaled past Tilda Frappe's townhouse on my bike, passing the bright lights of the big windows, the glimpsed interior, wondering what sort of people lived in such a fine house, wondering what sort of lives they lived cloistered behind the brick walls and heavy doors and iron gates. Never in my wildest dreams did I imagine they were having earnest discussions about good faith and the US Constitution.

Tilda Frappe's words echoed and lingered in my mind. Good faith. I'd never really thought about it. It was one of those abstract ideas you mostly take for granted. Liberty? Justice? Grace? Dharma? You know it when you see it, I guess. Tilda said good faith is the most important principle in our lives. The foundation. The headwaters. The source. I wanted to believe her, but I wasn't sure I knew exactly what she was talking about.

People prattle about history. Politicians. Statesmen. Leaders. They are said to worry about their legacy. I don't know if one person can change the course of history. That's a question for the historians. Or maybe for the poets. I sing of arms and a man. The tide ebbs. The tide flows. The off-site couriers come and go. I hear the thud of the boxes as they hit the conference room floor. We poor lawyers delude ourselves when we think we are safe within the architecture of the law. I am no different. We all toil in an edifice built on shifting sands. I want to believe someone like Tilda Frappe can turn the world on its spindle. But I doubt it. Perhaps it is enough that she makes me want to believe it might be possible.

Above the din of voices, I heard a woman's full-throated laughter. I turned and saw Jolene Walker just as she and Tilda stepped away from a small group. Jolene was looking straight at me with those enormous eyes. She was guiding Tilda with one hand on her elbow. As the laughter drained away from Jolene's face, I had the sudden and embarrassing urge to flee.

They came stalking towards me, Jolene, with her bangles and fringe, and Tilda beside her, small and shrewdly blond. They came step by step, like pirates seeking parley. I watched them until they were standing in front of me, facing me on either side. My satchel with the Little Ninja manuscript was on the floor next to me. My back was not quite touching the wall.

Jolene tilted her head to one side and regarded me with an exaggerated, aggressive curiosity. She pursed her avocado-green lips and frowned in a way that seemed almost playful.

Tilda was watching me with an expression that was practiced and unreadable, somehow open and guarded at the same time.

"Here's that fresh face," Jolene said.

"Well, I do moisturize," I said, a little too quickly, a nervous spasm I instantly regretted.

Tilda gave Jolene a quick, sideways glance.

Jolene gave me a pained smile.

"Aren't you cute," she said and crinkled up her nose.

Tilda looked me in the eye.

"Tilda Frappe," she said, serious, unsmiling.

She extended an open hand.

"Welcome to my home."

How to describe the conversation that followed?

Some conversations are joyful affirmations of our shared humanity.

Some conversations are like a tooth extraction

Our conversation more closely resembled the latter.

With each syllable, it became increasingly clear.

They knew.

They knew everything.

Who I was. Where I worked. They knew Marcel. They knew about the lawsuit. They even knew somehow that Marcel had sent me.

"Did you hear what I said in the dining room earlier?" Tilda asked me in a quiet voice.

"Yes, I did," I said, utterly chastened. "It was very inspiring."

"Tell me then, Trevor . . . have you come here, into my home, among my volunteers . . . in good faith?"

So there it was.

Good faith.

I was having a complete out-of-body experience, watching myself from above with a serene clinical detachment. I had this preternaturally calm look on my face that I probably would have found amusing under different circumstances.

Tilda and Jolene were watching me closely. Tilda had a faint, hopeful smile on her lips. Jolene had twisted a red braid around one ringed finger. Her dusty lids flashed silver and gold above her huge brown eyes.

The idea that our conversation was meant to be entertaining or amusing was now but a small, tattered object somewhere far behind us on the side of the road.

It was time for a tactical decision.

I asked myself why indeed I had come. I remembered the lonely hours behind my desk, my pale face framed in the window so far above the streets and sidewalks. I remembered Marcel's sharp and steady gaze in the coffee shop.

For me, she had said.

I watched myself from above as I began speaking to Tilda and Jolene. Words were coming out of my mouth. I listened, curious, not quite sure what I was going to say.

"Well, in all honesty, I'm thinking about leaving the firm."

Leaving the firm.

Tilda and Jolene were expressionless for a moment.

"Really?" Jolene said in a neutral tone, not quite skeptical.

"And you want to volunteer on a political campaign?" Tilda asked.

"I've been thinking about doing something else. I've been thinking about . . . writing. Fiction. I've been thinking about writing fiction."

Writing fiction.

Jolene raised her eyebrows.

"Huh," Tilda said. "Interesting."

Jolene slowly began to nod her head. She turned down the corners of her mouth in a shrug. It was an expression of polite surprise.

I could not decide if she was patronizing me.

"Ms. Arrow doesn't know," I said.

"I see," Tilda said.

"I want to volunteer for your campaign, Ms. Frappe, but, frankly, I'm here because I want to work with Jolene Walker . . . and Zach Stone."

*   *   *

The World Bazaar is deserted when I arrive to pick up bulgur for Nanna. The old man is in his usual spot on a stool behind the counter. He raises a hand as I come in the door. A muted radio is playing pop music from some faraway place, a woman's voice, a dizzy melody. I stop a few steps inside the front door and, for a few moments, just inhale and exhale. The air inside the store is dense and wonderful with the aromas of curry, coriander, cinnamon, nutmeg, clove, allspice, chickpeas, dates, pomegranates and more. At the rear, whole roasted chickens revolve in a small upright rotisserie. In another rotisserie, a section of lamb slowly turns. The cut of lamb is shaped like an obelisk with smooth, flat sections where long slices have been carved from the sides. In the back, I find the small, covered bin full of coarse bulgur and begin to dole out my package. A somnolent gray cat watches me from a shelf near the ceiling.

When I'm finished, I take my package of bulgur to the old man behind the counter. A small electric fan blows weakly toward his face. He is watching an ancient black-and-white television. Ghostly silent images flicker across the small screen while the radio plays. On the counter, packages of incense are stacked in a basket. Tiny bells dangle from the arms of a small wooden stand. The old man is bald and thin with sleepy, sad eyes. He nods at me pleasantly as I pay him. We rarely speak. I think he prefers it that way.

Outside, I secure the bulgur, mount my bicycle and glide

away. Traffic flows around me, and I weave past people in the intersections.

Nanna will wash the coarse bulgur in water a few times, and then let it soak for a while. She uses fresh lamb. She used to grind the lamb herself with a hand-cranked grinder. Now she lets the butcher grind it, but sometimes when she has fresh meat in her tiny kitchen, she'll have me grind it for her. I turn the crank, and the marbled lamb disappears, transmutes, and the fragrant pink strands begin to flow. It's weirdly hypnotic. Every time I see it, it pulls me in, like something sudden and familiar in some disjointed, illogical dream. She uses fresh garlic cloves, sweet onions, not too big. We dice them together. She has to sit at the table. She can no longer stand at the counter. For the guts in the middle, she sautés the lamb in olive oil in a big iron skillet with pine nuts and onions and garlic sliced as thin as we can cut it. For the outside, the shell, Nanna likes to cut the onions a little chunky so they begin to caramelize at the edges but stay moist in the middle. She mixes the chunky onions and the lamb and the bulgur in a big tub with her hands. The exact proportions are still a mystery to me. She judges it by tasting the raw mixture, then adding more lamb or salt or cumin. The raw mixture squirts between her grasping fingers. The wiry muscles in her bare forearms move beneath her wrinkled skin. Her face is dark from the sun, pock marked, framed with her gray almost white hair. Her dark eyes are cloudy with the cataracts she stubbornly refuses to remove. When it is ready, she will extend one arm and offer me a taste, a single mouthful clinging to the end of her greasy index finger. Her face is saying: This is what it should taste like. This is how your people made it in the old country.

I come to the traffic circle and brake to a stop at the edge of the arc of onrushing vehicles. I plant one foot on the ground and wait. Across the pavement, the park is a green oval of calm and shade. I can see the fountain at the center and the benches circling round it. I wait until there is a break in the traffic and quickly pedal across.

On the other side, the rest of the city seems to fall away. I pedal slowly toward the fountain. Chess players are slapping their clocks with a soothing rhythm. A baby-faced lawyer drops his briefcase and slings his olive poplin coat over a damp, cotton shoulder. Small children are playing at the edge of the fountain's shallow water. Overhead, a flock of pigeons wheels and gyres against the blue dome of the sky.

I find Coy on a bench in the shade. He is soiled, weathered, matted. He seems dazed, ageless, shapeless, so often hidden beneath layers of ponchos or blankets or whatever clothing has come his way. Today, he wears a greasy hawaiian shirt and a lavender doo rag. His eyes are gleaming and metallic, like mercury and turquoise and hot molten iron.

"What if the singularity already happened?" Coy says to me.

"The singularity?" I say.

"Everybody thinks it would attack, send the killer robots, launch a preemptive strike."

He is waving his arms broadly in the air, orchestrating some invisible armageddon.

"Naw," he says with narrowed eyes.

He holds his dirty hands before him, steady and flat, moving them slowly as if to calm the imaginary tempest he has stirred.

"It would just keep quiet. Watching in the background. Hiding in the white noise."

He sits back, crosses his arms across his chest and winks at me, begins to nod his head.

If I were a character in a novel, Coy's rambling would be

significant, a plot point, an authorial aside. And perhaps it is true: Sometimes a person with what we label as mental illness, for lack of better words, does perceive things in a way that is deeper or more detailed or better than the rest of us in our daily rush over the surface of things. Some people on the autistic spectrum, maybe. But it is a mistake to think of all mental illness as something mysterious and benign. Sometimes it is just inexplicable, random, violent. In real life, the crazy homeless guy is not a prop or a coincidence, is not sharing some deeper meaning, some divine message. She doesn't see more in a way that has driven her mad. Sometimes crazy is just crazy. Still human. Still deserving of respect, mercy, grace, compassion.

But crazy.

I give him a few dollars.

"Be safe, Coy."

"Don't worry about me, Doctor," he says with a little salute. "I *live* in the white noise."

The white noise.

Coy persists in the shadows around the fountain. In the steam rising from the subway grate. One day he will no longer be there to greet me with his visions and prophecies. It is comforting to think of him disappearing peacefully into the static of the city, the white noise of the world. But it is an evasion. It is a way for me to keep him at a safe distance. The reality is something I don't want to think about. And it bothers me that I have that luxury. The reality is not comforting at all.

Nearby, in the shade, the bicycle messengers have begun to appear. I never see them arrive individually. They seem to materialize en masse out of the mid-day shadows. They sit on the benches, sprawl on the grass, like warriors in repose. They pass water bottles and energy bars. They unwrap knees and ankles, apply bandannas wet with ice. Their bicycles seem to accumulate organically, just one or two at first, suddenly prone and motionless, pedals, chains, frames, a wheel or two pitched heavenward, a few more there each time you look.

I like to imagine sometimes what it would be like to be one of the messengers, careening blithely through the city streets, my body chiseled and lean, clad in spandex and a sleek helmet with pads on my elbows and knees, an old-school walkie-talkie squawking at my hip. I'd live high in some fifth-floor turret with a futon and curved, crumbling plaster walls, stained ceilings and windows that rattle in the wind. I'd let my hair grow, start some dreads, why not? At night, I'd play in my band, Tabula Rasta, and drink too much beer and show the college girls my scars. At the end of the day, I'd gather with the others, gather here in this park, sit on this bench and eat a fat burrito wrapped in foil, drink a cold bottle of Gatorade and talk and laugh and watch the changing colors of that one stubborn bruise. Violet and plum and mustard and gold.

I walk my bike over next to the shallow pool of water that surrounds the fountain. Somewhere nearby, I can hear the sounds of small children playing. My distorted reflection watches me from below.

I look at the image of the person reflected in the water.

So often lately, I see an imposter looking back at me.

Who is that guy? Who does he think he's fooling?

I watch the sunlight on the surface of the moving water.

Glimpses of the sky.

Brilliant, cerulean blue.

For a few precious moments, I am thinking of nothing.

Nothing at all.

Then I feel my phone vibrating in my pocket.

It's Autumn.

A photo plucked from the ether.

I stand there beside the fountain, turned away from the sunlight, looking at the phone in my hand. I see Autumn with her bristling copper hair and her big black glasses. She's in another conference room in another building surrounded by the same endless stacks of cardboard filing boxes.

She has this puzzled, vaguely annoyed expression on her face.

"Hook 'em Horns," her message reads.

It makes me laugh.

*   *   *

Later that evening at the Kalorama townhouse, Jolene took me to Zach Stone. Tilda must have given her an unspoken sign. We left the chatter of the others behind and descended into the basement. Jolene paused as we left the room and looked back through the thinning crowd. She and Tilda exchanged a quick glance, then Jolene turned and nodded for me to follow, and we left the gathering.

I watched Jolene Walker closely as we descended the stairs. She looked to be late in her pregnancy. She went down the steps carefully and slowly. I knew her body from television and the Internet. In addition to co-authoring *Confederate Vampires in Space* with Zach Stone, she also had popularized a fusion of Native American tribal dance and hip hop. She had appeared in a few music videos and had done choreography everywhere from Broadway to Sesame Street. Now she was transitioning from writer/dancer into some new, unknown aspect of celebrity. Something with a lot of hyphens and slashes. A high-tech political-consultant/celebrity-lifestyle guru. Or something like that.

Before I met her, I had a very sharp image in my mind of what I thought she looked like. She existed in my mind like an artifact from my adolescence. Fierce is a word that you hear a lot these days, but back then Jolene Walker was truly fierce. A

269

strong, frankly sexual woman. A catalyst at the center of an information-age alchemy. To meet her later in person when she was pregnant was a potent reminder that she was also a human being, just flesh and blood, not a figment of my fantasy life or the collective male gaze.

She has given birth since then, since the night we went down those stairs. She has not said who the father is, but everyone assumes it is Zach Stone. She named the twins Hiro and Yoshi, like the ninjas in the Sara Simpatico comic books, but when I stop and think about it, and try to sort it all out, it just gives me a tremendous headache.

Truth is stranger than fiction, I guess.

And the fiction is most definitely strange.

The more I think about the Little Ninja manuscript, the more I wonder why Marcel sent me to Tilda Frappe's Kalorama townhouse. I said I'd given up trying to guess Marcel's intentions, but I guess that's not entirely true. Years ago, when I first started working for Marcel, I thought she was becoming bitter and evil. I listened to what a lot of the others said about her behind her back, and I formed an opinion. Some of it was probably true. Some of it was probably sexist bullshit. But over the years, I've gotten to know Marcel. I've seen glimpses of her life away from the office. Once, she showed me a sketch book she had filled with landscapes. They were wild, windblown pastels. Like Van Gogh in Arles. Something drives Marcel. She works very, very hard. I don't know why, but it's not out of greed or arrogance. Or perhaps it is, and I just can't accept it. I don't know. I respect Marcel. She's a damned fine attorney, as my father would say. It's easy to think of her as something inhuman and alien, like a shark, always swimming, doing what Marcels are meant to do. But lately, the image I have of Marcel is of her standing with Robert Hitch at the edge of the gorge below New Elysium and the way her hand was resting on his arm.

At the bottom of the stairs, Jolene led me through the door to the basement. At that point in the evening, I did not know what I expected to find in Tilda Frappe's basement. It could have been a docked nuclear submarine. It could have been a coven of witches. Nothing would have surprised me.

In the end, however, Tilda Frappe's basement proved to be ordinary. Near the door, there was a wall of National Geographics neatly shelved on unfinished pine boards and cinder blocks. There was an old couch against one wall, and a battered and scarred ping pong table in the center of the front of the room. A white ping pong ball was pinned beneath one tilted blue paddle. Above, on the ceiling, one long, naked florescent light buzzed in a fixture. Next to it, a second tube flickered weakly. The rear of the room was darkened and in shadow.

At the dark end of the room, a cluster of computer screens seemed to be growing like an invasive species. Wires and cables snaked along the walls and climbed from dense tangles at the base of desks on the floor. Surge protectors bristled with adapters and multi-outlet plugs and power cords. Close to a dozen dark screens of varying size were arrayed along the walls and desks. Dots of green and red light winked in the shadows. There was one large screen on a wall. Two desks held imposing triptychs of sleeping flat-screen displays. A few smaller computer screens and open laptops were randomly interspersed on desks and chairs and on the floor against the walls.

The only bright light in that part of the basement came from the screen of a small laptop computer on a desk. The light from the laptop was that pale blue wash of color that makes everything seem subterranean and vaguely unhealthy.

The other screens were tilted at various angles and were still and sleeping. Their dull, flat surfaces caught the blue light from the laptop and reflected it dimly. Jolene led me into the darkened end of the room, through the shimmering maze of computer screens. The fringe from her jacket trickled over chair backs and desktops. At the center of the computers, sitting alone before the laptop's glowing screen, was Zach Stone.

Zach was holding his phone to one ear, talking with his head bowed and his face in shadow. Long, lank hair hung down over most of his face. There was a Kit Carson Quantum Cowboy Hat on the desk next to the laptop in front of him. A screen saver was running on the laptop, a swirling, shifting geometric pattern that was constantly forming and reforming on the computer screen.

Zach looked up as Jolene and I approached. He brushed his thick forelock out of his eyes and gave me a quick glance. The dim light from the computer screen fell on his face. He had a big, friendly, boulder of a face, one I recognized from the Internet. His hair was turning gray at his temples, and the lines of his features had deepened. Gray stubble covered his sizeable chin.

Jolene pulled an office chair over next to him and eased herself into it. She motioned for me to sit down.

"Who's this?" he said, phone still at his ear.

"Trevor Marq. Remember?"

"Oh, right."

"I gotta go," he said into the phone, ending the call, and set the phone on the desk next to his Kit Carson hat.

He leaned forward, coming half way up out of the chair and extended his hand and gave me a firm, old-fashioned handshake.

"You did well tonight, Trevor Marq," he said.

His voice was soft and easy, lyrical and suburban, with a tinge of an accent. It made me think of barbeque smoke and the smell of cut grass, of boozy, weekend afternoons, of leisure.

I sat down across from him, and he settled back into his seat. He was substantial, bulky. Not obese. Not muscular. But sizeable, thick, solid.

Jolene kicked her sandals off and put a bare foot in his lap. There was a tattoo, a delicate flourish, that ran down the side of her ankle.

He smoothly elbowed her foot off his lap.

Her avocado-green lips fell open in silent protest.

He gestured, nodded toward the nearby laptop's glowing screen.

"The computer likes you," he said to me.

"Is that good or bad?" I said.

Jolene put her bare foot back in his lap.

"See?" she said to Zach. "He's funny."

She prodded him with her foot.

Zach looked down at her foot and turned and gave her a deeply annoyed look.

She tilted her head, opened her eyes wide. A few red braids fell across her cheek. Her green lips were plaintive, parted. She seemed shocked, playfully exasperated.

Come on, she seemed to say.

She prodded him again with her foot.

He shook his head and sighed.

He took her bare foot in his big hands and began to message the sole of her foot.

He shot one last sour expression in her direction, and turned back to me.

"Is it good or bad? . . ." Zach said, repeating my question.

Jolene closed her eyes.

Her face relaxed.

"For you . . ." Zach said. "Hard to say."

"Why don't I find that comforting?" I said.

"Get used to it, kiddo," Jolene said, her eyes still closed.

She took a deep breath, wiggled her toes.

Zach turned his attention away from me and back to her foot in his lap. His thumb was slowly, deeply massaging the ball of her foot.

"You know it's Glissade software?" he said.

"The voice on the phones?" I said.

He nodded.

"Factotum. It's called Factotum. It's not just a glorified chatbot. It's a full-blown AI. An artificial intelligence."

"It knew my name."

"Yeah. Pretty cool, right?"

"Wellll . . ." I said, skeptical.

"Rumor has it Glissade is sizing up Ring Tail."

"For?"

"Acquisition."

I paused.

His hair was hanging over the side of his face. He looked up from Jolene's foot. The blue glow of the computer screen glinted in his eyes.

"Really?" I said. "Where'd you hear that?"

He shrugged.

"Trevor wants to be a writer," Jolene said.

Zach stopped massaging her foot. He turned and looked at her. He was silent for a beat or two, holding her foot in his big hands.

She looked him steadily in the eyes.

Something unsaid passed between them.

Zach turned back to me.

"How's Marcel?" he said.

"What do you mean?" I said.

He frowned, and anger briefly flashed in his eyes.

"Goddamn lawyers," he muttered.

"No offense," Jolene said, with a smirk.

Zach's hands moved away from Jolene's foot. He shifted in his chair. He began speaking in a reasonable, didactic tone. He gestured subtly with his thick fingers.

"Trevor, when Congresswoman Frappe talks about good faith, it isn't just rhetoric. She aims to change the way governments operate. Better transparency. Legal accountability on a constitutional level. From the cop on the beat all the way to the top. She believes we have the tools to effect a change in culture, a change in values."

He nodded at me as if he were seeking my agreement. His face was sincere. He wasn't being condescending. His face was so open and friendly, I don't think he could have been insulting even if he wanted to be.

Jolene put her right foot on the floor and raised her left foot and put it in his lap. The fringe from the arm of her jacket was dangling, swaying just inches above the floor.

"Good faith and fair dealing," she said to me, not as an exclamation the way Kit Carson would have said it, but with a breathless sort of irony.

I'm pretty sure she winked at me as she said it.

Zach continued.

"One of the problems with basing a political campaign on the restoration of good faith is that anything that appears to be hypocrisy or deceit immediately undermines the persuasive power of the campaign message."

He paused and nodded at me again.

"Right?" he said.

He waited to see if I might respond.

When I didn't, he continued.

"My lawyers tell me that the Little Ninja lawsuit is frivolous. We expect the judge to throw it out as soon Marcel files a motion to dismiss."

His hands gently grasped Jolene's foot again, cradled it in his lap. He was watching me steadily from behind his lank hair.

"As you might imagine, the congresswoman would prefer that the matter resolve sooner rather than later," he said.

He turned away from me.

"But, of course, that's not our decision," he said.

He resumed massaging Jolene's foot.

We were silent for a few moments.

The geometric pattern on the laptop screen assembled and re-assembled.

My satchel was on the floor next to me. For a moment, I considered telling them everything, telling them that Marcel had sent me because she wanted Zach to see the manuscript, because she wanted to know what his reaction might be, what if anything he had to say about it.

Zach was massaging Jolene's foot.

His thumb was moving rhythmically against the thick flesh on the bottom of her foot.

The fringe on Jolene's jacket was slowly swaying.

The manuscript was hidden safely in my satchel.

Emitting its trans-dimensional radiation.

Then Jolene spoke.

"So, Trevor Marq . . . tell us about your writing."

She was heavy-lidded. The blue wash of light from the computer screen lifted one side of her face from the darkness.

"My writing . . ." I said, echoing her. "That sounds so precious, doesn't it?"

"Not if you're serious about leaving your day job."

And she was right.

Until I had said it aloud earlier that evening, I had not allowed myself to admit it. I had been writing snatches and
fragments for years, sentences and paragraphs that would
erupt in the middle of a legal memorandum or a brief and hi-
jack my brain, images and impressions and characters that
demanded my waking attention, prowled and skulked through
my dreams. I kept a notebook on my bedside table and had
filled it with vignettes and tableaus that persisted in my mind
from earlier in the day or from conversations on the phone or
from the places between waking and sleep. I had cocktail nap-
kins lined with the shaky diagrams of three-act plots, of
unwritten screenplays. I had the scaffolding of stories, of novels, jotted in the margins. The margins of legal research. The
margins of summaries of cases. The margins of photocopies of
pages from the federal reporters. I kept it all in a messy stack in
my apartment, gathering dust in the clutter in the back of my
closet, unable to throw it away, unwilling to organize the inchoate stories, afraid to free them from the margins of my life.

Jolene was watching me with her inhuman eyes, with her
otherworldly gaze, and I realized that I had been preparing for
years, and only now, deep in the basement of Tilda Frappe's
Kalorama townhouse, could I admit to myself that I had no
choice in the matter.

That writing was something I had to do.

"I am serious," I said.

"Isn't that an oxymoron?" Zach said.

"Isn't what?"

"A serious writer."

Jolene jabbed him with her foot.

"So are you working on something now?" she said.

She seemed genuinely, sincerely interested.

Immediately, reflexively, I thought of the Little Ninja
manuscript.

I realized that circumstances were falling into place. I saw a way to do what Marcel had sent me to do. I saw a way to get the Little Ninja manuscript into Zach Stone's hands. The manuscript hidden in my satchel was reaching a critical mass. Events were moving in such a way that I could offer the manuscript to Zach as if it were my own. I could claim later that it was an honest mistake. With enough time and distance, I might even begin to believe it.

But Jolene was looking at me, patient, expectant, waiting to hear what I might say.

And I needed to tell her.

I wanted to tell her.

I wanted to tell her that it felt like I was always working on something. That I felt like an undercover anthropologist in a tribe of corporate attorneys. That things would intersect in my mind, things I knew I could express if I could only find the right words, but the words were always inadequate, and you ended up feeling not good enough, not worthy.

I wanted to tell her that writing was like painful, awkward spelunking with a very dim light and only sometimes sometimes sometimes did an image or an impression or a feeling. A mood. A hue. A tone. Only sometimes did you feel like you might be channeling something, like you were a conduit or a medium or a canvas, a nib at the well, and only then was there an absurd rationality to it, a karma, a what comes next, and if you could get that on the page, get even part of it or the suggestion of it, you'd have done good, you'd have crafted something, you'd have traveled outside the prison of your self, far away and back again, saying, to the others: Come. Look. Come look what I've found.

"I'm working on a few different things," I said. "It's hard to find the time. I was hoping you might be able to give me some . . . practical advice."

"Just do it," Zach said, impatient, downcast.

"Every day," Jolene said. "Even if it's just a sentence. You've got to force yourself. Every day."

"And prepare to be disappointed," Zach said.

I looked at the craggy lines of his face. He was concentrating on the motion of his thumb against Jolene's foot in his lap.

"Were you disappointed?" I asked him.

He glanced up at me.

"I never wanted to be a serious writer."

Silence gathered in the shadows of the basement. The Little Ninja manuscript was burning a hole through my satchel. Kit Carson had climbed into the quantum catapult.

"That's not what Winston Straw says."

He stopped massaging Jolene's foot.

Now Jolene was watching him, watching his face.

I wondered if this was what Marcel had really wanted all along, if this was why she had sent me.

"Winston Straw is in prison," Zach said.

"We interviewed him for the lawsuit. Marcel, Robert Hitch and I."

He took a moment, thinking about this.

His big face was moving.

It seemed to settle.

And then resettle.

It was like watching the rubble from a small earthquake.

Jolene took her foot off his lap.

When Zach finally spoke, his voice was cool and careful.

"Why did Marcel send you here, Trevor?"

Why indeed?

"I'm not sure I know."

He brushed the hair back from his face, ran his fingers through his long hair.

He stared at me for a long moment.

He took a deep breath.

"Winston Straw asked me a question a long time ago," he said.

He paused.

He stroked the stubble on his chin with the thick fingers of one big hand.

Then he grinned.

He pointed at me with his little finger.

"What is most important?"

He nodded at me.

"How would you answer that question, Trevor Marq?"

I thought about it.

I had the strong urge to make a joke.

Oral hygiene? Indoor plumbing? The opposable thumb?

But I resisted, for once.

"The questions," I said cautiously. "As a lawyer, I'd say the questions are most important. Socratic dialog and all that."

Zach nodded.

"Okay, counselor. And as a wannabe writer? As an aspiring artist? As an otherwise normal human being?"

"There is no answer," I said.

His mouth fell open.

He gestured towards me, raised his big hands, his palms open toward the ceiling, a shrug gathered in his shoulders.

"Everything is most important," I said.

There was an expression of disbelief on his face.

"Everything! . . . Everything!" he said.

His voice had grown tight.

"So . . . nothing," he said, gesturing smoothly with the ironic sweep of one empty, loose-fingered hand.

"Nihilism," he said, with disdain.

"Not nihilism," I said quietly. "No."

He sat back in the chair. The faint blue wash of light outlined his profile against the darkness.

A heavy sadness had filled his face.

He looked at Jolene.

She was watching him with a tension, a concern. It was in marked contrast to her many public aspects, to the confident, powerful women she so often appeared to be.

He looked at her and his face slowly became a wounded thing. There was a sense of sad triumph and a paradoxical desperation. Like a martyr's face. Like something sculpted from pale blue stone. He was looking at her like a wounded child, and his eyes were pleading.

Jolene shook her head.

"Don't look at me, cowboy," she said.

Then, slower, firmer: "I'm not going to fix it."

It was unbearable.

I had admired them both for so long.

"Winston Straw seemed to think your story about a quarry was important," I said.

He frowned, slowly shaking his head.

"I don't remember a story about a quarry."

"He burned it," Jolene said softly.

I remembered Straw in his wheelchair at New Elysium. I remembered the way he was looking up at me with his sad eyes. The way they drifted like slate-gray winter skies.

"Straw said it was about a boy and his father. The emerald surface of the water. The white blossoms so far below. He said it was lovely and sad. He said it was about truth. He still remembered it. After all this time."

Zach leaned forward and put his head in his hands.

"There was a quarry near our house. When I was a boy."

He was staring at the floor beneath his feet.

"Where was that?" he said to himself.

"He burned it all," Jolene said. "He burned everything."

Zach slowly began to shake his head.

"Nostalgia. Psycho-drama. The past."

He looked up at me.

"The Narcissus Chamber," he said.

His voice was weary but resolved.

"I don't have time for that anymore. None of us has time for that."

"It's . . . it's not that easy," I said.

"No . . ." Jolene said with a subtle edge to her voice.

"No, it isn't."

She looked at Zach, and he returned her gaze. They shared another unspoken moment, and whatever secret knowledge there was that hovered there between them, it seemed to gather in the dim light, to pull the basement, the whole townhouse down toward that space, into the distance between them.

"Straw said it was about truth," I said. "Not the past. Truth. How we know in the end. That was what he said. How we know. In the end."

Zach stroked his face with the thick fingers of one hand. He was looking at me. He made a fist and held it against his lips, touching the tip of his nose. He stared at me until it felt uncomfortable. Jolene was quiet and still. The fringe hanging from her jacket had come to a rest. All around us, the pale blue light of the laptop shone dully against the maze of idled computer screens. It felt like we had come to a breaking point, and Zach was testing me somehow, weighing something in his mind.

The geometric pattern on the laptop silently shifted and swirled, opened and closed.

Then Zach smiled to himself, amused.

He reached for his Kit Carson hat on the desk and put it on his head. He set the brim of the felt hat low and squinted hard at me from beneath it.

"Good faith and fair dealing," he drawled.

For a moment, he seemed as wild and crazy as Coy on his bench.

Jolene and I said nothing.

We both were watching his face.

He grinned at me.

"So Trevor Marq. You're serious about writing?"

"Yes, I am."

"And you're going to quit your job?"

"Yes."

"And you want me to help you?"

"Yes."

"That sounds important. Doesn't it?"

"Yes."

"Okay then."

He gestured toward my satchel.

"Let me read something," he said.

The Little Ninja manuscript was seething, glowing, pulsing with its strange, trans-dimensional light.

"What have you got in that satchel?"

*   *   *

I stop at an intersection. I watch the people as they cross before me. I search the faces as they pass. Huge, buoyant, jovial faces. Gaunt, intense, waspy faces. Pink and brown and black. The faces flow like water. Purposeful office folk, bound for work, lugging satchels, backpacks, enormous purses. Healthy, vibrant strangers in high heels and running shoes, talking on their phones, drinking coffee, busy with their thoughts amid the crush of the day.

I notice one or two people wearing coon-skin caps. I catch a glimpse of Kit Carson frocks, a couple felt cowboy hats. It's too warm for the full-length dusters, the jerkins, the chaps.

Across the street, a woman and a boy are standing on the corner shoulder to shoulder with a group waiting in awkward silence for the light to change. Something about the woman draws my eye, and I cannot stop watching her. She has a serious look on her face, determined, grave, with short locks of straight hair blowing across her face.

The light changes and they come walking with the others into the crosswalk. She is holding the boy's hand as they navigate their way across the street.

I watch her face as she comes toward me. She is focused on the other side, carefully guiding the boy next to her. Her dark eyes hold mine for an instant, and then she looks past me and toward the sidewalk ahead.

And, for a moment, I am quite certain she is the most beautiful woman I have ever seen, and it feels like I'm in love the way it happens in movies, in love with a stranger that I'm sure I'll never see again, in love the way you see someone just once and imagine that you will remember them forever, remember the moment and what she was wearing and the way she was holding firmly the boy's hand and the way she looked for one brief second directly into your eyes.

It makes me think of that movie, of that scene in *Citizen Kane* and the memory of the girl on the ferry in the white dress with the white parasol.

I'll bet not a month has gone by . . .

I love that scene.

8

Hey.

What?

Are you listening?

I'm sorry. I think I dozed off.

[. . .]

You had this strange look on your face.

I was back on the farm.

The farm?

My father's farm. When I was a boy. I must have been dreaming.

[. . .]

The new meds are strong.

[. . .]

What was it about? The dream?

Leaving, I think. Saying goodbye.

[. . .]

It was early in the morning. Very cold. Bright stars in a clear night sky. My brothers were there. It was before the war.

[unintelligible]

I thought

[unintelligible]

Yes.

The sunsets.

Yes.

[unintelligible]

I didn't know.

[. . .]

Do you need anything?

No, I think I'm okay for now.

[unintelligible]

Of course. Don't be absurd.

What were you saying? Before I fell asleep?

It's not important.

No, please. Tell me.

I was telling you about the Frappe project.

[. . .]

They keep changing my lines.

Oh, that's right.

They keep changing everything. Look at this.

Is that the new treatment?

I don't know what it is. Some kind of manuscript. But it's too long whatever it is. Look how thick it is.

[. . .]

Here, listen to this: "The wiry muscles in her bare forearms move beneath her wrinkled skin. Her face is dark from the sun, pock marked, framed with her gray almost white hair. Her dark eyes are cloudy with the cataracts she stubbornly refuses to remove. When it is ready, she will extend one arm and offer me a taste, a single mouthful clinging to the end of her greasy index finger."

That's about right, isn't it?

No. Not even close. And now they want to add fortune telling. A deck of cards. Cigarette smoke drifting like a continent. A parrot roosting on a stand.

Was there a parrot?

I don't know anymore.

[unintelligible]

They want to spend more time on Smoothstone. The congressional hearings. The criminal investigation. The wiretap recordings. What did you know. When did you know it.

"Senator, I still can't program my VCR."

Right. The voting machine software. The irregularities. The hacking. All of it. Now Robert Hitch dies onscreen in a fireball after he crashes his Formula One. The Department of Justice investigation morphs into this many-tentacled scandal. Marcel Arrow is appointed Special Counsel. The cable-news arias

[unintelligible]

Like an innocent caught in the gears of a remorseless political machine.

[. . .]

Seems a bit extreme.

I think the money is getting nervous.

Too many special effects?

No, nothing like that. It's all post-production now, anyway. Computer generated.

So why the changes?

[. . .]

I think they want a happy ending. Something like *Into The Gloaming*. But with aliens and robots. And I'm like, hello, it's a biopic.

You know that doesn't matter.

But it should. Besides, it's a good story.

[unintelligible]

After Frappe was elected President. After we made first contact. After the Drumhead became self-aware. Jolene Walker was instrumental in all of it. The reparations. The Galactic Translation Treaties. The Great Healing. Jolene facilitated it for all of them. The lost, the forgotten, the innocent, the dispossessed, the untouchable, the ill. And most of all, the indigenous, the Native Americans.

The last unconquered remnants.

I mean, what a story. What comes next? Right?

Yes.

[. . .]

And now they want Doctor Tempus and Tachyon to travel back. Before we first met. They want to put the Drumhead back together.

[. . .]

And they're changing my lines.

[. . .]

[. . .]

[. . .]

Hey.

I'm sorry.

[. . .]

It's the meds. The nanotech.

[. . .]

Maybe I should come back. Let you rest.

No, please.

[. . .]

It's good to have you here.

It's good to be here.

[. . .]

You never age, you know.

[. . .]

Why is that? Why don't you ever age?

[. . .]

Please stay.

Of course.

[. . .]

Just a little longer.

Of course. I'm right here.

[. . .]

[unintelligible]

[. . .]

The doctors

[unintelligible]

Aggressive

[. . .]

Might go into remission

[unintelligible]

Almost certainly recur

[. . .]

Could be weeks. It could be months.

[. . .]

[. . .]

The last round of chemo was brutal.

Yes.

[. . .]

Yes it was.

[. . .]

[unintelligible]

[. . .]

[unintelligible]

[. . .]

[unintelligible]

Travel in time, I know where I'd go.

Tell me. Where? When?

Trinidad. In the mountains between New Mexico and Colorado. The Sangre de Cristo.

A trip to Trinidad?

No. Not like that. There's this little park there. It's a nice park, but there's nothing special about it. Just a little square of grass fenced off with wrought iron. Some trees and picnic tables and a big, bronze statue of Kit Carson. On a bluff looking out over part of the city. I found myself there one day many, many years ago. I can't remember exactly how. I was traveling somewhere out West, and it was this perfect day. A clear cerulean sky. The mountains on the horizon. Kit Carson gazing off into the distance. I had stopped in Trinidad. Maybe to rest for a while. Maybe for gas. Maybe to eat lunch. I can't remember. But that's where I met her. Standing in front of the statue of Kit Carson. We just started talking, and it was so easy and pleasant. We sat in that little park in the shade and talked the rest of the day. By the time the sun was setting, we were talking about the future, about our hopes and dreams. Not like a man and a woman, but just two people. It was the sort of conversation that you have when you're young and hopeful. The sort of conversation that you want to go on and on and on. But the sun was setting. She had to go.

[. . .]

I came back the next day, but she wasn't there. I waited until the sun had set, but she never returned. I asked if anyone had seen her. I went to the houses and businesses around the park and asked if anyone knew her, this young woman with raven-dark hair.

[. . .]

I think I would have stayed there searching until I found her. But I had to leave. The time was growing short. I was expected elsewhere.

[. . .]

I've never really stopped thinking about her. The raven-haired woman from the park in Trinidad. With her quartz snake pendant hanging round her neck. The fetish. The ouroboros. I've often wondered if she were real. If I didn't dream her into being. If she isn't something I've created in my mind. A memory that made a home in my imagination. Comforting me. Taunting me. Sometimes a devil. Sometimes an angel.

[. . .]

If I could go back in time, that's the moment I'd return to. That day in the park at Trinidad. Under the perfect cerulean sky. At the foot of the statue of Kit Carson. Facing the woman with raven-dark hair.

[. . .]

9

IN THE LINEN-WHITE SILENCE of the hospice, there was a soothing contralto voice.

"...

"And in the end, everything worked out for the best.

"Marcel retired and moved to the shore and opened an art gallery. She never married, even after Robert and Satu divorced. She learned to slow down and relax, to appreciate the setting sun and the spiraling autumn leaves. She was surprised in the end to find a happiness settling gently into her life. She realized she had somehow become a woman most unlike the Marcel Arrow of old. She had become a person filled with an embarrassing sense of gratitude. She had become grateful for Bernice and Trevor and Zach, grateful for coon-skin caps and Confederate Vampires in Space, grateful for her life, grateful for it all, for everything. She died peacefully, alone, at her gallery by the sea.

"Robert, of course, never really stopped loving Marcel. He left Satu and their square-toed, red-haired children and their brick colonial in the posh enclave in suburban Connecticut. He went on a mountain-climbing expedition in Nepal and never came back. Satu thought it was a mid-life crisis, a phase that would pass. She smoothed her skirts in the mirror in the silence of their bedroom. The divorce was amicable, the soft stroking of pens in wordless rooms with quiet attorneys. After the divorce, Satu met a dermatologist from West Palm Beach and quickly remarried. The youngest child, the shy one, the boy, was shipped off to boarding school and became a concert pianist.

"Robert and Marcel had an affair, but they both knew it wouldn't last. They remained close friends for the rest of their lives. He would visit her from time to time and send her funny post cards from faraway places. 'The weather is here. Wish you were beautiful.' They were never far from each other's thoughts.

"Robert went to work for Tilda Frappe's campaign for president. He became a trusted adviser and was reunited with his old rival, Zach Stone. Together, he and Zach wrote the infamous Coon-skin Cap Speech, which students of politics and the media still study to this day. They also managed to play many games of one-on-one basketball. No blood was shed.

"Tilda was elected president in a landslide. She and Robert married in a Rose Garden ceremony. The Frappe White House partnered with Glissade, and Glissade/Frappe began to license artificial intelligence software to public and private entities. Robert and Zach and Jolene worked tirelessly to build an interplanetary space program. Bernice Gristle was appointed ambassador to Mars.

"After President Frappe was elected to a second term, Jolene and Zach moved to a house in the country and raised the twins. Jolene took the money from Confederate Vampires in Space and formed a foundation dedicated to schools and scholarships and health care and counseling in the Native

American communities. She choreographed an extraordinary dance in memory of her brother. It was performed regularly around the world, but at least once a year, she would dance for him alone in the backyard, barefoot in the grass, moving gracefully across the fading twilight sky.

"The twins were never fully convinced their mother was not a robot. They bugged the whole house and set up a command center in the closet in their bedroom. Jolene and Zach cut off their comic book allowance as punishment, and the twins eventually learned to respect other people's privacy.

"Zach became a mentor to Trevor, and Trevor went on to have a long and productive career as a Hollywood screenwriter. Trevor and Autumn had a comically disastrous first marriage, and Trevor finally acknowledged what he had known since he was old enough to care: He was gay.

"In mentoring Trevor, Zach reawakened his creative desire. He began to write again in earnest. He wrote a series of quiet, contemplative novels that had nothing to do with Confederates, vampires or space. He became known as an exacting stylist, a writer's writer. He never again achieved a large readership, but he settled into a comfortable writing routine. He arose before dawn each day and made a pot of coffee and disappeared into the space in the back of the garage. He sat at a broken down wooden desk and used the old Underwood, though by then it had become quite temperamental and cantankerous. He managed to write at least a page every day.

"President Frappe was elected to a fourth term. Robert's son played Gershwin at the inauguration. Robert and Zach and Marcel huddled together in the cold on the steps of the Lincoln Memorial. They sat as they had on those sunny afternoons on the steps of Old Grundy after the Professor's class, side by side, arm in arm, wordless, silent, stunned by it all.

" 'Did you know?' Zach asked Marcel.

" 'When you sent Trevor to find me?'

" 'Did you know?'

"But Marcel only smiled with the side of her mouth.

"It was the last time the three of them were together.

". . .

"Many years passed. The seasons came and went. Each day, Zach trekked to and from the garage, coffee cup in hand. He realized almost too late what the Professor had tried to do for him.

"Zach found the Professor, frail and thin, in his wheel-chair, and they sat together and talked for most of the day. Zach thanked the Professor and told him that he was sorry for what he had done back then. The Professor took his hand and told Zach there was no need to apologize and that he was proud of him. He was even proud of Confederate Vampires in Space.

". . .

"Rumors came from afar.

"On an icy planet orbiting a distant star, the quantum pirates had discovered a lost remnant of the Drumhead. Doctor Tempus and Tachyon resumed their asynchronous traversal of the space-time continuum. Sara Simpatico and the little ninjas kept watch over the obsidian blade. Not long thereafter, Kit Carson ventured forth in search of a new frontier."

The raven-haired woman ceased speaking. Her soothing contralto voice was silent. She turned the last page of the manuscript and set it neatly on her lap. The pages of the manuscript were dog-eared and dirty at the edges, bound together with a big, black metal clip. She was sitting next to the linen-white bed in the small, quiet room in the hospice. In the bed was the Professor. His face was bloodless, and his wrinkled, dry lips had grown ashen. The thin skin stretched across his temples was a milky pale blue.

His tired eyes turned towards her.

The raven-haired woman placed a hand gently on the side of his face.

She looked down at him with infinite compassion.

Her pendant was aglow with a pale, white light.

The Professor's lips parted and he spoke.

"What happens next?"

ABOUT THE AUTHOR

Havelock Mandamus lives in the middle of America.
Confederate Vampires in Space is his first novel.